Titia Sutherland was brought up in the country and has spent much of her adult life in London. She had a patchy education at various day-schools, and English was the only subject in which she received a good grounding. As a child she started many novels which were never completed, and she and her brother wrote and acted in their own plays. In her late teens she spent two years at the Webber-Douglas School of Drama and a short period in repertory before marrying a journalist. The birth of a baby put an end to acting. Following a divorce, she had a series of jobs which included working as a part-time reader for a publishing firm, and designing for an advertising agency.

She started to write when the children were more or less adult and following the death of her second husband. Her four previous novels, *The Fifth Summer*, *Out of the Shadows*, *Accomplice of Love* and *Running Away*, are also published by Black Swan. She has four children, enjoys gardening and paints for pleasure when there is time.

A FRIEND OF
THE FAMILY

Titia Sutherland

BLACK SWAN

A FRIEND OF THE FAMILY
A BLACK SWAN BOOK : 0 552 99650 5

First publication in Great Britain

PRINTING HISTORY
Black Swan edition published 1995

Set in 11/12pt Linotype Melior by
Phoenix Typesetting, Ilkley, West Yorkshire.

Black Swan Books are published by Transworld Publishers Ltd,
61–63 Uxbridge Road, London W5 5SA,
in Australia by Transworld Publishers (Australia) Pty Ltd,
15–25 Helles Avenue, Moorebank, NSW 2170,
and in New Zealand by Transworld Publishers (NZ) Ltd,
3 William Pickering Drive, Albany, Auckland.

Reproduced, printed and bound in Great Britain by
Cox & Wyman Ltd, Reading, Berks.

For my god-daughter Susanna,
with love

A FRIEND OF
THE FAMILY

Chapter One

The first occasion on which Kate Protheroe caught sight of Roly's car parked in her road late at night, she thought little of it. His number plate was momentarily illuminated by the headlights of her taxi as it turned the corner, and she had a vague impression of a shape huddled in the front seat; but the car was drawn up beyond the pool of light thrown by the street lamp and it was difficult to be certain. Glancing back curiously from her doorstep, she wondered where Roly had been dining and with whom, relieved to think of him taking an interest in someone other than herself. Every so often her conscience pricked her seriously where Roly was concerned. Minutes later, as she was about to close the bathroom blind, she saw the car cruise slowly past in the street below, and realized with faint surprise that he must have seen her at her front door. It was a little odd, she thought, that he had made no effort to contact her. Then, dismissing what was after all a trivial matter from her mind, she went to check on her son, Jake.

His door was ajar, letting in a shaft of light from the landing. She stood beside the bed where he lay sprawled, bottom upwards and uncovered, tufts of dark hair squashed against the pillow. He looked, in sleep especially, uncannily like his father, serving to remind her of Matt's absence. Their separation always attacked her acutely in the dark hours, making her irritable with her aloneness. Gently she pulled the duvet over the sleeping boy and crept away. Roly, as was so often the case, had been temporarily forgotten.

The mornings were always a rush. Jake's school and Kate's place of work lay in diametrically opposed directions, entailing a taxing trawl up and down the King's Road or along the Embankment. At a standstill behind a line of traffic, she felt her stomach knot up in frustration. Beside her, Jake grew pale with the apprehension of being late.

'I feel sick.'

'It'll wear off.' She glanced at him, wondering if this was an accurate assessment.

'I'll be late for Assembly.'

'Not very, if at all.' The lorry in front of them shot forward. 'Look, we're moving.'

Jake's hunched shoulders relaxed a fraction. 'Can I ask Toby back for tea?'

'No. You know the rule: nobody back for tea except Fridays, or the homework doesn't get done.'

'Boring,' he muttered.

'Ask him for Friday.'

'I'm going to Daddy for the weekend,' he reminded her. 'Aren't I?'

'For Saturday night,' she told him. 'We have to shop in the morning, buy you new shoes.'

'Mum!'

'Sorry, darling, but there it is,' she said, drawing to a halt outside the school. 'Here we are, with three minutes to spare.' She gave him a kiss. 'Off you go. See you later.'

He scrambled from the car, hampered by a bulging satchel, putting a horrified face back through the window.

'Swimming things!' he said. 'Where are they?'

'Oh *Jake*!' she sighed. 'You're old enough to remember for yourself.'

'I can't miss swimming, they'll be furious.'

'Helga will have to drop them off at school when she goes shopping,' she said resignedly. 'Now hop it.'

She watched him climb the steps with the last of the stragglers, a spare, bony figure, his arms and legs seeming to have outgrown the rest of him. The groups of mothers and child-minders scattered, some to their cars, others on foot with toddlers in pushchairs. One or two of them smiled and waved as she drove away, and she grinned back, conscious of their youth in comparison with her own advancing years. She was, at thirty-seven, probably the oldest mother amongst them. Awareness of the fact prevented her from bonding with them, joining in the swapping of child horror stories while they waited for their offspring to come out of school. They appeared so assured, so complete in the belief of their security, that she was convinced none of them suffered the traumas of a collapsed marriage. Intimidated by their cheerful confidence, she would grab Jake the moment he appeared, more often than not breaking up the friendly horseplay which signalled the end of incarceration, and propel him away grumbling.

Halted by traffic-lights, she stared at her face in the car mirror. Bare of the make-up which she never had time to apply in the early morning, she looked tired and, she reflected resentfully, old. Resentment seemed to have become her predominant emotion: towards Matt, towards her present existence with its fuzzy, undefined limits, even towards herself. It irked her that she should have the chief responsibility for bringing up their child, should always be the one to have to admonish, lay down the ground rules; while Matt, when he was in charge, had nothing to do but think up some form of new entertainment. Contrarily, she knew quite well that she would have hated the roles to be reversed. Jake was her anchor, the one stable element in an uncertain world and an antidote to loneliness.

She should have grown used to loneliness. Matt's absences, travelling and photographing in remote corners of the earth, should have immunized her. Instead, they had become the largest bone of contention between them; where once she had understood and accepted and encouraged, intolerance had taken over. She could no longer stand the empty husbandless stretches. The irony of finding herself in the same situation with a trial separation had not escaped her. Yet more ironic and harder to bear was the fact that he had stopped roaming for the time being, and was based in London, in a flat just across the river, working on a book. There were times when she felt he had arranged his life this way on purpose to annoy; acknowledging in more honest moments that whatever else, he was not devious and the writing had always been part of his plan. She had come to realize there were disadvantages to this mutually agreed parting, decided upon when the tension between them grew untenable and boiled over into open warfare. Arrangements over Jake were simple: Matt would have unlimited access to him. Regarding themselves, there were no guidelines, merely a tacit understanding that they should respect each other's privacy. Within such a nebulous structure, Kate found herself searching unhappily for a code of behaviour. Old friends, taking pity on her, asked her to dinner, nine times out of ten producing a spare man. It was not long before she learned that women living alone, never mind their status, were regarded as fair game. She had thought to leave behind unwelcome sexual tussles in her twenties; now she parried them with a blatant lack of response which worked quite successfully. It did not help the loneliness; she was left feeling unprotected and confused, and longing childishly to be cosseted without demands being made of her in return.

Her friendship with Roly was a direct result of her state of mind, she had decided recently. He had happened as if by divine providence in answer to her current needs, dispensing comfort and support and assuming nothing: apart from that one occasion not so long ago when her eyes had been opened to how he really felt. It had been, she realized, hopelessly insensitive of her not to guess, and she put it down remorsefully to self-absorption, and the fact that she did not want such a satisfactory relationship to end. The awkwardness had been glossed over, or so she thought. Now she was far from sure. Reflecting on it as she turned into her road, she found herself scanning the parked cars anxiously, half-expecting to see Roly's BMW amongst them. There was of course no sign of it: it was at night that he had taken to waiting, silent and anonymous in the shadows of the street. Three times since she had first noticed him, he had been there as she returned from an evening out. It was becoming habitual; she no longer dismissed it as an odd coincidence. The realization of being watched was unnerving, giving her a cold *frisson* between the shoulder-blades. That it should be Roly indulging in such an inexplicable exercise, staunch, amiable Roly, made it doubly macabre. More than once she had been on the point of tapping on his car window and asking him outright, in a light, joky way, what on earth he was doing playing at private investigators. But instinct, and an uncomfortable feeling she already knew the answer, had prevented her.

The detour home had made her late for work. The au pair, Helga, was ironing as Kate shot into the

13

kitchen to give instructions about Jake's swimming things; the ironed clothes lying in neat, segregated piles.

'Mr Roland was telephoning after you were gone,' Helga said.

'Oh? What did he want, did he say?'

'He was asking were you going to be out this evening. I said I thought not, because it is my evening for the aerobics.' A smile lightened Helga's perpetual severity. She approved of Roly. 'Perhaps he would like supper?' she suggested. 'I will buy food for two?'

'No,' Kate said, refusing to have her life arranged for her; and then, changing her mind, 'Yes, perhaps you better had, Helga, please. And don't forget Jake's gear, will you?'

Upstairs she hurriedly threw various items of make-up into her bag and left the house in a rush, picturing her friend and employer Isobel's irritability at her unpunctuality, thus setting the tone for the day. Taking the direct route down the King's Road to World's End, where Isobel ran her interior decorating business from a small shop, part of her mind was occupied with the day's work: chintzes and brocades, samples and measurements; while the remaining part toyed with the problem of Roly, which nagged like incipient toothache. In retrospect, she realized, she should never have allowed him to become so involved in her single-parent existence. She had admittedly suspected him of being slightly in love with her, but not to the extent of it becoming an overriding passion. Passion was not an emotion one automatically associated with Roly. Therein lay her mistake, she told herself; for she could think of no other reason for his sudden weird behaviour, nor how to deal with it. From the start, looking back, she had taken him shamefully for granted.

*　　*　　*

The meeting between them had taken place at his mews house in South Kensington. Kate's brother Charlie had introduced them; when in London he often stayed overnight at Roly's place and on this occasion he had suggested they should telephone Kate, and all have dinner together.

'You've never met her, have you?' Charlie said. 'She's quite pretty, I suppose. And she's having a rather grotty time. She and Matt — you know, Matt Protheroe — have split up for the moment. Might be kind to get her to join us.'

Charlie was mistaken; the minute he saw her, Roly knew they had indeed met briefly at a party, and recalled when and where. Kate, however, showed no sign of recognition, and he supposed resignedly, and not for the first time, that he was unmemorable. He looked at her standing in his living-room while she made up her mind what to drink, seeing a face that tapered to a point, and grey eyes spaced curiously wide apart, so that the whole effect was catlike. He could remember what she was wearing: a short dark skirt that rode up her crossed legs when she sat down, and a thin white shirt in some crisp material that was almost but not quite see-through. His heart thumped uncomfortably as he turned away to pour her vodka and tonic, and his hand when he passed her the glass was unsteady. The effect she had on him was unprecedented. In those few seconds he had become enslaved. Quite unaware, she was exchanging obligatory information with Charlie about their respective children and Roly listened, glad to have the chance to pull himself together, until, clumsy with nerves, he knocked his glass of wine to the floor. Kate had found the kitchen and returned with a roll of paper and a tin of salt, and on hands and knees had doctored the stain, while Roly hovered

15

over her ineffectually and Charlie made unhelpful remarks from where he was sitting.

'Good old Roly. His next trick will be impossible.'

'Shut up, Charlie,' Kate glanced up at Roly. 'It's nice to know someone besides myself is accident-prone,' she said, smiling at him.

They had walked to the restaurant along warm summer streets, where crowds from the pubs spilled out onto the pavements, shirt-sleeved and voluble over pints of beer. Seated beside Kate at dinner, he felt his inner turmoil slowly subside with the intake of wine and leave a sense of enchantment, as if he was capable of great achievement. He reached a stage where whatever he said seemed to him to be immensely witty; a fact which Charlie, sitting opposite, commented on, eyebrows raised and smiling rather superciliously in that way he had. But Kate had laughed obligingly, glancing at Roly with real amusement in her eyes. They entertained her with stories of how they had met at university, Charlie and Roly, and finally Matt who had arrived a year later. Their lives since had separated them to a great extent, but at the time they had formed a triumvirate socially if not studiously. Roly supposed they were an unlikely trio; one could not have found three more disparate men had one tried, and Kate echoed his thoughts.

'You're all so different,' she said. 'Charlie's pompous, Matt is basically a loner, and Roly is – ' she turned to study him, her head on one side – 'I don't really know you, do I, Roly? But you look kind, and you're a joker. A kind joker: I can't think of a better mix.'

'Thank you,' he said, gratitude and pride swelling inside him. Too often the butt of someone else's humour, he was genuinely touched.

'I resent being called "pompous",' Charlie observed without animosity. 'And what about *my* kindness

16

in giving you a slap-up dinner? Thinking of you, you see, alone and languishing. Fat lot of thanks I get for that.'

'Thank you, Charlie, for my nice dinner,' she said. 'Why haven't we met before,' she asked Roly, 'since you all know each other so well?'

Roly had been wondering the same thing. 'I hardly see Matt these days. I bump into him occasionally swimming at the same place. But he's away so much, isn't he, on his travels?'

'Yes,' she agreed, staring at her plate.

Sensing his tactlessness, Roly added hurriedly, 'We do such different jobs, our paths don't cross much, I suppose.'

'It took Roly nine years to pass his accountant's exams,' Charlie remarked unnecessarily, filling up their glasses.

'Well, at least I'm a bloody good one,' Roly said with unusual spirit.

'There you are, you see. He's always putting people down,' Kate said. 'It's a despicable habit, Charlie.'

Roly could not make out whether the banter between brother and sister sprang from affection or a clash of personalities; there was, he thought, a sharp core running through it. Being an only child, he had no experience of relationships between siblings. Certainly they differed completely in appearance, Kate with her pointed face and dark hair and quick gestures, and Charlie with his smooth blond blandness. Roly had never quite ceased to envy him his urbanity, comparing it wistfully with his own heavily built, bearlike form which, try as he might, refused to lend him self-assurance. He failed to achieve tidiness; suits crumpled on him, his fine, mouse-brown hair seemed to ruffle of its own accord, giving him the appearance of an ageing schoolboy. It had its uses, this bumbling air; clients

17

found it reassuring, like having their tax liabilities sorted for them by a favourite uncle. His work was the only area of his life in which he had complete confidence. People at social gatherings tended to bypass him for someone more exciting; and the girlfriends he had had seldom took him seriously after the first date. Since the ability to make people laugh seemed to him his only asset, he played up to it; had done so from schooldays as a form of defence against bullying. He did not particularly like the role of buffoon which life had thrust on him. Behind its camouflage another man yearned to emerge and be acknowledged; a serious-minded romantic subconsciously looking to love and be loved in return. Sitting next to Kate, the real self had never longed more acutely for recognition.

'I mustn't be too late,' she was saying. 'I have to be on time for work tomorrow or Isobel will kill me. We're doing up this flat in Eaton Square, and I'm meeting the owner at ten o'clock with armfuls of samples.'

'Terrifying woman, Isobel,' Charlie said. 'I don't know how you can stand working for such a rabid feminist.'

'She's all right if you know how to handle her. Besides,' Kate shrugged, 'we need the money; it's within my interests to get along with her. Matt isn't exactly flush at the moment.'

The mention of Matt gave Roly a faint shock; he had temporarily forgotten the existence of a husband, his mind wandering in pursuit of impossible goals.

'I'm not surprised.' Charlie signalled for the bill. 'You're running two establishments for one thing. Are you *any* closer to reaching a decision?' he asked.

'No,' Kate replied flatly. 'If we were, you'd know about it.'

'It's a very unsatisfactory way to live,' he said

disapprovingly, straightening the salt and pepper mills. 'I'm against these trial separations. They're far too nebulous to solve anything, and unsettling for children.'

'It's better than having rows in front of them,' Kate retorted. 'Jake's old enough at nine to understand. Actually, he sees more of Matt than he did while he was at home. Matt devotes whole weekends to him now, when it's his turn.'

'All the same, I wish you'd sort something out between you.'

'And I wish', she told him, 'you'd talk like a human being instead of a solicitor. I don't want to discuss it any more; we're embarrassing Roly.'

'Roly knows the score. He's not embarrassed, are you, Roly?'

'Just *stop*, will you?' she said in a tight voice.

'OK, OK. Only showing concern,' Charlie muttered distantly, scanning the bill with an eagle eye.

'We'll halve it,' Roly offered, glad of a change of subject.

He remembered thinking that the moment demanded a diverting wisecrack, and finding his usual fund had deserted him, driven out by a glimpse of the tension in Kate's pale face. If the brief exposé of her marital affairs had made him slightly uncomfortable, it had also given him an insight into her feelings. Behind her superficial sparkle, he detected loneliness, recognizing it easily as one of his oldest enemies. It opened up a field of opportunities: not that he thought then that he might make himself indispensable to her; only that she was in need of nurturing and that he was happy to provide it. He knew by experience that people automatically trusted him, regarded him as solid and reliable and generous; he was, as a result, much in demand as a godfather. The sexual encounters he had embarked on might have been unsuccessful, but he invariably remained friends with the women in question, many of whom became the mothers of his godchildren. He saw a way, with this modest flair of his, of seeing more of Kate, and gaining her approval if not her affections. He had not looked further than that; his whole objective being, at the time, not to let her disappear without trace.

He had felt like singing as they walked home, three abreast with Kate in the middle, little wafts of her scent drifting to him on the night air. She and Charlie seemed to have forgotten their weighted conversation, and were discussing when she should visit; Roly could tell by the way she hedged round the open invitation that she was not keen on going. Needing an outlet for his euphoria, he stopped to give his local tramp five pounds where he sat huddled in the doorway of the Midland Bank.

'It's highly likely he drives back to his semi-detached, two-bathroomed house in a Mercedes,' Charlie pointed out.

But even this piece of cynicism could not bring Roly down to earth. As he saw Kate to her car, opening the door for her and closing it again carefully, he was thinking: It is only the first time I shall be doing this, there will be many others.

'Will you have dinner with me one evening?' he had asked her through the open window; and she had replied with a smile she would like that, and that Charlie would give him her number.

'Good of you if you'd keep an eye on her,' Charlie said, yawning over a late-night brandy. 'I love her dearly, but she's obstinate as hell, and not much of a chooser.'

'Matt was an all-right choice, surely?' Roly asked.

'Oh yes. I'd have thought he was fine, but look where they are now. The situation bothers me, frankly: Kate swanning around in limbo.' He gave another huge yawn. 'At least she won't come to any harm with you,' he added. 'Good old Roly.'

Roly had found it difficult to sleep that night. People like Charlie, and he was in the majority, never looked beyond the surface presentation of a personality; 'Good old Roly' was how he was recognized and accepted. It did not occur to them that his emotions were as capable of escaping control as were theirs. Certainly his stayed on the rampage until the early hours of the morning, his heart racing, before he fell into a light and sweaty doze. But he woke feeling amazingly well, and lay for a while in a state of anticipation, visualizing a whole new aspect of his life hitherto undreamt of.

Over the following months, from that late-summer introduction through to early spring, Kate's friendship with Roly had flourished; establishing itself quite quickly into a comfortable routine of meeting up at least three times a week. Reflecting on it now, Kate supposed he had become a habit, and, according to her mother, all habits were bad. But such a relationship had been insidious; his attentions so warm and undemanding, it was easy to become complacent about them. She contributed her share of hospitality, cooking supper for them when he was not taking her out. On the evenings at home, she did not bother much about the way she looked after a while, and was apt to slop around in leggings or jeans and baggy sweaters, with little or no make-up on her face, confident of his continued faithfulness. From the start she had been completely relaxed in his company, which would not have happened had she found him physically attractive. Looking back in guilt, she realized that; but at the time he had seemed perfectly happy with the way things were: an affectionate but sexless arrangement. Occasionally,

after he had aimed an inept kiss at her mouth, or
she had caught him gazing at her with spaniel's eyes,
she thought it odd that he did not make stronger
attempts to get her into bed. But she had dismissed
the query rapidly, putting it down to the fact that
he was probably slightly neuter. He was, after all,
everything she needed, and more, and she accepted
him gratefully with open if platonic arms. How could
I? she asked herself in retrospect. How could I have
been such an insensitive bitch?

Whether they were going out, to a film or the
theatre or dinner, or staying in for one of her suppers,
he seldom came to the house empty-handed: a bunch
of flowers wrapped in white paper or a bottle of
wine were invariably laid down unobtrusively on
the kitchen table. She came to rely on him, ringing him at work saying she would be late home
and could he pick up the meat, or the groceries,
or whatever was needed. And he washed up the
saucepans for her: even Matt, who was a New Man
in theory, had balked at saucepan cleaning in practice. But out of Roly's many endearing qualities, the
one that touched her the most was his fondness for
Jake. Once Jake's instinctive suspicions had been
overcome, and they did not last for long, a bond
was forged between them that sprang from Roly's
natural affinity with children.

Kate had introduced them on his second visit to
the house, prising Jake from the television and his
viewing of *Raiders of the Lost Ark.*

'This is Mr Bliss, darling,' she said. 'Switch off
and say hello.'

Jake did both with a marked lack of enthusiasm,
holding out his hand mechanically, his dark eyes
guarded. Roly took it solemnly.

'Please call me Roly,' he said. 'I hate the Bliss
part.'

'Roly is a friend of Daddy's and Charlie's,' Kate

explained. 'They were at university together.'

This information somehow cleared the wariness from Jake's face. He stared at Roly in astonishment. 'Are you really called Roly Bliss?' he asked.

'My real name is Roland Bliss,' Roly admitted mournfully. 'I can't imagine what possessed my parents to land me with it.'

Jake nodded. 'It must have been awful at school.'

'They called me Roly-Poly, of course. I was a fat boy anyway, you see, so it was God's gift to them.'

Roly did not mention worse humiliations, like the 'taking the piss out of Bliss' war-cry.

Kate said, 'I'd better finish off getting supper. Look after Roly, Jake, and pour him a drink when he's ready.'

'Can I stay up?'

'No. Bed in ten minutes,' Kate's unequivocal reply came from the kitchen. 'But you can show him your word processor if you like.'

Jake looked at Roly enquiringly. 'Would you like to see it?'

'Very much.'

Jake's room was crammed with the paraphernalia of a nine-year-old, modern technology overlapping remnants of the nursery; Beatrix Potter and *The Wind in the Willows* rubbed shoulders with posters of Grand Prix racing drivers and model cars. The word processor sat in pride of place on a table by itself.

'Daddy gave it to me last Christmas,' he said. 'Would you like to have a go?'

'Better not, I'm rather inept. I might wipe out your entire program. Give me a demonstration.'

Jake sat down self-consciously and tapped away at speed with two fingers. Roly stood and watched over the boy's shoulder, asking questions about technical matters which to Jake were probably elementary.

'What do you use it for most, school work or fun?'

Jake stopped tapping. 'Well, I write my diary on it, it's great for that. And thank-you letters when I have to. There are masses of things I use it for, really.' He swung round to face Roly. 'Don't you have one?' he asked.

'Not of my own. We have them in my office, of course.'

'You really should get one,' Jake advised earnestly.

'I expect you're right. It would be good for writing a book.'

'Do you write books?'

'No,' Roly admitted. 'I make up stories but they're in my head only. For my godchildren,' he added.

'What sort of stories?'

'Fantastical ones about pirates and dragons and buried treasure. Then there's one about a certain Captain Diehard who sets out to capture space pirates. He's a kind of space James Bond, and he takes his children with him, two boys, one who's good and the other terribly naughty.'

Jake wriggled on his chair, eyes shining. 'Will you tell me?'

'You might be too old, it might not interest someone who's into computers,' Roly said doubtfully.

'It would, it would! Please.'

Kate called up the stairs, 'Bed, Jake, I'll be up in a minute.'

'I'll tell you a bit until Kate comes,' Roly promised.

Kate had found them deep in the adventures of Captain Diehard, Jake's face rapt above the duvet, his eyes riveted on Roly whose bulky frame weighed down the side of the bed. Sitting where Matt used to sit as part of the good-night ritual; the thought struck her painfully, and then passed.

'I hate to be a killjoy, but time's up,' she said.

'Five more minutes,' pleaded Jake.

Roly got up heavily and straightened out the dent he had made. 'More in our next instalment,' he said.

'Does that mean you'll come again?'

'I hope so.'

'Good.'

'You've made a hit,' Kate said as she and Roly went downstairs.

'Well, I don't know about that—'

'I do. Jake regards any visiting male as a potential threat to Matt's territory.' She smiled at him. 'You seem to have passed the test first time round.'

He flushed with pleasure. 'I like children,' he said simply, wishing Kate's affections could be so easily captured. That was an altogether more complex matter, demanding caution since he was a novice and had little idea as to how to proceed, and even less as to where it might end. But those were the early days, the times of optimism when his heart had wings and anything seemed possible.

Kate's parents lived near Guildford in one of the few remaining acres of countryside that had avoided being built over by motorways and housing estates. Since the separation from Matt, Kate had seen a great deal more of them than during the years of togetherness, using their home as a bolthole for herself and Jake. If, as occasionally happened, she felt guilty about her lack of family commitment in the past, she would remind herself that that was, to a great extent, her mother's fault. She had never approved of Kate's choice of husband, mistrusting his means of earning a living, which seemed to her haphazard. Secretly the only careers she understood or thought of as satisfactory were those that entailed the hours of nine to five behind a desk, and, of course, the

Army, which, despite an element of danger, was at least straightforward. At the nearest whiff of anything artistic she shied away like a startled horse, labelling it unreliable; reliability being top of her personal list of desirable qualities. Her relationship with her son-in-law had always been an uneasy one; she did not know what to make of Matt, and his natural charm only increased her suspicions. When Kate and he parted, she seized the opportunity of pointing out it merely confirmed what she had always suspected: that he was untrustworthy and selfish, and careless of Kate's happiness. Kate would have been less irritated if her mother had clearly admitted to disliking him.

It had been, she now knew, something of a mistake to bring Roly into the family circle; but at the time it had seemed a good way to repay his continuing kindnesses to her. She had taken him to lunch with the parents one Sunday, and once or twice subsequently until he was automatically assumed to be a permanent fixture in her life; at least by her mother. Her father, reticent by nature and a retired solicitor, never assumed anything and seldom asked questions. His wife, Prue, found in Roly all the makings of a satisfactory second husband for Kate, who read the workings of her mother's mind with amusement. Prue was undoubtedly planning a divorce with far more enthusiasm than she had shown for her daughter's wedding. Meanwhile, Roly was spoiled even more disgracefully than Jake. His favourite puddings having once been discovered, were put before him at every visit. He was taken on tours of the garden borders by Prue, her arm linked cosily with his, without her realizing he was not horticulturally educated and could not tell a tulip from a rose. His innate good manners saw him through these tête-à-têtes, murmuring a pleasantry here, a query there. Far more embarrassing for him were the gentle enquiries into Kate's affairs, and the snide remarks about Matt: 'I never thought he was right for her; she needs a more stable existence.' He did not know how to answer; Matt was a friend, however long-lost, and as such deserved loyalty. On the other hand, Roly was conscious of the fact that, given the chance, he would himself behave disloyally with Kate. He managed as a rule to turn the conversation to another topic when the pressure from Kate's mother became too great.

On a raw day in November Kate had wandered down the garden to help her father make a bonfire, rather unfairly leaving Roly at the mercy of Prue. The autumn smell of dampness and burning vegetation reminded her for some reason of childhood as she raked the leaves into heaps. The smoke rose straight upwards in a slow spiral in the stillness and from the nearby copse the voices of Jake and his friend Toby could be heard, faint and spasmodic. The afternoon stuck in her mind because her father had broken his role of not interfering in his children's lives by asking out of the blue: 'What are you going to do about this Roly fellow?'

She stopped raking. 'Do? I wasn't planning actually to *do* anything. He's a good friend, that's all.'

'He's in love with you; you must realize that, surely.' George Brownlow prodded the bonfire with his fork, inducing it to burn. 'I don't think you're being fair to him.'

'He knows the situation,' she said. 'I'm sure he doesn't expect any more than what we already have. It suits us both,' she added, suddenly uncertain.

'You mean it suits you,' her father replied drily.

She watched him leaning over the smoking pile of leaves; a tall, slightly stooped figure with receding grey hair that seemed to her to have remained the same as far back as she could remember. A tolerant, infinitely comforting man easily confided in, who nevertheless could make one feel quite small when he made it his business to do so.

'Are you suggesting,' she asked, 'I shouldn't see him any more? If I didn't have friends, life would be intolerable, especially right now.'

'I'm not suggesting anything of the sort; merely that you should let this particular one know where he stands.' He turned his head to look at her. 'That is, if his feelings aren't reciprocated, and I don't think they are in your case, are they?'

She shoved her cold hands deep in her anorak pockets. 'I don't really *know* what his feelings are,' she said obstinately. 'I can hardly make mine clear under the circumstances, can I? I'd look a complete fool.' When her father did not comment, she went on, 'You don't understand Roly like I do, Pa. He's a born carer, at his happiest looking after people whom he thinks need propping up. I come into that category, I suppose. But he's not the type to fall headlong for someone: I think he's rather frightened of that sort of a relationship, as a matter of fact.'

'You were never much of a judge of human nature, Kate,' her father remarked mildly.

Childishly hurt by the accusation, she snapped back, 'I suppose you think Matt was a mistake, then?'

He pulled out a handkerchief and mopped his forehead. 'That's something only you and he can decide. I hope not because I'm fond of Matt, but I've no intention of interfering in that department.'

'Only between myself and Roly?'

'I'm merely trying to prevent you laying up a store of trouble for yourself.' Forking more leaves onto the fire, he said over his shoulder, 'Let me cite you an instance in which I was involved not so long ago. A couple were in the process of getting a divorce. She was the guilty party, had left home to live with her lover, and I was acting as solicitor for the husband. He was hurt and bewildered by his wife's defection. But there was nothing in his attitude to suggest he might make vindictive reprisals; an amiable, straightforward sort, it seemed to me.' He was silent a moment.

'So, what happened?'

'He started by breaking into the lover's home where he ruined his wife's designer clothes with a pair of kitchen scissors. After which he did irreparable damage to their car, and, to cap it all, dug up a whole load of scandal concerning the lover and offered it to one of the tabloid newspapers. Finally he found himself facing a libel suit and made an attempt on his own life: an abortive one, as it turned out.'

'Lord! What a happy little saga,' Kate said, 'but I don't see what it's got to do with Roly and myself.'

'Just an illustration of how mistaken one can be over someone's character.'

She picked up the rake and began to draw the pile of leaves towards her in long, thoughtful sweeps. 'There's no comparison,' she said with a laugh. 'Roly and I aren't married, for one thing, and for another, I can't imagine him going berserk with scissors, or in any other way. The man in your story doesn't sound remotely like him.'

'There are similarities, nevertheless,' her father answered, 'or I wouldn't have bothered telling you. And one doesn't necessarily have to be married to suffer unbearable frustration.'

The silence that followed his remark was broken by the raucous chorus of rooks coming home to roost in the tallest trees of the copse. The children's voices could still be heard as they pursued some ploy of their own. Roly appeared, walking towards Kate and her father, as four-square as the rose-red house behind him in sweater and flak jacket. He looked friendly and solid and quite unneurotic.

'Anything I can do to help?'

'You could be a darling and call the boys in for tea,' Kate told him. 'They're building a camp in the wood.'

'What fun! Right up my street. I'll go and inspect.'

When they were alone, she said to her father, 'There you are; he's just one of the boys at heart. I honestly believe that half the attraction in being with me is Jake and the bedtime stories.'

'There's none so blind as those who will not see,' he replied.

'You really are in a "beware the Ides of March" mood,' she said mockingly; and then, because she was deeply fond of him and noticed worry lines between his eyes, she kissed his cheek. 'I have listened and duly taken note, Pa. I'll watch it, I promise.'

She decided privately that his opinions were exaggerated, if not way out of line; and yet she could not entirely forget them. He was seldom wrong in his assessment of people; she knew that by experience. The day became a marker, the point at which she had stopped accepting Roly's devotion unquestioningly and begun to analyse it. Various signs of emotion he displayed, and which she had taken to be just part of his make-up, such as the way he shook when he touched her, suddenly took on a new and uncomfortable significance. She realized with a shock that she had looked on their relationship as automatically platonic without considering his own instincts; dismissing the bearlike hugs, the fumbling search for her mouth on parting, as rather clumsy expressions of affection. Facing the reality of her attraction for him she found difficult. She did not want the comfortable situation they had formed between them altered in any way. Roly, like Jake, had become a buffer against an uncertain world and given her reassurance; Roly as a lover was out of the question. Aware that she should explain tactfully her lack of reciprocation, and the sooner the better, she hesitated for fear of losing him altogether. Still he made no positive declaration, encouraging her to put off the making of her own. They drifted on through the weeks of winter; it was some time before she did anything about it.

While Kate had been having her peace of mind disturbed by her father, Jake and Toby were building a house in the tangled undergrowth of the copse. They had got as far as two tripods with a stick balanced between them.

'We need two more forked sticks at either end,' Jake said. 'Four in all.'

'Why?'

'Because the roof's got to be sloping, dumbo, so's the rain'll run off it.'

'It won't run off bracken,' Toby pointed out. 'It'll leak anyway.'

'Not if we put on enough of it.' Jake searched the ground for suitable building materials, kicking aside bracken and brambles with his gumboot. 'Come *on*,' he said. 'I'm not doing all the work.'

It was difficult to find sticks of equal length. The structure when erected was decidedly lopsided.

'We ought to have Roly helping,' Jake observed eyeing it critically. 'He's good at this sort of thing. Now for the bracken.'

'Is Roly your uncle?'

'No. Just a friend.'

'I suppose he's your mother's boyfriend,' Toby said.

'No, he's not,' Jake told him fiercely.

'Then why is he always round at your place?' Toby asked, pursuing his enquiries relentlessly.

31

'I've said, he's a friend,' Jake threw down an armful of damp bracken. 'She doesn't have boyfriends. She's married to Daddy.'

'Your father isn't there, is he, though?'

'Only for a bit. He'll come back. They're having a trial something-or-other, that's all. Because of the rows.'

Jake did not in fact know what would happen, it was only what he fervently wished. The good thing about his parents living apart was that he saw a lot of Matt, and what they did together was usually fun. But it did not make up for being shuttled backwards and forwards from one to the other, leaving his mother alone gave him a weird, uneasy feeling that she would disappear in the meantime, that someone would spirit her away. He mistrusted any strange man who came to the house in case he should turn out to be the 'someone'. Roly did not count. Roly would not do a mean thing like that, and, besides, he was his father's friend as well.

'I bet Roly and your mother do "it" together when you're not there,' Toby said with streetwise certainty.

Jake knew what 'it' meant, his father had explained about sex. Privately he thought it sounded revolting, and quite unthinkable in connection with his mother. Rage rose hotly inside him.

'They don't!'

'Do! Do! Do!' chanted Toby, grinning.

'Don't.'

'Do!'

'Shut up! Shut up! Shut up!' Jake flung himself at Toby, who staggered, tripped and fell backwards on the mushy floor of the wood. Jake pummelled mercilessly with his fists. 'Take it back!' he yelled. 'Bloody well take it back!'

Toby was giggling helplessly. 'Shan't!' he gasped. A fist collided with his nose. The laughter stopped.

He put a hand over it, gazing in astonishment at Jake's face inches from his own. 'That hurt. It's probably broken.' He wriggled under Jake's knee pressed into his abdomen. 'Let me up!'

'Say you're sorry.' Jake knelt harder, red with anger and exertion.

Toby mumbled unintelligibly.

'Can't hear. Louder!'

'Sorry.'

Jake withdrew reluctantly, feeling his temper subside and ebb away, leaving a flat dreariness in its place. He did not like fighting. The afternoon was spoilt; the house they were building looked silly and childish in its skeleton stage.

Toby came up behind him, feeling his nose gingerly. 'Is it bleeding?'

'Don't know,' Jake said without looking. 'Don't care if you bleed to death.'

'Come off it. I've said I'm sorry. Shake?'

Jake turned, hesitated, shook the muddy paw extended to him. Mates were mates, you could not afford to lose them.

Roly appeared, brushing his way noisily through the undergrowth. 'Livingstone and Stanley, I presume,' he said cheerfully.

'Who?'

'Part of history. Maybe they don't teach it any more. I've been sent to announce tea. Is this the camp headquarters?' He examined the collection of sticks. 'Not bad. Not bad at all. It'll look better still when you've got the roof on.'

This was achieved in record time with his help. The tattered shreds of the afternoon's fun were miraculously pulled together. They returned to the house dirty, happy and half an hour late for tea.

*   *   *

It was not until mid-March that Roly's reticence finally gave way and his real feelings for Kate cascaded out unchecked and without warning. He did not intend it to happen in this fashion; had in fact planned a quiet, civilized discussion about where their relationship was leading, imagining it over and over again in his mind. But he had not bargained on the strength of his emotions, which had been fermenting inside him, battened down under a precarious lid of self-control for the past six months. It had got to the point where Kate seldom left his consciousness; sleeping, eating, breathing, he lived with her in his thoughts. Even at work, desire for her was a dull ache in the background. He developed a jealousy for anyone who claimed her, apart from Jake; those faceless friends whom she continued to see regularly, unaware of his pain. Merely making himself indispensable was no longer enough; like a drug, she was in his bloodstream, and he wanted her to himself, permanently. Such was the state of his mind that he was able to gloss over the fact of her marriage. After all, she had admitted she was ambiguous in her feelings towards Matt: 'The trouble about separating is the losing touch,' she had said, 'and when you do see each other all the wrong emotions come to the surface, like resentment.' Roly tried unsuccessfully to understand. In Matt's place, he would never have agreed to leave her alone, could not have borne the parting.

Since it was not planned, the timing of his outpouring of love had not been propitious. Kate was recovering from a heavy cold, they had seen an Alan Ayckbourn play which had not lived up to its reviews, and stood afterwards in sleeting rain searching for a taxi. Returning home, she went immediately to have a hot bath, while Roly heated up soup which they ate on their knees in the sitting-room. He had never seen her look so vulnerable, crouched in front of the gas fire, wrapped in an oversize towelling robe, eating her soup like a child at bedtime. It was this childlike quality that got to him, caught at his heart and caused a welling-up of feeling that practically stifled him.

'I think I'll try a whisky,' she said, sneezing.

'I'll fetch it.'

'Thanks.' She sank back in the armchair.

When he returned with two drinks, she was asleep against the cushions. He put down the glasses quietly, then, lowering himself heavily to kneel in front of her, leaned forward and kissed her. Her eyes shot open, wide and startled like a cornered cat. She struggled to sit upright, but his arms and torso caged her in while his mouth jolted from hers and slid down to bury itself in the gap in her dressing-gown. He groaned.

'Roly,' she said in an even voice, 'get off me, please.'

Punch-drunk with her proximity, he eased himself backwards to sit on his haunches awkwardly, but he hardly noticed the discomfort. Nothing could stop him now.

'Kate, darling Kate, I love you and I want to marry you.'

She gazed at him with an odd mixture of astonishment and relief. 'It's not possible. I'm already married to Matt, remember?'

'But you've been separated for nearly a year; you can't love him,' he insisted. 'There's always divorce.'

'I've no intention of getting a divorce,' she said quickly, 'at least until I see how things are working out.'

'I'll wait. I don't mind how long it takes.'

She took a deep breath before saying, 'No, you mustn't, Roly, because I'm not going to marry you.'

'Never? Whatever happens?'

'Whatever happens,' she repeated.

He felt the awful stab of rejection, together with the realization he was going about this in all the wrong way, and it was too late to switch tactics. In for a penny, in for a pound.

'I shouldn't have asked,' he said. 'Stupid of me when you're confused.'

'I think it was very sweet of you to ask me.' Kate touched his hand.

'Sweet?' he said. 'You don't understand, I'm hopelessly in love with you and I can't carry on in the way we've been doing: so close and yet miles apart. I want us to be lovers, Kate; that's what I'm trying to say.'

She was silent, staring down at her hands laced together in her lap. 'I didn't realize,' she said at last. 'Let's have those drinks: I think we need them.'

He heaved himself to his feet to fetch the glasses, all the time talking, unable to prevent himself once the floodgates had been opened. He could not recall afterwards exactly what he had said, only the gist of it.

'I've been wanting to say this for months, but I didn't dare; frightened of losing you, I suppose. You're with me the entire time, there isn't a moment when you're not in my mind. I'm not much good at expressing myself as a rule, but with you there's no difficulty: I can articulate with the best of the poets. I don't expect you to feel the same for me, darling Kate. But please say there is at least a particle of love in return—'

'Please stop,' Kate said in a voice strangled with catarrh and nerves. 'There isn't an easy way to say this, so I'll come straight out with it. I don't love you, Roly; that is, not in the way you obviously want me to. You're my very best friend, and I'm terribly fond of you, but I'm not in love with you. I'm sorry,' she added, gesturing helplessly.

In that moment, Roly's world fell apart; he felt his body literally sag under the impact of the words as if from a physical blow. This is how it must feel to be shot, he thought fleetingly. He saw her pointed face, pale and full of pity, heard her say how a great deal of it was her fault for being insensitive; and he was suddenly consumed by an anger which left him as quickly as it arrived. He caught sight of himself in a wall mirror, large and rumpled and pathetic.

'It's not your fault,' he said, pulling the last remnants of dignity round him like a shroud. 'I've made a fool of myself; all par for the course.'

'Oh, darling Roly, of course you haven't.' Her face creased on the verge of tears. 'If anyone's behaved idiotically, it's me.' She got up from the armchair and took a gulp of her drink. 'What would we do without whisky?' she said with a weak smile. 'It was made for occasions like this, when nobody knows what to say next. I suppose,' she stared hard at her glass, 'you'd rather we didn't see much of each other from now on?'

'Is that what you want?' he asked. 'Because personally it would make me miserable.'

'It's not what I want; you're my one prop. I'd miss you dreadfully, and so would Jake. But I feel I've monopolized you when you might have been out there meeting other people.' She hesitated. 'Other women,' she ended in a rush. 'Single ones without problems.'

He looked at her, unable to believe that she could be so unaware of his agony as to suggest such an easy solution. 'You don't understand,' he said.

'I'm trying to. It was you who said you couldn't go on the way we were.'

So he had; that was in a moment of wild hopefulness for the ultimate. Faced with the prospect of losing her altogether, there was no choice left to him. With a superhuman effort to appear calm and rational, he took her hand and gave it a quick squeeze.

'Can we forget all I've said this evening? Look on it as a moment of temporary derangement and start again as if nothing had happened?'

She hesitated, frowning. 'Are you sure that's wise?'

'What's wisdom got to do with it?' he said. 'It's what I'd like more than anything, if you agree.'

She nodded a little uncertainly.

'I promise I won't behave deplorably again,' he added.

'I wasn't thinking about that,' she said, collecting the soup bowls and carrying them out to the kitchen. 'Would you like some coffee?' she called to him.

'Not for me, thanks,' he said cheerfully from the open doorway. He swallowed the rest of his drink in one, all at once conscious of a desperate need to escape, to be alone where a pretence of normality was not necessary. A lump in his throat, composed of bitterness and despair, threatened to reduce him to ignominious blubbing.

'You need your sleep,' he told Kate when she returned. 'I must be going.'

'Must you?' She eyed him, her head on one side, her expression anxious: summing him up. 'You *will* be all right, Roly, won't you?'

'I'm fine.' He sketched a kiss on her forehead. 'A pity about the play. I got that wrong, too, didn't I?'

'It was funny in bits.'

'Dinner on Tuesday, perhaps?' he suggested, blundering towards the front door.

And then the door snapped shut behind him and he found himself outside, walking away from her into the biting east wind. The dampness on his face might have been rain or tears; whichever, it no longer mattered. He walked with his head lowered, like a bull weakened and distracted by the wounds from the picador's darts. The thought of his silent and empty house repelled rather than beckoned him home. On impulse, he took a taxi to a small club in Shepherds Market where the call-girls met in off-peak moments, and there he sat until the early hours, drinking his pain into temporary oblivion.

Chapter Two

In the kitchen of his flat in Battersea, Matt Protheroe was teaching his son poker. Jake's face was set in concentration as he scrutinized the list of rules beside him, jotted down by his father.

'See you!' he challenged.

Matt laid down his cards: two aces and the rest valueless. Jake slammed down his own.

'Full house!' he said in triumph. 'At least, I *think* it is, isn't it?'

'Two kings and three tens. I'll say it is, you devil.' Matt scooped up the kitty and put it in front of his son. 'And that's cleaned me out. How much have you made?'

Jake counted. 'Thirty pee,' he said, grinning.

'It's my expert tuition. You're getting very good at keeping an inscrutable expression.'

'What's inscrutable?'

'Dead-pan. Giving nothing away.' Matt got to his feet and crossed to the window. 'It's stopped raining. Let's take ourselves out.'

'Where to? Rowing on the lake?'

'Good idea, if you'd like to.'

'Great. Will I need a life-jacket?'

'I shouldn't think so,' Matt replied. 'It's the park, not the Solent; the water's probably no more than a foot deep.'

'Mum says—'

'Yes, I know and she's right, of course. She wouldn't approve of gambling, either. So that's two lots of rules we'll have broken, but I won't let you drown.'

'Shall I put the cards away?' Jake asked, guessing the answer.

'No, leave everything and go and get a sweater. We'll tidy up later.'

Jake obliged happily. 'Tidying up' was something that got postponed indefinitely in his father's establishment. Crockery and cutlery piled up by the sink. Sunday newspapers were strewn carelessly over floor and furniture, and there were stacks of books on every available flat surface. Only the large desk where he wrote was kept immaculate, pages of typescript neatly in order beside the word processor. Matt claimed he had a blitz once a week and restored the place to pristine glory, but Jake had never seen it. Life was too short to worry about a bit of clutter, so his father said; and there was no-one to argue with him like there had been when he lived at home. Forever impatient to move on to the next project, he seemed to exist at a permanent gallop. Kate called it having a low boredom threshold, whatever that meant; certainly Jake was not bored in Matt's company, there wasn't time.

In the slip of a room where he slept when staying the weekend, sharing it with a row of filing cabinets, he dug a jersey out of his overnight bag. Framed photographs hung on the walls, the product of his father's travels. They hung in fact on every wall of the flat like an art gallery; pictures of birds and beggars, slant-eyed children and old gnarled men and women, mountains and rivers and spectacular waterfalls. Jake thought them brilliant and never tired of Matt telling him stories of the places where each one had been taken. Having an

41

unusual and talented father gave him quite a lot of one-upmanship at school, where he embroidered Matt's life-style shamelessly, depicting him hacking his way through snake-infested jungles and shooting impossibly hazardous rapids. He had inherited Matt's old camera, but not his expertise. After several trips to Richmond Park and lessons from Matt in setting the distance and the light and shade mechanism, he still managed to cut the heads off a herd of deer and make the trees fuzzily out of focus. No, cameras were not for Jake. It was his father's writing that interested him. He was drawn like a bee to nectar by the desk and the computer and the neat and ever-rising stack of Matt's script; longing to touch the crisp white pages and to read the black professional lines of print. There was no law against him doing so: 'Read it,' Matt had said carelessly. 'As long as you keep the pages in order.' But there never seemed the chance for a good read, with his father constantly on the go: like now, with Matt calling to him to hurry up.

They walked to the lake through the park, where the trees were a froth of new April foliage, and cherry trees dripped fat clusters of pink blossom. Jake had to take two steps for each one of Matt's, who walked as quickly as he did everything else. Anyone observing them would have been in no doubt about their relationship: the similar slight, bony shape, the same thin faces with dark eyes under thatches of nearly black hair. A tattooed attendant held the rowing-boat steady while they clambered in, and shoved them away from the jetty with Matt at the oars and Jake sitting in the stern. A stiff breeze chopped the olive green water into wavelets that slapped against the sides.

'Can I row?' he asked when they were truly launched.

'Move to where I'm sitting,' Matt said. 'That's right; now I'll move to the stern. Put the oars back in the rowlocks, and off we go.'

It was not as easy as it looked. Jake struggled to get the two blades even in the water and pulled, and they proceeded slowly across the lake in an ungainly zig-zag.

'Take shorter strokes,' Matt told him. 'Don't dig so deep in the water.'

Jake did his best to comply, skimmed the surface, showered his father and lost an oar. Matt leaned over and caught it as it floated by.

'I'm no good at this,' Jake said in a defeated voice.

'Nonsense. Anything worth learning takes time,' Matt observed, changing places to sit beside him. 'We'll each take an oar until you've got the hang of it.'

After a quarter of an hour Jake tried again on his own, this time with success. 'I've got it! I've got it!' he shouted as they drove a straight course through a flotilla of ducks. 'Though I don't know if it's worth it,' he added. 'I don't get much chance to row.'

'You never know when it might come in useful. I've spent a good many hours in boats of all descriptions over the last few years, including canoes and rafts. It's as well to know what you're doing.' Matt relaxed on the hard wooden seat, one eye alert for the hazard of other craft. 'But then, you probably won't choose my way of life.'

Jake pictured a huge turbulent river and white water frothing round boulders, and a raft spinning down it like a cork, Matt controlling it expertly with nothing but a pole. His heart leapt in admiration. Then he remembered Kate's expression as they saw his father off on yet another flight, her face all screwed up from minding his going, and he thought of a pile of white typing paper.

'I want to be a writer,' he said.

43

'My kind of writing?' Matt enquired with interest.

'I don't think so. I'd like to write stories, ones I've made up in my head; not real ones like yours.'

'Fiction, in other words.'

'I expect so,' Jake agreed uncertainly.

'It's quite an ambition,' Matt remarked. 'A great deal more difficult to manage than travel. My background and characters are already there in the places I've visited. All I have to do is knit them together and try to make it amusing.'

'I've started, sort of.' Jake let the boat drift while he thought about it. 'I'm putting Roly's stories on the word processor.'

'Are these the famous Captain What-not sagas?'

'Captain Diehard,' Jake corrected him. 'He's terrifically good at making them up. I suppose it's cheating, really, my writing them down, because they're not mine at all; but I use my own words.'

'Roly,' Matt murmured thoughtfully. 'A spinner of yarns. It's a side of him I don't remember, although he could be very funny. You see a lot of him, don't you?' he asked casually.

'Yes. Whenever he comes to supper or takes Mum out. He does that quite often. He's great; much the nicest of Mum's friends.' Jake wanted to say: It's not the same as having *you* there all the time; when are you coming back? But he didn't, in case the answer was – never. 'You don't mind, do you?' he said instead.

'Mind?' Matt said, smiling at him. 'Why should I mind? I'm happy to know Mum isn't sitting around moping.' Privately he was surprised at Kate's choice of Roly as constant companion, and more than a little relieved that it was not some charismatic bastard on the prowl for an easy lay. 'He's a good chap, is Roly,' he added. 'Just the person to see she's all right. Pull on your left oar: we're in danger of ramming another boat.'

Jake glanced over his shoulder and started to row. 'Actually,' he said, 'I haven't seen him for a bit; he doesn't come round quite so often. I must ask Mum why.'

His father made no comment, thinking to himself: so that's how things are; the poor sod has fallen in love with her. Jake saw his eyebrows lift in quizzical understanding, and felt excluded from some sort of adult secret. A light drizzle had begun; Matt glanced at his watch.

'Once round that island, and then home, I think. Birgitta is going to drop in to cook us lunch, with any luck.'

Birgitta was already there when they arrived back, standing in the kitchen stirring something on the gas with a wooden spoon. She was Swedish, tall, with blond hair to her shoulders and a pair of long legs clad now in narrow white jeans. Turning down the flame, she gave them a dazzling smile, showing even and slightly prominent teeth.

'Hi, I'm making a really English lunch today, especially for Jake; lamb cutlets and cauliflower with that horrible white sauce you like.'

'Great! Thanks, Birgitta. What's for pudding?'

She flourished a cardboard cake box triumphantly. 'Meringues! These I haven't made because I don't know how, but they look good. It will be ready in ten minutes.'

'That's my girl.' Matt gave her a friendly slap on the bottom before disappearing to check for messages on the answerphone.

Jake had grown used to Birgitta being around the flat at odd moments. She wasn't the only girl, there were at least two others who appeared occasionally; all of them pretty and fun and willing to cook a meal, which Matt persuaded them to do with no apparent effort on his part. Jake guessed the idea was to provide him with a proper lunch instead of junk food, so that if Mum quizzed him about his diet, he could give a satisfactory answer. Sometimes, if the weather was bad, the girls would stay on in the afternoon and play cards, but more often than not Matt would dismiss whoever-it-was charmingly while he and Jake went off on a ploy of their own. Jake felt a bit sorry for the girls being made use of, although it was for this reason they did not seem to pose a threat. He thought it was unlikely any of them would stand in the way of his father deciding to come back home; they were not important enough, and that was all that mattered. Birgitta was there more often than the others. He could see her scent bottle on the glass shelf above the basin as he gave his hands a token wash before lunch. She had a habit of leaving it there more or less permanently, and Jake wondered if she and Matt ever did 'it' together; but the idea was so weird and awful to him that his mind shied away from the subject. His mother was a far bigger worry to him in any case: he did not quite understand why. Roly was the great stand-by; nothing really bad could happen to her so long as he was constantly with her.

After lunch it started to rain in earnest, and Matt reopened the poker school. Birgitta proved to be a skilled player and took everybody's money, but she insisted on returning Jake's thirty pee to him. Later they switched to Scrabble, Jake and Matt howling with unkind mirth at her spelling, and the game grew noisier and more ridiculous as the afternoon wore on. It was at moments like these that Jake had secretly to admit there were advantages to parents living apart.

Kate held the shop door open and watched her customer sail out and away with a feeling of immense relief. She let the professional smile slip from her face abruptly and began the task of tidying up after an hour and a half of trying to please. The centre table was piled high with sample swatches and pattern books, all of which had to be replaced in the correct order on rails and hooks. Monday mornings always seemed to bring difficult clients; this one had been indecisive, unable to choose between blues and yellows or pinks and greens for her bedroom curtains, and equally unresponsive to advice. Kate's head ached; holding a batch of materials over one arm, she switched on the electric kettle in the alcove with her free hand and called down the stairs to Isobel.

'Coffee.'

With or without the hassle of clients, Mondays were extra stressful, particularly when preceded by a weekend of having to see Matt: an inevitable part of his collecting and returning Jake. Ideally, they should never meet. A year had gone by almost to the day since they separated, and yet she had not adjusted to the arrangement. There was something painfully unnatural about the circumstances – the strained snatches of conversation, the offer of a drink, seldom accepted, the departing backview forever disappearing – that brought the worst out in her. It was as if they had become strangers, had never lain in the same bed, made love, joked, laughed, quarrelled harmlessly or gone through childbirth together. She felt frozen out by coldness, miserably alone and horribly aware of still wanting and needing him. Before each of their brief encounters she would school herself to be cheerful and non-aggressive, but for all her efforts, the resentment would build up in her, making her snappish. And for what purpose, to what end? They were no nearer coming to a decision about their future than at the start. Before long there would have to be a discussion, she knew that, and both dreaded and welcomed it.

Isobel appeared from the basement office, clutching a bundle of invoices. 'Did you order the Colefax & Fowler chintz for Lady Geddes? I can't find any trace of it here.'

'I'm sure I did,' Kate said, knowing quite well she had forgotten. She hid her lying expression over the kettle, spooned instant coffee into two mugs and added water. 'I'll check directly I've cleared the mess away.'

'There's no sign of it on the PC,' Isobel pursued her, probing relentlessly.

A short pause; Kate's head throbbed dully. It suddenly seemed easier to confess her sin than try to flannel her way out of it.

'There wouldn't be,' she said, handing Isobel one of the mugs. 'I rather think I completely forgot. I'm sorry.'

Isobel seldom lost her temper; sarcasm was her weapon. She eyed Kate coldly down her high-bridged, aquiline nose which was intimidating in itself. 'Then perhaps you'd better go and do it now before you have another memory lapse,' she said, starting to hang samples on the rails with swift efficiency.

Kate disappeared to the haven of the office like a junior schoolgirl ordered by a prefect to find a mislaid tennis racket. That situation had indeed once been reality, for she and Isobel had shared a term at school together, she in the lowest form of all while Izzy lorded it in the Sixth. Nothing had changed, Kate decided; Isobel still adhered to the original pecking order, although given to sudden bursts of disconcerting kindness. Kate carried out her mission and returned to find Isobel drinking her coffee and staring thoughtfully out of the back window.

'Would you say,' she asked, 'that I'm overworking you? Loading you with too much responsibility?' It was said without sarcasm.

'No, of course not, Izzy. It's what I'm here for, isn't it? Why do you ask?'

'Because you're all over the place lately, darling; distracted, the mind elsewhere. Would you agree?'

'What you mean is, I'm bringing my troubles to work,' Kate said. 'I didn't realize it was so obvious. Are you giving me the sack?'

'Don't be moronic, darling. You're a partner, not my employee.'

'Only a small part of a partner,' Kate pointed out. 'You pay me a salary.'

'Stop splitting hairs, and let's sit down for a moment, for God's sake.' They perched opposite each other on the upright chairs used for clients. 'Of course I don't want you to leave, silly girl; I'd merely like to know what's wrong. Even if not directly connected with the shop it's having its effect.'

Kate sighed, longing for one of her very occasional cigarettes and knowing it was out of the question in Isobel's company. 'I'm tired of living a semi-detached existence,' she said; 'being married with none of the bonuses. I expected to find deep relief when Matt and I parted: no more hassle, no more rows. And I suppose for a short while it did seem rather peaceful without him. But it didn't last, and now each day is more difficult to get through than the one before, like wading through mud wearing gumboots.' She traced the pattern on a square of chintz with her finger, absently. 'If we were to get back together again, it probably wouldn't work. The basic problems would still be there; as it is, I can't even be nice to him. So it's stalemate, you see.'

Isobel made a 'hmph' noise. 'I'm probably the last person to give you advice: I never had that problem with my husbands. The first one bolted and the second I made redundant without hesitation. But you know the story.' She studied Kate calmly across the table. 'I suspect it's the sex you miss?' she suggested.

'No, it's not,' Kate said firmly. 'At least, only partly. It's Matt I miss. I really liked being married to him; so much so I couldn't bear him being away half the time.'

'He won't change, if that's what you're hoping,' Isobel pointed out, 'and neither will you. If it were me, I'd admit defeat; but I don't suppose for a moment you'll agree.'

'I can't,' Kate protested, 'throw away eleven years of marriage just like that.'

Their life together had not always been an endless series of departures and homecomings. They had met at a photographic exhibition; a mutual pick-up, homing in on each other in instant recognition. At the time, she was working as girl Friday for an interior design magazine, and he as an all-purpose reporter for an evening newspaper. Within weeks she had left the flat she shared with two girlfriends and moved into his own, rather more basic home, incurring her mother's alarm and disapproval. Those early, unencumbered years seemed blissful in retrospect: difficulties such as the shortage of money and the crumbling state of the flat did not matter when they were young and inseparable. She taught herself to cook and he took studio portraits, mainly of children, to supplement their income, so that the sitting-room was invariably littered with cameras and white boards and squeaky toys to keep toddlers amused. The work bored him, and when they could afford it, they went on cheap bucket-shop holidays abroad, where he could indulge in the kind of photography at which he excelled: of people and places and poverty. He exhibited, won an award, and was taken on by one of the Sunday papers to edit their travel section. That was how the serious travelling had started. Shortly afterwards they had married, and moved to the house in Denbigh Street where Kate still lived: a startling wedding present from Matt's father, domiciled with his third wife in France and hardly ever seen or heard.

For a long time Matt's absences had not worried her; she was bursting with pride and enthusiasm for what he was doing. Besides, occasionally she would go with him, finances and the prospective territory permitting, putting up with often primitive conditions for the sake of excitement and participation. Then Jake had been born, a much-wanted baby, Matt keeping his promise and arriving back from Peru in time to hold her hand and urge his son into the world. She had been too engrossed in looking after this squash-faced, dark-haired replica of Matt to have time to think about anything else; and Matt, when he was there, did his fair share of nappy-changing and getting up in the middle of the night. Childhood followed on babyhood, followed by school, and she went back to work, in order to clear her head of domestic woolliness rather than from necessity. Matt had increased his workload, writing articles for various travel and photographic magazines, and in spare moments making notes for his intended book. Their life had seemed complete.

So where did it all go wrong? she wondered. It had not been a sudden thing, more a slow and insidious trickle of dissatisfaction which infiltrated her morale, starting around the time when Jake was five. She wanted another baby before he grew any older. 'Wonderful idea!' Matt said vaguely in answer to her suggestion, and disappeared into his darkroom or to type away at his notes. But nothing happened, not for want of trying. She became anxious, and in her anxiety developed a tendency to blame him: his constant long-haul trips were making her tense and preventing her from conceiving. She began to dread his going; to feel that if she watched just one more aircraft take off with him aboard it, she would fall to screaming. Only a percentage of his travel was on behalf of his newspaper: the rest was for his satisfaction alone, and the fact irked her. What she had once applauded as being romantic and enterprising, she now saw as selfishness. She confronted him, starting by trying to explain how she felt and ending up losing her temper. 'What do you expect me to do?' he asked, exasperated. 'It's my work, my life. I can't just drop it for something else.'

'What about *my* life, *Jake's* life?' she had shouted at him. 'Or don't we count?'

It was the first of many rows; one-sided, for Matt refused to fight by her rules, withdrawing into himself instead, his thin face white with suppressed anger. They could have, should have, halted there; drawn breath, discussed the situation like adults and perhaps reached a compromise. But she had been like a dog with a bone: once having started to gnaw, she found herself unable to stop. She hated herself for this senseless destruction, hated him for making no attempt to prevent it. There came a time when there was no turning back: too many unforgivable words had been exchanged for either of them to declare peace. And now that a year had lapsed, and she felt secretly ready for a tentative move towards reconciliation, he was unreachable; fenced off behind this awful barrier of coldness, defying her to hurt him again.

'I don't want to throw it all away,' Kate repeated to Isobel, 'but I can't think how to revive it. I no longer have access to Matt's mind or to what's happening in his life. For all I know he may have found someone else. There are other women—'

'How do you know for sure?'

'Jake,' Kate said. 'He doesn't mean to, but he lets things slip out: you know how it is with children.'

'I don't, but I can imagine,' Isobel said drily.

'There's someone called Birgitta . . .' Kate's voice trailed away.

'Well, you surely don't expect him to live like a monk, do you? It's too much to ask of any normal man. Not that there is such a thing, in my opinion.' Isobel held the theory that all men were shits. She leaned her chin on well-manicured hands and regarded Kate. 'You could of course retaliate and find yourself a lover.'

Kate thought about the possibility and discarded it without bothering to reply.

'On second thoughts, perhaps not,' Isobel agreed to this silent dissent. She rose to her feet with an air of bringing the conversation to a close. 'Nothing stays the same,' she added. 'Fate has a way of crashing in and rearranging things whether you like it or not. I'm not sure whether or not that's any comfort. Meanwhile,' she picked up some of the samples still lying across the table, 'friends are a sound investment. What about that amiable and harmless man you had in tow? Roland – something?'

'Roly,' Kate sighed, reaching for the empty coffee mugs. 'Even Roly,' she said, 'is not without his problems.'

Twice a year, in the spring and autumn, Roly gave a drinks party. It would be May in two weeks' time and he was checking the guest list, seated at his desk looking out on the mews. The evenings were drawing out and at seven-thirty the street lamps were not yet lit. Later, much later, when it was dark, he would leave the house. Meanwhile, he might as well keep busy rather than watch indifferent television while he tortured himself with imaginings of Kate.

He did not particularly want to give a party; but he realized the importance of friends if he wished to keep his sanity, and recently he had neglected them. Before his dreams had been shattered, Kate had occupied his life and thoughts to the exclusion of other people; and afterwards, after that dreadful night when she had killed all hope with a few gentle but deadly words, he had lost the incentive to contact anyone. However, he always had people in for drinks around this time of year, and he found routine oddly comforting: something to do, no doubt, with being brought up by a grandmother. If he had been called upon for reminiscences of school holidays, he would have recited a list of rituals: meals on the dot, church every Sunday, bed at half-past seven until he was thirteen, and so on. There were other memories evocative of childhood, of course: a large country house smelling of beeswax and sweet peas, a garden with sloping lawns and a cedar tree, bare feet leaving prints in the dew on summer mornings, a shaggy pony who bit and refused to be caught, bread-and-butter pudding and Granny's chocolate cake which sagged deliciously in the middle. It had not been a bad upbringing, merely a remote one devoid of companionship. He remembered a constant ache of longing not only for someone to play with, but for a tangible show of affection. His grandmother had not been unkind, but she came from a generation that did not believe in demonstrativeness, and any hugs and kisses that were going were confined to the cook when she was in a good temper. There had been children at the Rectory for a while, a large and wonderfully unruly mob with an untidy garden where he joined in hectic games of football and hide-and-seek; but the Rector had been moved to another parish and Roly was left to his own devices. Once, he recalled, his grandmother had allowed him to invite someone to stay in the summer holidays; a boy from school named Saunders, and virtually his only friend. Homesick and doubtless scared of the

54

autocratic old woman, Saunders had wet his bed, and although Grandmother was surprisingly understanding about it, he had not been asked again.

Roly added another name to his list, and wondered whether a more normal childhood with conventional parents would have altered him as a person. Would he have married at the age of twenty-eight or thereabouts, to an equally conventional girl, and had several children of his own by now; rather than waiting until forty to become hopelessly obsessed with someone out of reach? He nibbled the end of his pen, watching the growing darkness outside and the lamps now shining orange on the cobbles. There were still two hours to pass before setting out in his car for Denbigh Street to take up his vigil. His thoughts strayed to his mother, who had been elusive in the extreme. One of a group of actresses who had never quite made it to the top but were nevertheless seldom out of work; she would make infrequent and short-lived appearances at his grandmother's house, loaded with unsuitable presents for him and upsetting the even tenor of the household. His grandmother disapproved of her daughter-in-law, blaming her, mostly in acid silence, for the break-up of her marriage to her son, Roly's father, whose total absence was a mystery to Roly for most of his childhood. Later he had learned there had been some kind of insider-dealing scandal, ending in a short prison sentence and his father's disappearance to start a new life in South Africa. Lack of a father did not worry Roly: you do not miss what you have never had.

He idolized his mother, putting the press cuttings and photographs she sent him in an album and watching her with nervous excitement whenever she appeared on television, however small the part. She represented another world; an unbelievably exotic world that he hardly understood but longed to be

55

a part of. Her visits were dotted about the growing-up years like special occasions: long-awaited and quickly over. He dogged her footsteps while she was there, dragging her on walks to see his private hideouts. They must have looked an odd couple, he decided in retrospect: he an overweight little boy squeezed into jeans a size too small – she never got the size right – and she teetering across the lawn in high heels. Bored with the country, she would pack him into her small scarlet sports car and drive to a pub where she fed him packets of crisps and Coca-Cola, and let him have a puff of her cigarette. 'One day before long,' she would say, ruffling his hair, 'I'm going to make enough money to put my roots down, and then we'll be together. You'd like that, wouldn't you, sweetie?' And she would hug him to her, enveloping him in a cloud of scent and false hopes. It did not happen, of course; whatever her temporary home, and whoever she shared it with, and both were constantly changing, Roly was not included. Her roots had only been dug in recently at sixty-five when she bought a small flat in Ladbroke Grove. He visited her there every so often; still attractive at seventy, she had lost none of her independence, occasionally playing granny roles in television dramas and boasting to him of a lover. He found the last idea vaguely distasteful; no longer, thank God, in thrall to her, he saw her for what she was: a gaunt and ageing woman who had shifted all responsibility for her child onto the shoulders of another old woman. The magic of her was a mere memory; the fact of her defection had taken its place, and his adulation transferred elsewhere.

It was strange, he thought, that he had been brought up by women and yet remained largely ignorant of how they ticked. In his late teens, when he learned to drive, he had been invited to houses within striking distance, where he lumbered amiably about a tennis court or a croquet lawn amongst groups of what his grandmother called 'young people'. He had never grasped the rules or technique of the mating game that seemed to come naturally to other men of his age. Watching them chatting up the Carolines and Camillas and Serenas, he tried to learn the secret without success. Innately shy, he would resort to the clowning that was to become his shield against ridicule. After all, one might as well be professionally ridiculous and have people laugh with rather than at one, if that was to be one's lot in life. Born before sex education became the norm in schools, he knew little about the mechanics of it; emerging from an interview with the headmaster when he was twelve almost as mystified as when he went in. An afternoon spent with Elaine around the same age had been far more instructive. The daughter of his grandmother's gardener, and a year older, she had explained in basic English and with a certain amount of demonstration, hidden away in one of his lairs beneath a vast rhododendron bush. Nothing much had happened, but it was the cuddling he remembered, the warm comforting proximity of another human being. Later in life, when he found occasional solace in the arms of a friendly prostitute, he would be reminded of the Elaine incident, experiencing the same sense of undemanding well-being in which he was not expected to prove himself. Until he met Kate, and she had become the focal point of his existence.

In many ways, nothing had changed between them. For a while after the disastrous evening of rejection, he had kept his distance and cut down on their meetings, too embarrassed and distraught to face them. But she had smoothed over his awkwardness by the simple expedient of behaving as if nothing had happened, and gradually they had slipped back into their old arrangement of seeing each other once or twice a week. This friendly simplicity that was so much a part of her charm, now secretly hurt him; stressing, as it did, the yawning difference in their feelings. The changes that had taken place were all within him. The longing for her was still there in all its aching intensity; but without hope to support it, it had turned into a sort of stubborn determination to hold onto what he had of her. The possibility of there being another man in her life had grown in his mind until it became a compulsion to find out. There was little he could do about it if it proved to be fact; but in a strange sense it would be a relief to have his rejection explained in this way rather than for reasons of his own inadequacy. So far, and he had been watching the house for some weeks, her home-comings had been unrewarding. She usually returned from an evening out on her own in a taxi; occasionally by car, when a man would see her safely through her front door and depart immediately with a wave; the actions of a polite host, no more. But the act of prying on her, he discovered, was addictive as a drug and he had become hooked; finding a curious mixture of excitement and masochistic self-loathing by hiding in the shadows, waiting to be hurt afresh.

Glancing at his watch, he realized he was sitting in darkness. He switched on his desk lamp and debated eating supper at home or at the local restaurant. In the end he made himself a mushroom omelette and a green salad and ate it in front of the television, getting in on the second half of an incomprehensible American detective series. When that was finished he cleared away, put some papers in his briefcase ready for the next morning, and, at ten-thirty, left the house to drive to Denbigh Street: his hands growing clammy on the steering-wheel and his heartbeat quickening the nearer he came to his destination.

* * *

Kate stood in her bra and pants searching listlessly through her clothes cupboard for a suitable dress. The recent conversation with Matt had left her feeling drained and frustrated, as if she had been talking through plate glass and getting no reaction. For some reason it had taken courage to ring him; but one of them had to make the first move towards a proper, constructive meeting, and since he showed no signs of doing so, it had fallen to her out of a driving necessity.

'Hello, Kate,' he had answered; and she wondered how he always managed to sound friendly and cool in the same breath.

Promptly losing her nerve, she said, 'It's half-term at the end of May. I'd rather like to know whether you want Jake for part of it. Otherwise I'll take him somewhere, probably down to Ma and Pa.'

There was a pause. 'Can you give me a day or two before letting you know? There's a chance I may be away.'

'Oh? Where?' The question slipped from her involuntarily.

'China: if I go at all.'

'I thought you were writing,' she said, feeling a shadow of the old wrench of parting.

'I am, but there are one or two places I want to revisit.'

'I see.' Nothing had changed, she thought, nor was it likely to. Taking a breath, she said, 'There *are* things we should discuss, Matt.'

'Such as?'

'Us, principally. And there's Jake's education. He'll be eleven next birthday: it's time we decided on the next school.'

'I agree,' he replied pleasantly. 'Why don't we have a talk the next time I collect him?'

'No,' she said, getting quietly furious. 'None of this can be discussed in front of him, particularly

59

about us. I want a proper meeting, just the two of us, please.' She added, 'It's a year since we separated, in case you hadn't realized.'

'I had, actually,' he told her. 'Let's meet, by all means. But we won't achieve much if you're going to lose your temper.'

'I am *not* losing it.'

'Oh?' he said maddeningly. 'I thought I could already detect it in your voice. Let's face it, Kate, you do have a very short fuse these days; that's half the problem.'

And with good reason, she muttered to herself silently. What about the other half, his pig-headedness, his refusal to budge an inch in her direction? She took another deep breath.

'The last thing I want is a row,' she said with careful control. 'All I'm suggesting is a calm discussion to try and sort out the future. But it's no use if you're not interested—'

'Why shouldn't I be?'

'You don't sound it.'

'Don't you think,' he said, 'this conversation is becoming rather childish? I'll come round and we'll go out to supper one evening, OK? Only do you mind if we postpone it for ten days or so? I'm on a tricky chapter of the book and I'd like to get it finished.'

'I don't mind,' she answered untruthfully, dreading the outcome of their talking and hoping to get it over with immediately.

'That's settled, then. I'll call you.' He hesitated. 'Everything all right otherwise; Jake and so on?'

'Quite all right, thank you.'

'Good,' he said. 'See you, then,' and the receiver his end of the line clicked down like a curt dismissal.

She took a dress off its hanger and laid it on the bed, eyeing it dispiritedly. It had been silly of her to make the call before she was due at Roly's party; she was no longer in the mood for it. The distance between herself and Matt seemed all at once unbridgeable, sapping any hope and confidence she might have had for sorting themselves out. What did she expect to achieve anyway by discussion? What point was there in getting back together if the same arguments, the same recriminations were to be repeated over and over again? It was blind folly to imagine they could return to the blissful days of early marriage. Starting again meant starting where they had left off, and that required compromise and forgiveness which she had begun to doubt either of them could muster. A year apart lay behind them, dividing them psychologically as well as physically; communication confined to the minimum. Heaven only knew what emotional changes Matt had experienced in that time. Looking back, her own year stretched away from her bleakly, twelve months of keeping going, of not moving backwards or forwards, like treading water to stay afloat. She had a sudden enormous longing for something cataclysmic and wonderful to happen that would propel her out of this rut and open up a whole new vista. And pigs might fly, she told herself as she wriggled her hips into the narrow black dress. Happiness was not bestowed by divine right; count your blessings, she continued to lecture, which in her case were Jake, a job she enjoyed, an attractive place to live and enough money to survive without sleepless nights.

She closed the zip on the dress as far up her back as she could reach and regarded the result critically in the tall looking-glass; deciding that it looked rather naked with its shoe-string straps for a chilly May evening, but that she did not have the energy to change, nor to put her shoulder-length hair up, which was what the outfit demanded. She added large pearl-cluster earrings, then went upstairs to Jake's room to say good night.

'Wow!' he said, turning from the word processor to gaze at her; adding flatly, 'Your bosoms show.'

'Fasten the zip for me, please, then they won't.' She squatted beside him while he fumbled. 'There. How's that?'

'Better; only it does look rather like underclothes, that dress.'

'Don't, Jake. You're making me nervous.' She bent to kiss him and he flung his arms round her in a hug.

'You look great, honestly,' he promised. He felt quite happy about her going because the party was Roly's, and she would be taken care of. 'Helga and me are going to watch a creepy old movie.'

'Helga and I. If you're going to be a writer, smarten up the grammar. You'll have bad dreams.'

'I shan't.'

'Any messages for Roly?'

'Tell him I'm putting the last Captain Diehard story on the word processor and I need some more, please.' He laced bare feet round the rungs of the chair. 'I wish he'd asked me to the party,' he said.

'You'd be terribly bored,' she told him.

'Is Daddy going to be there?'

'I don't think so.'

'He's Roly's friend, so he should be.'

'I must go,' she said, dodging the impossibility of explaining why not. 'Don't stay up too late, darling.'

The last of Roly's guests drifted away at nine-thirty, leaving behind them the hush of a room recently packed solid with bodies and suddenly vacated. Kate stayed to the end because she had promised to do so, offering to help Roly clear up. Now, it appeared there was no need; the two girls who had produced very good small eats were moving about the room retrieving glasses and piling them on trays.

There was something infinitely depressing about the aftermath of drinks parties, Kate thought; one spent a lot of time and money preparing for two and half hours of unmemorable conversation, with nothing to show for it at the finish but dirty glasses and aching feet. Only three other guests remained, slumped on the sofa like beached whales: her brother Charlie and his wife Stella, and a man called Niall Hunter whom Kate had recognized from the past without being able to place him. Roly was still standing, restless and rumpled from the strains of playing host. 'Did it go all right, d'you think?' he was asking anxiously. 'Did they have enough to drink?'

There were murmurs of reassurance. Kate sat down in an armchair and eased the shoes off her feet, wondering whether, if Roly was not in need of assistance or her company, she could make a getaway without hurting his feelings. Charlie was talking about them all going out to dinner which she did not feel inclined to do. Not that she had anything against Charlie and Stella, but she had been pinioned in a corner with her sister-in-law for a large portion of the evening and had exhausted all suitable topics of conversation. In Stella's case, these were mostly confined to affairs of the village where they lived, and of which she was a staunch pillar. Mostly she talked and Kate listened, with the occasional 'Really?' or 'Heavens!' thrown in, while descriptions of fund-raising for the church roof and the village hall, and plans for the July fête flowed on and on; until her eyes had glazed over and wandered for a moment to the head and shoulders of a man. The face, too young for the completely grey hair that topped it, was vaguely familiar. Disconcertingly, he stared back at her and she looked away hurriedly, in time to hear Stella say, 'And when are you going to come down to us? It's truly ages since we've seen you and Jake.'

Thoroughly cornered, Kate said, 'It would be

lovely. How about the weekend after next? I haven't got my diary on me, but I'm almost sure—'

Stella had found her own and was already writing in it. 'There! I've put you down for Sunday.' She touched Kate's arm, her brown eyes full of commiseration as if Kate was facing a serious operation rather than a marriage problem. 'We *do* worry about you, you know,' she said.

'There's no need. I'm fine,' Kate assured her robustly, and wondered how on earth she was going to persuade Jake, who found Stella's and Charlie's twin daughters boring, that the visit was a necessary evil.

Roly had rescued her eventually, easing himself between chattering groups and propelling her away to meet a man and a woman having a heated argument about hunting. They casually acknowledged Kate's presence before continuing where they had left off as if she was not there, leaving her free to gaze around the room. The man with the grey hair had disappeared; the familiarity of him nagged at her gently, her memory refusing to divulge any clues as to where or when she might have met him. He was not easily forgettable; his nose, in particular, badly broken at some time in his life, gave him a certain pugilistic attraction. Deep at the back of her mind she connected him with something reprehensible, but that might easily have been due to his looks. She became aware of someone at her elbow proffering a bottle of champagne and turning, found him standing over her. Startled, she watched while he filled her glass.

'You don't remember me, do you?' he said without preamble.

'I do, actually, but I can't think from where—'

'You were sharing a flat with a friend of mine, Sally Beamish. Rather a long time ago.'

'Of course.' Kate had a sudden recollection of

bachelor-girl days, and Sally, a pale waif-like blonde with straight silky hair and a propensity for unhappy liaisons. 'You're Nigel – no, Niall – is that right?'

'Niall Hunter. And you are Kate Brownlow.'

'I'm Kate Protheroe now.'

'Ah yes. Married to Matthew Protheroe.'

'How did you know?'

'Someone must have told me,' he said. 'I read his articles from time to time.' He looked at her as though summing her up. 'You haven't changed,' he added. 'Not a fleck of grey in the hair, hardly a line on the face, even smile lines. But then, you didn't smile much as far as I remember, or certainly not at me.'

'Probably not,' Kate retorted, stung into retaliation by these personal statements. 'I was worried about Sally.'

'You disapproved?'

'Of what you were doing to her, yes. You gave her a hard time.'

'There are two sides to every story. Sally was a born victim.'

'That excuse ranks as nil,' Kate said. 'I lived with her, remember?'

It all came back to her now; Niall Hunter appearing at the flat when it pleased him, drinking their limited supply of drink and cadging meals; Sally watching him with adoring eyes, hopelessly besotted; until quite abruptly he wasn't to be seen again, without explanation. There had followed evening after evening of Sally willing the telephone to ring and bursting into tears when it did, and it was not for her; and then her pregnancy scare, for although she was on the pill, she was forgetful about taking it. It turned out to be a false alarm, but not before they had gone through a week of hell, when the flat was scattered with sodden tissues and Kate had mentally castrated Niall a dozen times. Poor Sally's gullibility in falling for so obvious an uncaring bastard had irritated her, but she had understood it. There was a certain animal attraction attached to the wretched man, which Kate had grudgingly admitted to herself in more honest moments. Why this incident, which had happened so long ago, should bother her now she could not imagine. She put it down to what Matt had termed her 'short fuse', and reminding herself that this was Roly's party and she should behave, took a sip of her drink.

'You look rather professional with that bottle,' she remarked. 'One hand behind your back and so on.'

'I *am* professional. My firm is doing the catering this evening,' he replied. 'I must press on, but we'll meet up again'; and giving her a last appraising look, he turned his back and was gone, moving expertly round the packed room.

Now, she wriggled her stockinged feet in their welcome freedom and listened while Charlie tried to plan the rest of the evening without success. No-one, it seemed, wanted dinner; reluctantly, he and Stella disappeared to find their own amusement, closely followed by Niall Hunter, and Kate and Roly were left alone.

'I thought,' he said while they washed up the last few glasses, 'that it would be more peaceful to have supper on our own; just the two of us.'

'I'm too tired, Roly, and not really hungry; too full of those marvellous vol-au-vents.'

'We needn't go out. I could make scrambled eggs here.'

'Thanks, but not tonight.'

'That's all right,' he said, folding the tea towel carefully; 'not to worry.' But she could see by the droop of his shoulders that he was disappointed. How horribly easy it was to make him feel rebuffed. It was this vulnerability that prevented her from tackling him on the subject of his nocturnal prowling as she would have liked to have done. His shadowed observance of her coming and going had escalated; hardly a late evening's return to her house went by without her noticing the parked car, his shape huddled in the front seat. Such irrational behaviour was disturbing; she had begun to be scared, not for herself but his state of mind. Facing him with the facts seemed the most likely deterrent, but this was definitely not the right moment; not that there was *ever* a right one, she reflected sadly.

'Tell you what,' she said, 'I'm dying for my one cigarette of the day. Let's sit and have a post-mortem of your party while I smoke it.'

He brightened a little, made mugs of coffee, and they sat drinking it in the lamplight and discussing his guests.

'The food was delicious,' she said.

'It wasn't bad, was it?' he agreed. 'I've never used caterers before, but it saves a lot of hassle. Well worth the extra expenditure. Niall Hunter's firm; the chap with grey hair and a crooked nose, if you happened to notice him.'

'Yes,' she said. 'I've met him already, years ago,' and explained briefly, leaving out the details. 'Is he a friend?'

'Not a friend, exactly; more of an acquaintance. In fact,' he took her empty mug from her, 'I don't care for him much. And he's got a dodgy reputation where women are concerned,' he added.

'Let this be a warning,' Kate said, smiling.

'Why the interest?' he asked suspiciously.

'Oh, Roly!' she sighed. 'It was meant to be a joke.' Putting a hand on his arm, she said, 'You used to be a great joker. Don't lose it all, please.'

He rubbed his eyes between thumb and forefinger. 'No, no, you're right. I suppose I'm tired.'

'Of course.' She got to her feet. 'I shouldn't have

stayed.'

'Kate . . .' His voice was strained.

'Yes?'

'Nothing,' he said. 'It isn't important. I'll walk you to a taxi.'

She gathered up her bag. 'Come and see Jake soon. He needs another story from you. He's putting them all on computer and making them into a book.'

When her taxi drew up outside her house, a man was standing by the front door, pushing something through the letter-box. He ran lightly down the steps as she reached the pavement and she saw it was Niall Hunter.

'What are you doing here?' she asked, far from pleased and with a nasty intuition that he might become intrusive.

'Putting an invitation through your door,' he replied, lounging against the basement railings and smiling at her.

'What sort of an invitation?'

'Not a social one. My flat needs refurbishing, and since I gather you are an interior decorator, I thought you might like to give me your ideas. For a price, of course,' he said.

'I'll have to ask my partner,' Kate replied dismissively. 'We're very busy.' She looked at him in the semi-darkness. 'Why didn't you telephone me? Why bother to come round?'

'I don't have your number, only your address.'

'You seem to have an awful lot of information about me,' she remarked crossly.

He grinned. 'I met a helpful woman this evening – your sister-in-law, I think – who gave me your address but stopped short at the phone number. Of course, if I'd know you were coming home so quickly, I could have asked you in person.' He paused. 'But

I imagined you having a long and enjoyable dinner with Roly,' he said blandly.

Damn Stella for rabbiting on, thought Kate.

'I was tired, and so was Roly.' She searched in her bag for her keys and drew them out pointedly. 'Which is why I am about to go to bed.' She marched up the steps. 'Good night, Niall. I'll let you know about your flat, if you're serious.'

'I'm serious about a lot of things,' he said, 'that I'm not given credit for.'

'Such as?' She put her key in the lock.

'Friendship, for one; particularly between you and me.'

'That will be difficult,' she said from the open doorway, 'considering we have a personality problem.'

'Now you've lost me: explain.'

'I don't mean to be rude,' she said, about to belie her words, 'but I really don't like you very much.'

'The fact hadn't escaped my notice,' he answered, unperturbed. 'And I want to rectify it if you'll give me the chance.'

'Listen.' She leaned wearily against the lintel, wondering why she bothered with this unedifying exchange. 'I have marriage difficulties, a son to bring up, a demanding job. I certainly do not need any further complications in my life, and something tells me that you would be one of them.'

He sighed. 'That's a great pity,' he said. 'I could prove otherwise if you'd let yourself get to know me better.'

'Give me one good reason why I should.'

'Because it's a very necessary preliminary,' he told her, 'if we are to become lovers; which of course we shall.'

'You're mad!' The breath knocked out of her, she grasped the door preparing to slam it, remembering a sleeping Jake just in time. 'And another thing: you

69

can forget about your bloody decorating!' she hissed into the night.

A light laugh was all she received in reply. He was already unlocking his car door without a backward glance.

Chapter Three

Two weeks later, Kate was working on a design of Niall's flat. Coloured sketches of interiors, or visuals as they were known in the trade, were not a new concept, but it had been her idea to introduce them into Isobel's business and one that she had embraced enthusiastically. The late afternoon was warm and still, and Kate sat in the garden, her paints and brushes spread out around her on the wooden table, engrossed in her work. She enjoyed seeing the colours of walls and curtains spring to life; took a pride in detailed accuracy. Up at the other end of the paved rectangle, Jake was hitting a tennis ball, attached by elastic to a solid pole, against the back wall with the repeated and hypnotic twang of a racket. If the elastic snapped as it had been known to do, the ball was likely to break a window or wreak havoc amongst the pots of paint, but it was a risk Kate was prepared to take. After all, the garden belonged to both of them and he needed to let off steam after school. It sounded to her as if he were whacking the ball with particular ferocity, perhaps working off the mood he had been in for several days; not exactly morose, but silent and withdrawn like his father when faced with a problem. His angst sprang from an unfortunate first encounter with Niall; she was aware of that and sympathized since most of the blame lay with Niall, but felt singularly unable to cope with the situation, apart from preventing it happening again.

The affair with Niall which had begun ten days previously, was totally unintentional on her part. Nothing could have been further from her mind, or indeed from what she could have sworn were her desires. She had not desired him at all. If she felt anything for him, it was a mild contempt mixed with a grudging admission of a certain limited attraction; hardly a propitious basis for a love affair. Even now, it seemed as though what she had done was purely accidental, an automatic response to despairing over her marriage, to feeling the gap between herself and Matt forever widening. That, she had told herself, was no excuse. She had committed every solecism which only a fortnight ago she herself would have condemned; slipping into bed with someone she scarcely knew while still attached, emotionally and technically, to the father of her child; and all without coercion. She was far too old to plead seduction. There was no redeeming feature about what had happened; not even that of having fallen hopelessly in love. She had been determined to end it before it had time to escalate, to write it off as a moment of stupidity. This, she now realized, would have been a great deal easier to achieve if she had not enjoyed it. The fact shamed her: there was something ultimately sleazy about enjoying sex with a man one mistrusted.

She drew a fine stroke of pale yellow paint within the pencilled lines of the curtains, and wiped the brush dry on a rag. How much better it would have been if the situation had not been allowed to come about in the first place; if she had stuck to her resolution and refused the redecoration of his flat. On the night of Roly's party, when she had shut the door on Niall and his galling prediction, and her initial temper had died down, she dismissed

72

him from her mind as not worth another thought. Over the next two days he kept up a persistent on-slaught of telephone calls which she parried firmly and equally persistently. Until, unwisely, she had happened to mention it to Isobel, passing it off as a mildly funny story. Isobel had regarded it in quite a different light.

'Really, Kate! Turning down business because you don't like the clients is a sure-fire way to bankruptcy. I suggest you think again, darling.'

'I suppose *you* wouldn't handle it, then?' Kate had said.

'Oh! Don't be so feeble,' had been Isobel's crisp reply.

So Kate had found herself, after a telephone call to Niall in which she made it clear that it was only at Isobel's instigation, searching for his flat in a tree-lined avenue of Hampstead. He occupied the whole of the first floor of a large converted house, self-contained behind his own front door, which he opened as she struggled up the stairs with armfuls of patterns and swatches held in front of her like professional armour. He was charm itself, ushering her inside with words of gratitude and relieving her of the load she was carrying. All the brash assurance he had previously displayed had disappeared, care-fully tucked away – or so she suspected – behind an altogether gentler and more open persona.

'I really am grateful,' he said more than once. 'I've been meaning to give this place a face-lift ever since I moved in, and I don't know where to start.'

They toured the flat, pausing in each room while she made assessments and suggestions. The rooms were sizeable with moulded ceilings and tall sash-windows, the décor unexciting rather than in need of repair. He agreed readily with all she said, and she was slightly startled that money appeared to be no object. It was easy to become enthusiastic about the decorative possibilities of the place; before long her reservations were forgotten and her thoughts entirely occupied by colour schemes and textures. They returned at last to the living-room, and she started to drape materials over the sofa while he made coffee for them both.

'You don't have to decorate everywhere,' she said, taking the proffered mug from him. 'The flat is in good nick. The spare room, for instance; you could live with magnolia paint on the walls in there, and the bathroom.'

'Perhaps,' he said. 'But the curtains must go. I bought them with the flat to save time, and they're appalling, you must admit.'

'It's going to cost you an arm and a leg,' she warned him.

'In for a penny, in for a pound.' He smiled at her, and she noticed for the first time his eyes, pale blue and set curiously wide apart. 'Send me an estimate and if I don't have a heart attack, we'll go ahead.'

She drank some coffee. 'Catering must be lucrative,' she observed.

'Not bad. It's not my sole source of income, as it happens; I have other projects,' he said without elaborating.

They spent another hour choosing from the materials spread out over the sofa, standing side by side while she tried to stifle a mounting awareness of his closeness by moving away to hold up patterns against the existing curtains. It was twelve-thirty before they had finished and she had been able to gather everything together with a sense of relief. 'I'll have to come back to measure up,' she told him.

'Any time,' he said.

'I'll call you when I get back to the shop and I've got the appointments book in front of me.' She sounded particularly brisk and efficient.

He had seen her to her car and helped her load the back seat with her things.

'Have dinner with me,' he said, bending to the open window.

'No, thanks, Niall.'

'Lunch, then?'

She glanced at the pale eyes, the thick grey hair, the crooked nose, and away again quickly.

'I owe you an apology,' he said, 'for the way I behaved the other night. I'd drunk rather too much and got carried away.'

She put the car into gear. 'Not to worry. I didn't take you seriously.'

'None the less, I was being quite serious,' he said.

She had returned to the shop feeling satisfied with the way she had managed the morning's assignment. Isobel would be pleased at the amount of work it entailed, Niall had been more likeable than she had imagined possible, and apart from that transient and unwanted *frisson* she had felt at his proximity, all had gone smoothly. She did not make the mistake of believing him to be a changed character, but she no longer dreaded any further visits to his flat. She went back there the next day to measure for curtains and covers, taking Kevin with her, who was employed as general helper and van driver. Niall had had to leave for work, having let them in and handed her a spare set of keys with the request to lock up after her.

'Christ!' Kevin said, looking at the large double bed in the main bedroom. 'Makes you wonder what he gets up to, don't it? Bonking for Britain, I reckon.'

'Very droll,' Kate replied. 'Do get on with it, Kev, please.'

'As the bishop said to the actress,' he said; master of the clichéd rejoinder.

There was no real reason for returning to the flat after that, until curtains and covers were ready to be hung and fitted weeks later. Any queries concerning the work could be conducted over the telephone, such as his final decision about the few short-listed patterns of materials she had left with him to mull over. She had not foreseen these being used as an excuse for further contact, but he had rung her the same evening.

'I can't make up my mind,' he told her. 'I need a final consultation with the expert. How about a drink and dinner in return for your help?'

'I don't see why eating and drinking should be necessary,' she answered dauntingly. 'And I don't believe a word about your indecision.'

'Very well, then, I'll start again. I should like to give you dinner, Kate, as a "thank-you" for the trouble you're taking on my behalf. How's that?'

'It sounds incredibly pompous,' she said, but she could not help laughing. 'In any case, you're going to be paying for my services, remember.'

Nonetheless, she had given in. What the hell, she thought; there could be little harm in accepting as long as she was not expected to repeat the exercise. They settled for the following evening.

Matt had telephoned an hour before she was due to leave. The call was ill-timed; subsequent events would most likely have taken a different turn if he had only waited a day. The very sound of his voice made her feel immediately guilty, as if she was planning an underhand assignation instead of an innocuous meal with an acquaintance. He suggested they made a date for their meeting; she had a sudden longing to say, 'Oh yes, please let it be now, tonight. Don't let's wait.' As it happened, they compared diaries calmly and arranged a day two whole weeks ahead. Then he had dropped his bombshell. He had, he declared, decided to postpone the trip to China until the summer holidays, when he would like to take Jake with him if she agreed. It would be a wonderful opportunity for him, he pointed out, and one that might never arise again. How did she feel about it? Kate, hit by so many conflicting emotions she could hardly breathe, told him in no uncertain terms. It was a hare-brained scheme, Jake was far too young for the rigours and possible dangers of such a journey and what on earth was Matt thinking of? Their respective receivers went down on a cold note of dissension. She sat where she was for a second or two before the lump in her throat became tears, then locked herself in the bathroom for privacy and cried silently for a long time.

Her misery, transcending even concern for Jake, sprang from the fact that nowhere in Matt's scheme of things had she been included. She remembered the early days, the expeditions they had undertaken together in harmony, and wept for their passing. In excluding her from the proposed trip, he was tacitly claiming his rights as a single male parent, underlining more clearly than any bold statement that there was no place for her in his life. Crouched in the bathroom, she had felt the last of her hopes shrivel up and disintegrate.

Only an innate sense of obligation had prevented her from cancelling the evening, she recalled. She dressed in a rush without the time or inclination to care about what she chose; and the make-up she had applied to disguise swollen eyelids proved a failure.

'You've been crying,' Jake said, eyeing her beadily from his bath.

'Just hay fever,' she lied as she kissed him good night.

She poured herself a whisky, and drank it while she waited for her minicab, feeling incapable of normal conversation without it. It took the edge off her nervous exhaustion, leaving her numb and slightly light-headed. As she was driven through streets dappled by late sunshine, she tried to concentrate on soothing images like the chestnut trees in full pink and white flower, and Niall's future décor. But her mind kept turning to the glorious prospect of bed and oblivion in sleep, and how to get through three hours of enforced sociability. A hard little knot of anger crept into her consciousness, a resentment against men in general for their egoism and their manipulative childishness. It was a more positive emotion than despair; but she sensed her self-control weak as water, waiting to evaporate at the least provocation. Outside Niall's front door, she tried to arrange her features in a suitable expression of amiability before ringing the bell, her lips stiff under the ready smile.

It had not taken him in for a moment, this pretence of normality: she could tell by the long, considering look he gave her before leading the way into the living-room. A bottle of wine in a Perspex cooler stood on the glass sofa table, a bowl of quails' eggs beside it. The eggs were arranged on a bed of fig-leaves, white and gleaming against the green. There was also a blue-and-white pottery jug filled with pinks. He had obviously taken trouble, but she was too tired to query the motive behind the gesture.

'What a treat!' she said brightly, sinking into a corner of the sofa.

He held up the bottle. 'A glass of Chablis? Or would you like something stronger?'

'Wine would be fine, thanks.'

'In my opinion,' he said, pouring into long-stemmed glasses, 'there's nothing to beat whisky when life has dealt you a back-hander.'

She coloured up, thrown off balance by his perspicacity, and fiddled in her bag for cigarettes and lighter.

'Oh, I agree,' she said, 'but in my case, it's just been one of those days, that's all.'

'Have an egg,' he suggested, pushing the bowl towards her. 'It's better for you than smoking.'

In order to forestall any more probing on his part, she launched into a light-hearted description of a working day with its quota of tricky clients, muddles over orders and Isobel's capricious temperament. As it happened, the shop had been remarkably peaceful for once; she was merely trying to be amusing and, listening to herself prattle, probably failing, although he smiled in the appropriate places. Her repertoire faltered and finally petered out. The quails' eggs seemed to have lodged somewhere inside her, and she felt rather sick. He was still smiling as he rose to refill her glass.

'What's so funny?' she asked.

'I was thinking,' he said, 'how you've changed. I've never heard you so conversational.'

'You hardly know me,' she pointed out.

'True. I was remembering back to years ago when we first met. You scarcely opened your mouth except for the odd monosyllable.'

'There was a reason for that, as you know. You've changed as well.' She waved a hand at the table with its signs of hospitality. 'You used us like a restaurant when I was flat-sharing, and never even contributed a bottle of plonk,' she said, finding a certain relief in the revival of the old antagonism.

'Didn't I? How shameful,' he replied lightly. 'I was always a mean bastard, and those were the penniless days. But I'm trying to make up for it now and I didn't mean to start a sparring match.' He stood looking down at her seriously with the same expression of consideration. 'I very much wanted the evening to be a success, but something tells me I've got the timing wrong. You've hardly touched your wine.'

Please don't let him be sympathetic, she thought. Incipient tears welled in the background, threatening to make a fool of her. 'I had a drink at home before I came,' she confessed, deciding on honesty. 'It was probably a mistake.'

'Were you really dreading having dinner with me to that extent?' he asked with irony.

'No.' She hesitated, picked up her glass and took a sip. 'There was a crisis; at least, it most likely wouldn't seem to be one to anyone else but me.' The wine was extremely good. She drank again. 'Somehow it knocked me off balance.'

'Do you want to talk about it?'

'Not really. Other people's marriages are very uninteresting.'

'That depends,' he said, 'on the person involved. *You're* interesting to me. You arrive here bug-eyed and miserable, and I'm curious to know why.'

'Is it really so obvious?' she asked, sighing.

'Too obvious to ignore.' He leant over and touched her cheek lightly and swiftly before settling himself in an armchair beside her. 'So what has Matthew Protheroe been doing to you to cause you grief?'

Loyalty to Matt struggled with a sudden longing inside her to break down and explain. She stared hard at the remains of her wine, saw Niall's hand, fine blond hairs on the back, as he filled the glass.

'He hasn't done anything,' she said. 'It's something he said. I had hopes of us getting back together again, and now, after talking to him, I haven't any left. I won't bore you with the details.'

He sat relaxed, one long leg slung across the other. 'Whether to end or mend a marriage, or any relationship, come to that. Never easy,' he observed. 'My own attempt at marriage came to a halt a long time ago; it was a mistake in the first place.'

There was a coolness in his tone that reminded her of the man she had originally known rather than the one he seemed to have become. 'You're divorced?' she asked.

'No. Charlotte doesn't recognize divorce. She's

Catholic, and adamant on the point. Not,' he added, 'that the question has arisen. I've no plans to re-marry, and neither has she, so far as I know. We get on with our lives separately, and she brings up our two children. It works.'

'Do you see them?'

'Not much. They're abominably spoilt.'

The telephone rang, and he excused himself, saying he would answer it in another room. She had found the brief assessment of his marriage depressingly cold-blooded; it bore no comparison to her own history. At least within that, there had been love, whatever the outcome. For a short while she had felt a warmth in his apparent concern which had almost tempted her to open up. Now she regretted being there, tried to think of an excuse to leave early. Defiantly, she topped up her glass and carried it to the window, to gaze out on the tree-lined street, cast with evening shadow. She leaned her forehead against the pane, feeling it cool against her skin. A family, man, woman and small boy walked slowly by below her. They stopped a moment to let the boy climb up on the low wall of the house opposite, then moved on. Jake used to do that, she recalled, Matt holding his hand just as the father was doing now with his own child. His free arm rested round the woman's shoulders; he said something and she laughed. Kate watched them until they were nearly out of sight, at ease with each other, symbolizing harmony. And then, to her mortification, the tears started to slide down her cheeks, spilling unchecked from beneath closed eyelids. She groped blindly for a handkerchief that was elsewhere, in her bag by the table. She heard Niall's footsteps cross the room, felt his hands on her arms turn her towards him without speaking, and buried her face in his chest, past caring. Anybody's shoulder would have done at that moment, she thought later: his merely happened to be available.

He let her stand there for several seconds, wetting his pale blue shirt-front, before leading her to the sofa and sitting down beside her. He placed her rescued glass on the table, found a handkerchief in his pocket and put it in her hand. She leaned against him with a muttered 'thank you', mopping at her face and feeling the last of her tears receding.

'Poor baby,' he said, kissing the top of her head.

'I'm sorry,' she said in a muffled voice. 'I've ruined the evening, your shirt; everything. I shouldn't have come in the first place.'

'I've no regrets.' He smoothed the hair away from her forehead absently. 'I've got to know you a great deal better without barriers. In a way,' he added, 'I'm envious of you.'

She struggled to sit upright. 'Envious? Why?'

'Because, tough as it is for you, you obviously care much more about another human being; and that is an experience that has passed me by completely. Something lacking in me, I suppose.'

'At least,' she said wearily, 'you're in no danger of falling apart like I've just done.' She reached for her bag. 'I'd better try to do something about my face.'

'It's not necessary, even the mascara streaks have gone, unless you still want to be taken out to dinner, and I imagine you'd rather not?'

'I'm not hungry. Do you mind?'

'I'm disappointed, but there'll be other times.' He held her face in both hands and studied her. 'You look rather appealing; very young and scrubbed,' he said, bending his head to kiss her. 'Would you like to go home?'

She hesitated, ashamed to admit, even to herself, the sudden urgent longing for human contact.

'Not immediately. May I stay for a while?'

'You should eat a little,' he told her.

'Do you have some soup?'

'Home-made; carrot and coriander, in the fridge. Will that do?'

'Lovely.'

While he disappeared to prepare it, she went to the bathroom. Her face in the looking-glass above the basin stared back at her, blank and colourless, as if washed clean of all expression. She felt very little any more; the hopelessness had gone, and all that remained was a muted ache of resentment like a fading bruise.

They ate the soup, doctored with sherry and accompanied by warm crusty bread, from the sofa table; carrying the bowls to the kitchen when they had finished and stacking them in the dishwasher. This small domestic act had given her the perfect opportunity to leave, while she was standing in the unseductive glare of the kitchen and away from the subdued lighting of the living-room. 'May I call a taxi?' she had asked, her hand on the telephone.

He put his arms round her. 'If that's what you want,' he said.

'I don't know what I want,' she said, 'and you're not making it any easier for me.'

'You may regret it if you stay.' He released her so that he could look into her face, keeping her hands imprisoned in his. 'I don't want to be accused of taking advantage of you in a vulnerable state.'

She laughed weakly. 'That sounds like a line from a Victorian novel.'

'So? They talked a certain amount of sense, the Victorians.'

Neither of them spoke for some time after that because he had started to kiss her in earnest, and the psychological moment for her escape had passed.

He had been a far more considerate lover than she would have guessed. Later, lying curled beside him in bed, she realized with surprise that she had enjoyed every aspect of his loving. She felt no remorse, only puzzlement that the pain which Matt had caused could have been so easily cured. She had refused Niall's offer to drive her home, wanting to avoid any discussions about future meetings. Unexpectedly pleasing as the evening had been, or perhaps because of it, she fully intended it to be the last. Seeing her into a taxi, he had spoken of this being a beginning, not an end; but she had taken it to be the kind of remark inevitably made at such moments without validity. Leaving a strange bed and pulling on her clothes to go home alone in the early hours of the morning was an experience she had never had to face, and she found it curiously desolate. It was not until she was checking on a sleeping Jake that the first pangs of shame hit her.

Nonetheless, against all her better instincts she found herself having dinner with Niall a few days later. This time there were no tears and they ate in a restaurant, but otherwise the evening followed the same pattern. Only then was she forced to admit that she was addicted; not so much to Niall himself as to the sensations he had rekindled which had lain dormant in her for months. She had not foreseen the serious stumbling-block: not only was he uninterested in children, he in fact disliked them; and by the time it became obvious, she was caught in an emotional trap.

The design for his drawing-room was finished. She laid it to one side and started to put the tops on jars of paint. The thwack of Jake's racket had stopped, and he came to loll against her, peering over her shoulder at the painting.

'Who's that for?' he asked. 'Is it that man?'

'His name's Niall,' Kate said calmly, 'if that's who you mean.'

Jake kicked a pebble across the paving. 'Bloody Niall,' he muttered. 'I might have known.'

'Jake!'

But he had already gone, disappearing through the open door to the house like a rabbit down its burrow.

The taxi drew up at ten to two, waited while Kate opened her front door, then moved away into the night. The street was clear as daylight under a full moon, and Roly slid lower in the driver's seat of his parked car as she fumbled with her key. He need not have worried: she looked to neither right nor left. After she had disappeared, he took a small notebook from the glove compartment and wrote in the date and the time, adding it to a column of similar entries. The last two timings were considerably later than the others, shooting from the eleven-thirty mark to the early hours. Something had happened to alter the pattern of her evenings. His mind raced this way and that, tortured by imaginings of the faceless, nameless individual who lay behind the change. Quietly he started the engine; it was only a matter of perseverance before he would discover the identity; a question of waiting for Kate to drop a name into the conversation over one of their suppers together, or of waiting as usual in the shadows until she was escorted home. He guessed intuitively at a new stage in the game he played, lending extra stimulus to his masochistic pain. Occasionally, in the light of a mundane working day in the office, he wondered if he were not going mad. But with the coming of darkness he was invariably back in the grip of the same restlessness, driven by an insatiable urge to keep her in view. He doubted whether he could have stopped now had he seriously tried; the habit had become an obsession. The times he spent with her were a glorious respite, a few hours in which he could pretend nothing had altered between them and that she belonged to him, as he had once imagined.

'Mr Roland telephoned when you were out last

night,' Helga told Kate. 'It is strange; he is always ringing when you are not here.'

'Just coincidence, I expect,' Kate said. 'He calls a lot.' But she knew why, and the reason bothered her, as it always did if she allowed herself to think about it.

Matt glanced at his watch, saw with relief it was time to pack a bag and switched off the word processor. Normally he wrote quickly, preferring to catch ideas as they occurred to him and edit after each chapter. For most of that day, however, he had sat staring at a blank screen, and the pile of script, while already satisfyingly thick, had not increased in the last hours. Such mental blocks had become quite frequent recently, particularly since the arranged meeting with Kate. Not only had that been unproductive; it had made him contemplate the whole structure of his existence, which he had carefully avoided doing for months. He had managed to persuade himself that life without Kate was perfectly feasible, even enjoyable at times: the ostrich approach to an insoluble problem. An hour or so spent in her company had destroyed his supposed peace of mind and left him with the sour taste of dissatisfaction. He had found her enigmatic and strangely philosophical; he had never known Kate to be either. This uncharacteristic attitude unnerved him. Up until the present he had felt that, given the genuine desire to do so, the door would always be open for his return. Now he was far from certain.

In his bedroom, he stuffed his bag with suitable clothes for the weekend, adding a paperback which he probably would not touch. An hour later, he was heading for Wales along the M4, filled with a feeling of release as he left the last of the plate-glass office buildings behind him. Escaping to open spaces was invariably his way of dealing with pressure, and on this occasion his destination was a cottage in the hills rented by a group of friends for a stag-party. Five of them: one married, one separated, two divorced, and one about to marry for the second time. We do not have a very good track-record, Matt decided. As a rule he enjoyed solitude, preferred it to gatherings, but there were moments when his own company seemed unbearable, and this was one of them. He looked forward to three days of uncomplicated male companionship, to long walks and in-jokes and evenings spent drinking too much without the stigma of being alone. He drove with the car windows down under a sky of scudding clouds and patchy blue, and taped jazz in the background competing with the rushing wind. His thoughts wandered to Jake who had phoned him in the last few days, and thereby inevitably to Kate.

'When am I coming to stay with you next?' Jake had asked. He sounded untypically belligerent, which Matt had guessed was a cover-up for dejection.

'The weekend after this coming one,' he answered. 'Nothing wrong is there?' he added. 'Is Mum all right?'

'Yeah, she's fine,' Jake said laconically, with just the slightest stress on the word 'she'. 'But I wanted to know when I was going to see you. Can I come on Friday, to make it two nights?'

'Of course, I'd like that. We'll think up something special to do.'

'I don't mind about it *not* being special,' Jake told him. 'I like talking most of all. I've got to go now. See you, Daddy.' He rang off abruptly.

The conversation, brief as it was, disturbed Matt. It did not take great powers of detection to conclude that all was not well in Jake's life. What were he and Kate doing to him? He supposed he should have queried this long ago, although Jake had seemed to accept the situation with remarkable equanimity. But then, he was a great concealer of feelings, like Matt himself; a crisis of some kind was needed before he would reveal his real emotions. Matt was conscious of missing out on whole areas of Jake's growing-up; episodes and experiences encompassed in day-to-day living which would imperceptibly mould him into the adult he was to become. Being apart from Jake, seeing him only at spasmodic intervals, was one of the worst aspects of the separation. He also knew that it was not a good enough reason in itself for having a second attempt at the marriage. Kate and he had to find their own way back together again if it were to succeed; it would take compromise and a change of attitudes on both their parts, and a willingness to forgive innumerable hurts. Judging by their meeting, they were nowhere near achieving any of these aims. It did not surprise him; he was aware, when they were planning where to go for the evening, that he had managed to upset her, and traced it back to his mention of the proposed trip to China. He had expected objections, but not the angry burst of opposition she had given vent to down the telephone.

Kate was ready and waiting in the hall when he came to collect her, as if she did not want him encroaching further on her territory. He had keys to the house in Denbigh Street, but he never used them: it always felt strange to be ringing his own doorbell. She was wearing white cotton trousers, an oversized shirt and espadrilles, and her dark hair drawn back into a shiny knob. If she was aiming at severity, it failed: she looked about nineteen, and he had a strong impulse to bundle her into his arms and kiss the breath out of her, obliterating the whole dreary business of estrangement.

'I've booked a table at the Thai place round the corner,' he said. 'You like the food, don't you?'

She glanced at him and away. 'I do, but not tonight.

Can you cancel it? I don't feel like anything formal; I'd rather walk somewhere and eat at a pub, perhaps.'

A bloody unpromising start, he had thought to himself as he phoned the restaurant; nor had there been much improvement. They drove to Hammersmith and walked by the river, past houses flaunting newly planted window-boxes full of geraniums and petunias, until they reached the place where the houseboats were moored. They leaned on the wall, still warm from the sun, and looked down on the mud-flats of low tide; side by side yet divided, each of them wary of making the first move towards an amnesty. The constraint stopped him from putting his hand over her own brown paw lying so close to his, as he would like to have done. They started to discuss Jake's education which brought its own disagreements, but at least they were familiar and could be wrangled over on safe ground.

The two grandfathers, Kate's father George and Matt's father Magnus, had offered to share the financial burden of Jake's further schooling; an offer which Matt refused to accept. Pride prevented him: it seemed an admission of failure on his part to rely on others for the education of his son. Kate did not agree.

'I wish you'd think again,' she said now. 'We can hardly manage the present school fees. The next lot will be beyond us, and Jake isn't scholarship material. What's the alternative?'

'A good state school,' he replied. 'There *are* the well-run ones if you choose carefully.'

'State schools are a lottery; you don't often get a choice,' she pointed out. 'Jake would be lost in a large comprehensive; he's not used to the system.'

'He's tougher than he looks. Other children survive, and even go on to university.'

She flicked a piece of lichen from the wall with her nail. 'I want more for him than mere survival. I don't understand your attitude; you don't seem to care.'

'Darling, that's not fair.'

The 'darling' slipped out involuntarily, out of place in this exchange of words. 'I care as much as you do. But I believe that Jake is our responsibility, not George's or Magnus's, and we must do our best for him within our limits.'

'Fine words,' she said mockingly, 'but they don't exactly help Jake. What's wrong with grandparents helping out? It's happening all the time in dozens of families. The truth is,' she added, 'it's only your pride standing in the way. You feel it's a reflection on your ability to cope.'

The accuracy of the remarks stung. 'So maybe I do. Is that so odd? You haven't lost the art of sticking the knife in, have you?'

'I'm sorry,' she said surprisingly. 'As a matter of fact, I understand, even if I don't agree. This is getting us nowhere; let's start again.'

Her unusual magnanimity took him aback. He hesitated, querying its cause. 'What's *your* ideal where Jake's schooling is concerned?' he asked. 'Neither of us wants him at a boarding-school; at least we're agreed on that.'

'A day school where the teaching is good and the classes a reasonable size,' she said. 'For which, of course, one has to pay. Isn't that really what *you* would like for him?'

'In theory, yes.' He smiled faintly. 'I'll have to write a bestseller and follow it up with several others to make it possible.'

'Get writing, then,' she said, returning the smile.

He straightened up. 'Let's wander in the direction of the pub. I could do with a drink.'

As they walked slowly back, he said, 'I suggest we look at various schools, both private and state, and find out what is available. Then we can compare, and come to a decision.'

'We know about St Paul's, Jake's on their list; we

90

decided when he was a baby, if you remember,' she said, as if there were no comparison to be made.

'How hopeful we must have been,' he commented.

'We were,' she said pointedly. 'About everything.' She put a hand on his arm almost pleadingly. 'Promise me you won't turn down the grandfathers' offer without thinking about it again.'

Her face was turned towards him, the forehead creased in anxiety. 'I promise,' he said.

With the question of Jake's education shelved for the time being, they were faced with their own futures. They had walked in virtual silence as far as the pub, he recalled, and chosen a table outside on the narrow terrace overlooking the river. He ordered two large whiskies in an attempt to break down inhibitions brought about by a year of separation. He did not know how to begin. Watching her face, the slight uptilt of her eyes, the pointed chin, remembering a hundred similar evenings from the past, it was easy to persuade himself that nothing had changed; that a few adjustments to the way he ran his life would solve everything. In reality, he knew it was not so simple; they had lost touch with each other in more senses than one. He was still in love with her, he realized, and could not decide whether this was a help or a hindrance.

It was she who broke the deadlock by glancing at him over the rim of her glass and saying, 'It seems unreal, somehow, sitting here as if nothing had happened, and yet wondering what on earth to say.'

'Like strangers,' he agreed, grateful they were in accord; 'only worse, because we're not.'

'It would be easier if we were,' she said. 'We'd never stop talking, making an enormous effort to charm one another.'

'Is that what we did?'

'I expect so,' she said with a little smile. 'Everyone does.'

'Perhaps that's the secret of a successful marriage: to continue the charm to the end.'

'A nice thought, but unrealistic.'

'How sad. It sounds as if you're becoming a cynic.'

'Philosophical, perhaps; not cynical,' she insisted.

He stared out across the river that was slowly turning grey-blue with encroaching dusk, puzzled by her unusual air of calmness. He was used to a Kate whose reactions were swift; movements, temper, mirth all triggered off in a split second. It was she who had been eager to instigate a discussion which seemed now to be drifting as aimlessly as the water in front of them. Made vaguely uneasy by the enigma, he groped for an opening sentence that would force them into facing facts.

'A year is a long time to be apart,' he said. 'Do you feel it's served its purpose?'

'In what way?'

'In allowing us our own space; giving us both time to rethink, and to decide whether we stand a chance of starting again. Wasn't that the general idea?'

'I suppose so,' she said. 'Personally, I'm not sure *what* it's done for me. My thinking was mostly fogged over by incredible loneliness: I've loathed every minute of it.'

Distressed, he put his hand over hers where it lay on the table. 'I haven't exactly been having a ball either,' he said. 'I imagined you to be better off in the circumstances than me: you've always been more socially inclined. Where were all the friends?'

'They were around, but that's not the point.' She left her hand where it was, warm and inert beneath his.

'I gather Roly Bliss was amongst them,' he remarked casually. 'I would have thought he'd be an asset.'

'A mixed blessing,' she replied briefly. 'Jake likes him. I gather you haven't exactly been alone?'

'More often than not,' he said with equal brevity, and swallowed the last of his drink. 'I miss you, Kate. I miss being married to you,' he added. 'Are you willing to try again?'

She turned her glass on its stem absently. 'If you'd asked me that when you phoned me two weeks ago, I would have said "yes". Now I'm not certain.'

'What happened to change your mind?' he asked, guessing at the cause.

'Your plans for China.'

'I don't understand why that should have upset you,' he said. 'If it was the idea of my taking Jake, you had only to disagree.'

'It wasn't exactly that.'

'Then—'

'Work it out for yourself,' she said with a touch of her old asperity.

'Oh! For God's sake, Kate, stop playing games.'

'You really don't understand, do you? And that's the whole problem: you never have.'

She raised her head and looked at him, and for the first time he caught a glimpse of real hurt in her eyes. 'I don't figure in your plans, and I felt hopelessly excluded. What was the point of planning to get back together again while you were acting as a single entity?'

The simplicity of her explanation silenced him. He sat staring at his empty glass, thinking over the complexity of women and his own apparent insensitivity. 'I'm really sorry,' he said at last. 'It never struck me you would want to come.'

'You could have asked,' she replied.

'Is it too late? We could all go, providing we can scrape together the money.'

'I'd rather wait to see what we're going to do with our lives,' she said. 'It's more important.'

'There *will* be changes. I'm concentrating on writing in the hopes it will succeed and that travel

93

can take a back seat,' he told her. 'Please don't let a stupid cock-up of mine jeopardize our chances.'

She shook her head without speaking; a gesture of acquiescence, he supposed, although he could not tell what she was thinking. 'Do you *want* me back, Kate?' he asked.

'Give me a week or two to get used to the idea,' she said.

'More time? We've had twelve months—'

'I'm not ready; I need to tidy up my mind, I want to be sure.' She looked away from him as if to pluck assurance from the darkening water. 'I don't think I could bear things to go wrong between us a second time.'

'They won't if we're both determined they shan't,' he said with confidence.

'We're not the same people. Too much has happened to each of us that the other knows nothing about,' she said elusively.

The possibility that she might have fallen in love with someone else struck him painfully, taking him unawares. Watching her profile, he wondered why it had not occurred to him before.

'Speaking for myself, there's little to know,' he remarked lightly. 'Nothing, that is, that I wouldn't happily confess to my great-aunt. But I'd rather you told me now if there's a serious impediment on your side that's likely to rock our boat.'

She wrapped her arms across her chest as if suddenly chilled. 'No confessions, remember, by mutual agreement.' Giving him a smile, she added, 'I'm in a muddle, that's all. You know I'm prone to getting my life in muddles, and more so in the past year.'

'If that's all,' he said uncertainly.

'I'd like to disentangle it. May I?'

'How long?'

'I'm not sure. A week or so,' she repeated.

'And afterwards', he asked, 'where does that leave us?'

'With a decision,' she said. 'I promise.'

And that was how the discussion was left, he recalled, as the route to Wales disappeared effortlessly beneath the car wheels: open-ended and littered with unanswered queries. He still did not know whether she loved him; she had withdrawn at the precise moment he realized how much a part of him she was and always would be. It was as though they were dancing some sort of complicated minuet, alternately retreating and advancing and getting it wrong. They had completed the evening over plates of cold roast beef and salad for which neither of them had the appetite, making the kind of stilted and desultory conversation to be expected from two people out of emotional kilter. They had talked about Roly for quite a while, he remembered; Kate had wanted to know whether he was the type to become obsessional, confirming Matt's guess that the poor sod had fallen for her. But the subject had not held his interest for long; whoever else she might have become involved with, it was unlikely to be Roly.

Perhaps, while they were sorting out their own lives, he and Kate should have considered Jake: his education alone had been mentioned. The most vulnerable of them, he was also the one without a say in their final decision. It struck Matt now, his eyes on the distant, uneven line of hazy blue which denoted the Welsh hills, how grossly unfair it was to be a child and denied a voice; and his heart contracted with a mixture of pity and regret.

Chapter Four

Sunday lunch with Charlie and Stella, postponed by Kate for as long as possible, was not without incident. In fact, Jake had quite enjoyed bits of it, even though there was a price to be paid at the end of it. Going home in the car with Roly driving, his mother's face wore that stiff and unsmiling look which meant she hadn't forgiven him. The fuss that had been made at the time was out of all proportion to the crime, in Jake's opinion. After all, no-one had been hurt. All he had done was to lock his cousins in the woodshed; losing the padlock key had been unfortunate, but they had found it, hadn't they, after an hour's search.

There was never much to do down there. The trouble was, girls were so limited unless they were special, and Jake only knew one of those, who actually liked games of espionage, and damming streams, and even playing football. The cousins were unbelievably limited; they were interested in riding their fat pony who refused to be caught, and that was about all. He had eyed their very white T-shirts and their neat pony-tails of fair hair while they were having lunch, and longed to roll them in a muddy patch. Afterwards, they had gone down to the paddock and spent hours trying to catch the pony; Imogen with a halter behind her back and Lucy holding out lumps of sugar. Boredom had spread through Jake, making him yawn and yawn. They gave up at last, and mooched around in the garden, turning down his suggestions of climbing the cedar tree or exploring the adjoining farm buildings. 'We're not allowed to.'

'What do you do when I'm not here?' he asked.

They looked at each other in that maddening, secret way of theirs. 'Ride Blossom,' said Lucy.

'Or go for bike rides,' Imogen added. 'Not on the main road though.'

'Why don't we do that, then?' Jake demanded.

'We've only got two bikes.'

So that was that. What happened next was the girls' fault: they deserved it. Out of the blue Imogen announced, 'Your mother and father are going to get a divorce.'

Jake froze, sick with horror. 'They're not,' he retorted. 'What do *you* know about it?'

'They are. I heard Mummy and Daddy talking.'

'They only said *might* about the divorce,' Lucy said, who was slightly more honest. 'They weren't absolutely *sure*.'

'Well, you're wrong, wrong, wrong!' Jake had yelled, feeling as if his world was about to fall apart. 'They'd have told me if it was going to happen.' And jumping up from his prone position on the lawn, he had stumped away, fighting back tears. His back was turned on the girls, but he thought he could hear them whispering.

Fury stopped the crying. He hated them. He started to think up every imaginable torture possible to get his own back; starving them to death in a dungeon sprang to mind. That was how the idea had come to him. He walked back to the house and begged for string off Stella, who had found a whole ball of it, saying she'd like it back, please, and not in a tangle. Fat chance.

'We're going to play political prisoners,' he told the girls in a masterful voice that brooked no arguments. 'I tie you up and put you in the woodshed, and if you can get free in ten minutes, I let you out and you can make me the prisoner.'

'Supposing we can't get free?' said Imogen.

'You can tie me up anyway,' Jake lied. 'After ten minutes.'

'It sounds stupid.'

'I don't like the woodshed,' Lucy said.

Only lethargy had led them to give in. The shed was away from the house in a corner of the kitchen garden, and there he had trussed them together like a pair of chickens, back to back with wrists and ankles shackled, and pushed them inside. 'I'm timing you,' he called through the locked door; and then he had taken the key like any sensible guard would have done, and gone to lie in the sun at the end of the lawn. Ten minutes passed before the muffled squeaks and cries had begun and grown steadily in volume as the prisoners realized they had been abandoned. He lay on his back and gazed up at the sky through the cedar tree, listening with gleeful satisfaction to the sound of their desperation.

It was tea-time before his nefarious scheme was discovered. He had planned to let them go by then anyway, but the key had fallen out of his jeans pocket and had to be searched for, so their release came much later. Lucy was crying, and the grown-ups were furious; all the same, it was worth it. The atmosphere was frosty with disapproval as they piled into Roly's car; Roly alone giving him a sympathetic wink. There was not much talking on the way home, Jake sitting in the back watching his mother's grim profile. It was unlike her not to see the funny side of things eventually, but all she said was: 'That was a particularly nasty trick of yours, Jake. Lucy has asthma, and it could have been serious. I don't know *what's* got into you lately.'

'I'm sorry,' he said, seemingly for the hundredth time.

He knew what she meant, though. Nothing had gone right ever since that man Niall Hunter had suddenly appeared. Kate was not the same, either; it was as if he had cast an evil spell over her. She seemed reluctant to mention his name when Jake asked where she was going. 'Niall and I are having an early dinner,' she would say carelessly, without looking at him, or: 'Niall's got tickets for a theatre.' It never *was* early. Jake tried to stay awake, listening for her return, but he would invariably fall asleep before he could hear the front door open and shut. Niall had not come to supper at the house since that first time, when Jake had been allowed to stay up late with dire results. He had not talked to anybody about it, not even his friend Toby, who wouldn't understand the awfulness of the situation and might blab at school. He felt he would burst if he did not confide in someone, and Roly was ideal. An opportunity presented itself later that evening when Kate had disappeared to the kitchen and they were left alone.

'She's still cross,' Jake said.

'She'll get over it,' Roly observed comfortingly. 'I expect she's tired.'

'Do *you* think what I did was so bad?'

'No, not really. But women look at these things differently. Why don't you show me how you're getting on with Captain Diehard in book form?'

'OK.'

In his bedroom, Jake said, 'There's something I want to tell you. D'you promise not to let on to anyone else?'

'I promise.'

'Mum's got this new boyfriend. At least, I suppose

99

that's what he is; she goes out a lot with him, and it's making her kind of different. All jumpy and snappy which isn't like her as a rule.' His face creased in anxiety. 'It's all his fault, I know it is.'

'What is his name?'

'Niall-um-Hunter. Mum says you know him, but he can't be a *friend* of yours, Roly, because he's a real creep.'

Roly sat down heavily on the end of the bed. 'I don't know him well,' he said. 'I wouldn't call him a friend.'

Something in his tone made Jake look at him closely. He was pleased to see that Roly was taking the matter seriously; his round, normally cheerful face was strangely blank.

'I take it you've met him, then?' he asked.

Jake nodded. 'He came to supper,' he said darkly.

It was Jake who had opened the door to him; Kate was changing, which was an ominous sign in itself, as was the carefully laid supper table up one end of the drawing-room. She never bothered for Roly; they ate in the kitchen. Niall, after a brief mention of his name, had strode into the house as if he owned it, taking Jake's politely proffered hand and dropping it swiftly. 'Where is your mother?' he had demanded. Jake had explained that she would not be long, pointed out the tray of drinks on a side-table and told Niall to help himself, as he had been taught to do. Watching the man pour a large measure of whisky into a tumbler and add a splash of water, he felt a prickling sensation in the hairs at the back of his neck, like the rising of a dog's hackles. Dislike had been instant, hand in hand with the conviction that here was the threat to his mother he had dreaded all along, in the shape of a tall, grey-haired man with cold blue eyes and a weird nose.

Niall had turned, taken a gulp of his drink and surveyed the room, ending up with Jake. 'Don't bother to wait,' he said. 'I expect it's your bedtime.'

Kate had come into the room at that moment, bubbly and breathless, just as Jake was about to make an indignant retort. Things had gone from bad to worse from then on. He hadn't wanted to have supper with them, but his mother seemed to expect him to and he usually stayed up later on a Friday, anyway. It was fine when Roly was there; they joked, and told stories and made a lot of noise. That evening was altogether different.

'So you're allowed to stay up for supper?' Niall had remarked, raising one eyebrow in a particularly nasty way; and Jake had seethed inside, and kept his mouth shut in case he were tempted to be terribly rude.

'It's part of growing up,' Kate replied for him. 'I'm a believer in Jake joining in when it's possible.'

He shot her a look of gratitude. She sounded calm, but her eyes were shiny and her face pink which meant she was irritated.

Getting through the meal was dreadful; the food, salmon trout followed by strawberries, stuck in Jake's throat. Niall asked him which school he went to, making it sound as if he suspected a remand home, and thereafter ignored him; while Kate made desperate attempts to draw Jake into the conversation. No-one was at ease; the talk went in a series of jerks like a car's engine stalling. No sooner had he swallowed the last of his strawberries than Niall eyed him across the table and said, 'I'd like to have some time alone with your mother, if you've finished. Do you mind leaving us?'

There was silence. Jake, burning with the injustice of a complete stranger giving him orders, stared at his mother and waited for her help. Kate's eyes were brighter still with suppressed anger.

'That's *my* decision alone, thanks, Niall,' she said in a tight voice. 'Five more minutes, Jake,' she added

101

smiling at him. 'Would you give Niall some more wine, please?'

Jake's self-control vanished. He pushed back his chair, stood up and grasping the bottle, poured wildly past the glass and into Niall's lap. Two pairs of astonished eyes gazed at him; he could have sworn his mother was trying not to laugh.

'Don't worry: I'm going,' he said.

'You little sod!' the man muttered under his breath.

'Jake, what about saying sorry?'

But he had already gone, Kate's voice reaching him as he stumbled up the stairs. 'Sod yourself!' he shouted in the confines of his bedroom, hoping it was audible down below. He had been far too angry to cry.

There was a wry smile on Roly's face. 'Presuming it was white wine,' he commented, 'I imagine it was well chilled?'

'Really cold,' Jake agreed.

'How satisfactorily uncomfortable: a willy with frostbite.'

The remark struck Jake as hilariously funny. He doubled up with laughter, falling helpless on the bed beside Roly and rolling about, his stomach aching, until the spasm passed and the sombre mood returned.

'The funny thing was,' he said, 'Mum didn't seem really cross with me about what happened. She tried to explain about Niall, saying he wasn't used to children, which seems a feeble excuse. It hasn't stopped her seeing him, though,' he added gloomily.

'It may be unimportant; one of those passing friendships,' Roly observed; but he said it without conviction. 'She gets lonely without your father, you see.'

'She's got *you*,' Jake pointed out. 'I wish Daddy would come home, I'd like to tell him about bloody

Niall, but it might make him stay away for ever. They may be getting divorced anyway,' he said in a low voice. 'The cousins told me: that's why I locked them up.'

'I doubt if the girls are a reliable source of information.' Roly rose to his feet. 'As for Niall, he is probably just one of many people whom Kate has got to know. Don't worry,' he said, putting a hand on Jake's shoulder. 'If things get worse, you can always talk to me, and we can drop arsenic in his wine next time round. Now, show me how the Diehard adventures are coming along.'

Jake had to be content with this advice. His fears were not entirely dispersed, but the fact of them being shared made him feel better. There was something infinitely consoling about Roly; the very bulk of him, like a friendly and caring bear, was reassuring.

Kate's mood of grim disapproval had vanished when they descended to the kitchen for a spaghetti supper. Her face had ironed itself out and she was smiling. Before Jake went up to bed, she hugged him close without saying anything, as if trying silently to communicate that, despite recent ructions, she loved him the same. He lay curled under the duvet, visualizing her cat's face in the darkness. He supposed she was pretty, although it was hard to tell about your own mother. In a muddled way, he thought he understood that she needed someone other than himself to stop the loneliness. His father having left made no sense. Next weekend was to be spent with Matt. Half-formed plans to get them back together again went round and round in his mind until he drifted into sleep.

In the tree-lined street in Hampstead, at a discreet distance from the entrance to Niall's flat, Roly watched and waited. Reckless in his compulsion, he had followed Kate there in the daylight of a June evening, risking recognition each time she glanced in her mirror. He was, in truth, past caring.

During the past week, the watching and waiting from the shadows of Denbigh Street had been unproductive: Kate had hardly left her house. Roly did not doubt the verity of Jake's information, but he needed to corroborate it for himself; and what better way was there than to go straight to enemy territory, possibly to catch a glimpse of the rat emerging from its lair. So he envisaged Niall: an oversexed rodent, predatory and dangerous. The thought of Kate literally in his clutches filled Roly with revulsion as he imagined groping hands and worse. There was no magnanimity in his thinking, no hint of the fact that Kate's life was her own, and she should be allowed to lead it as she pleased. Not so long ago he had believed it would be a relief to be able to put a face to her unknown pursuer. How very wrong he had been.

Kate had already disappeared inside the house; he had seen her let herself in, wearing a short blue dress, vivid as a kingfisher. She had a set of keys; damning evidence of a close relationship. Roly had only visited Niall's flat once, but he remembered it was on the first floor. A lamp was switched on, dimly visible through the living-room windows. He slid further down in his seat and wondered what to do next, considering amongst other things, finding a coin-box and telephoning Matt to apprise him of the situation. But it was not a serious consideration; such an action could only damage Kate, which was unthinkable. She was not to be blamed; vulnerable and mixed-up, she had to be a sitting target for the likes of shits such as Niall.

The best approach, Roly realized as a grain of sanity penetrated a haze of mangled emotions, was to talk to her; find the right moment to warn her gently but firmly of Niall's sleazy reputation. She might not listen, but he could at least try. Jake, he knew, would whole-heartedly approve of any attempt to remove Niall from the scene. Remembering the boy's tense face, dark eyes full of apprehension over matters only half-understood, Roly ground his teeth. Attached as he was to Jake, it was almost possible for Roly to believe that he was acting purely on behalf of an anxious child: almost, but not quite. Desire for Kate was too strong, and denial had turned it into a fierce possessiveness. No-one should be allowed to succeed with her where he had failed.

His thoughts were arrested by the sudden appearance of the two of them. He had imagined them ensconced in Niall's flat for the evening. They hesitated on the pavement as if discussing a point; he towering head and shoulders over Kate, she with her face tilted upwards towards him, the line of her neck and chin accentuated. How adorable she looked! Niall was in an open-necked shirt, a pale jacket slung casually over one shoulder. Jealousy rose like bile in Roly's throat as he watched. If he had been in possession of a gun, he would have attempted murder at that precise moment; headlines flashed through his brain: 'Accountant in mid-life crisis commits GBH.'

Without warning, they turned and started to walk towards him, jolting him into confusion at the ignominy of possible discovery. He ducked, lowering himself clumsily into a semi-kneeling position on the floor by the dashboard. There had not been time to close the window; he could hear their voices as they drew nearer. The gear lever dug into the pit of his stomach painfully as he held his breath, shut his eyes and waited. Their footsteps stopped unexpectedly; he anticipated Kate's cry of astonishment as she gazed in on him grovelling on all fours. Then, there was the sound of car doors opening and shutting, the starting-up of an engine, and finally the manoeuvring before it pulled away and faded from earshot.

He let his breath go in relief. Slowly he emerged from his agonizing posture and flopped into the driving seat like a beached whale. Beads of sweat stood out on his forehead; he stared resentfully at the empty space ahead where Niall's car had been parked. As usual on these obsessive vigils of his, nothing had been achieved, save, on this occasion, confirmation of Kate's liaison. A wave of self-pity swept over him as he drove home, intensified by a sneaking sense of his own ridiculousness. Whisky had never tasted so good as the generous measure he poured himself on reaching the reassuring confines of his living-room. He drank it with his feet up on the sofa, and felt the nerves in his stomach gradually quieten, and an element of confidence creep back.

'Change of tactics,' he advised himself out loud as he refilled his glass. 'I *shall* speak to her when I get the chance; she can't know the half about the bastard. I owe it to Jake,' he added righteously.

Late one night Kate sat at her bureau in the drawing-room and prepared to write to Niall. It was not the best of times, tired as she was from an unenjoyable evening out, but the letter could not wait; it was necessary to get it down on paper while the contents were still fresh in her mind. She realized as she picked up her pen that she should be declaring an end to their affair, clean-cut and final, rather than the feeble compromise she planned. There was a reason for this, but not a very good one. Finishing a relationship of no great depth, and where nobody's feelings were likely to be wounded, should be simple. It puzzled and irked her to find it was not so.

Their relationship – dreadful word, she told herself, but what else did one call it? 'Liaison' was as bad, and 'love affair' was inappropriate – never firmly established, had gradually deteriorated. It was not surprising; started as if by accident, it was not built to last. She had drifted into it in a moment of abject misery, and he had provided consolation on that very first evening, unexpectedly successfully. She had not intended it to become an affair, but the beginning had done much to restore her confidence, worn thin by the bleak months without Matt. The delight of being wanted was heady stuff after such an interval, as addictive as a drug. So she had discovered when, realizing that the situation was far from making her happy, her instinct was to end it. Quite regularly she made the decision to do so; and then Niall, sensing her withdrawal, would switch on the considerable charm of which he was capable. Time and again her resolution would waver and disintegrate, and she knew the reason why. If this relationship failed, there was no certainty of replacing it with something more admirable. To be wanted, even in Niall's unreliable fashion, had taken on a rather shaming importance.

Uppermost in her mind was the recent discussion with Matt. There had been a reversal of their roles; for months it had been she who ached for their marriage to be given a second chance, while he had remained evasive and noncommittal. Now, without warning, he had taken the initiative, suggested his returning, asked her for an answer which, only a few weeks previously she would not have hesitated in giving. Struck by an attack of cold feet, she had begged for time. She did not understand the change in him, even less in herself. He had unexpectedly thrown open the door and she was frightened to walk through, plagued by apprehension of the future. They had swanned into marriage, blissfully oblivious of possible failure; a second attempt, fraught as it would be with hindsight, was a different matter. She was not sure she could handle it; and yet Matt was an essential part of her, as she had found during a year without him in which she had existed rather than lived. What am I waiting for, she asked in sleepless moments of the night, ashamed and impatient at this inability to act positively. She had promised an answer, and she was supposed to be tidying up her life, clearing away obstacles, the most significant of which was Niall. After the evening she had just spent with him and a collection of his friends, she was in the right mood for decisive action; if it had not been for the weekend in Paris, proposed and agreed upon early on, before she knew him for what he was.

He had changed; or to put it more accurately, she supposed he had reverted to the type who had played havoc with poor flatmate Sally's life. It was naïve of her to have imagined he had a 'nice side' to him. People like Niall never really altered; they merely assumed a caring attitude when it suited them, as easily as slipping into fresh clothes. The kindness he had briefly shown Kate, and the apparent admiration for her work, had largely vanished to be replaced by something altogether tougher and more demanding. He had rapidly become sure of her and made no attempt to hide the fact; criticizing everything about her from her dress sense to her lack of enthusiasm for his friends, and, worst of all, the way in which she was bringing up her child.

It was this last condemnation which alienated her: the others were mere pinpricks in comparison. Nothing infuriated her more than accusations levelled at Jake; she alone had the right to criticize his behaviour. She had not, however, ticked him off about the incident with the wine bottle; he had been given plenty of provocation, in her view. Niall's coldness towards children was one of his least attractive traits, and its discovery had gone a long way to killing her feelings for him. Unfortunately, he was at his most gentle and likeable in bed, where she no longer had any compulsion to be. There was little else to bind them together, no common thread or interest or sense of humour, beyond a fondness for the theatre: it was hardly enough. She found herself parrying his demands on her company, making excuses, struggling to distance herself from him. And to think, she reminded herself now, none of this would have happened if it had not been for one ill-timed, misguided telephone call from Matt.

The excursion to Paris had been idly discussed, but not planned; no definite dates fixed, merely an idea thought up in a moment of comparative harmony. She had hoped the concept had been conveniently forgotten by Niall, but that piece of wishful thinking was shattered at dinner. They had gone in a party to one of Curzon Street's gambling clubs, his favourite type of entertainment, she had discovered, and one that up until this evening she had managed to avoid. She had suspected it would prove to be her idea of a nightmare, and she was correct. His friends did not vary much; designer-clad women with slightly overweight men sat round the table discussing the problems of finding a reliable nanny, and the disgraceful cost of berthing one's yacht in the South of France. Unable to comment on an alien world, Kate ate peacefully in almost total silence, which she knew would irritate Niall enormously. At the end of dinner, the rest of the party drifted away to the casino, leaving Kate and Niall alone. He drew two air tickets from his inside pocket and laid them on the table.

'What are these?' she had asked, staring at them with a sense of foreboding.

'Tickets, Kate darling. What do they look like?' His eyes had a self-congratulatory gleam in them. 'I decided it was time to make arrangements for our

Parisian weekend. You thought I'd forgotten, didn't you?' he added perspicaciously.

She coloured. 'You might have discussed it with me. I don't even know the dates you've fixed on.'

'June twenty-third, a fortnight from next Friday.'

'I'm sure that's Jake's Sports Day,' she said, hedging wildly.

'You and your commitments.' He sighed.

'*My* commitments? What about yours?'

'I don't let them rule my life like you do. The catering is in safe hands; I delegate, you see,' he told her. 'You should learn to do the same.'

'That's not fair,' she hissed at him across the table. 'My life's different. You can't take off at the drop of a hat when children are involved. I have to arrange for Jake to be properly looked after.'

'You have a nanny.'

'No, I don't. Helga's an au pair, a mother's help, part time.'

'What about your admirable husband?' he suggested with a touch of sarcasm.

She stared at him unbelievingly. The immorality of using one's husband as child-minder while indulging in an illicit weekend seemed to have escaped him totally.

'I really don't think I can go,' she said.

'If you can't,' he answered coldly, 'then I'd like to know. I can find someone else to take up the ticket; it would be a pity to waste it.'

His eyes were like blue ice, and a little frightening. He disliked being thwarted.

'Then do so,' she snapped, undaunted. 'I hate being taken for granted.'

He lowered the coffee cup poised halfway to his lips, and put out a placatory hand to touch her wrist. She watched his expression change from the truculent to the appealing, and sighed inwardly.

'Perish the thought,' he said softly. 'It was meant as

a surprise.' Leaning forward, gazing at her earnestly, he added, 'Please come, Kate. There's no-one else I want to take.'

She straightened her back, and tried to sound brisk and in command. 'I'll have to let you know,' she said.

This conversation should never have been allowed to take place, she realized. She should have snatched the opportunity of telling him about a possible new start to the marriage, and she had let it slip by; another example of her recent indecisiveness. There was time enough in the next hour to regret it. She had accompanied Niall reluctantly downstairs to the casino, where he handed her a supply of chips and left her at one of the roulette tables while he disappeared to play cards. Gambling held no interest for her; she stood watching the seated players placing their bets with deft, practised fingers, raking in their winnings and accepting the losses without a quiver of emotion, and wondered where the fascination lay. There was surprisingly little glamour attached to them; if one were prepared to risk thousands on the turn of a wheel, she reflected, one might as well look good doing it. Her only other experience of casinos had been a small example in France on one of Matt's trips. Slightly sozzled on wine and sun they had recklessly thrown away a meagre handful of francs in a very different atmosphere of levity and good humour. The thought of it now made her sad. Her feet hurt and she was, she realized, extremely bored. These factors, compounded with the ignominy of being unceremoniously dumped on her own, led to a last impulsive gesture. Without bothering to count their value, she had placed every chip she held on the number three. It never occurred to her she might win. Her mind was elsewhere, fixed on the letter she had decided to write Niall, when the ball rattled to a stop in the wheel; her attention had to be drawn by the croupier to the neat pyramid of chips being pushed across the table towards her.

She had cashed them in for what turned out to be a shockingly large amount of money and went in search of Niall, who refused to accept it. He had taken back his original stake at her insistence: 'if it makes you feel better,' he said. 'Buy something incredibly sexy with the rest.'

'I shall give it to charity,' she replied coolly, incensed by the sexist remark.

She had gone home in a taxi alone; her choice, and one to which he did not put up much resistance, eager to continue the evening's gambling. It occurred to her that this was the undisclosed source of extra income about which he was so vague.

She had left the wad of notes in her wallet, ready to be banked the next day, made a mug of coffee and thought long and hard about what to do with the money. Eventually she made out a cheque for half the sum to Cancer Research, and turned to the task of the letter in an untypically feminist state of mind. A faintly puritan streak in her, perhaps inherited from her mother, made her feel her gains were ill-gotten; on the other hand, they insured her independence. She would go to Paris on her own terms, she wrote to Niall, separate bedrooms, an early flight home on the Sunday, and her accommodation financed by herself. Most men would find such rules unacceptable; in all likelihood he would cancel the whole project, and she would be spared the stress. In any case, no-one could mistake the letter for anything other than a brush-off, the beginning of the end. She closed the envelope, searched for a first-class stamp and found there were none left. When she raised her head, Jake was standing in the open doorway in his pyjama trousers, hair tousled and dark eyes heavy from sleep.

'Darling! What are you doing out of bed?'

'I had a dream, then I went to the loo and saw the light was on down here.' He came and lolled against her, half-comatose. She put her arm round him. 'Roly rang,' he said. 'He wanted to know whether you'd be here tomorrow. He needs to talk to you about something special.'

'I'll call him.'

'Mum?'

'Yes?'

'Is Daddy coming back? Ever?'

'I hope so – I'm sure – look, it's too late to talk about this now,' she said, giving him a hug. 'We'll choose a better moment. All right?'

'You'll forget.'

'I shan't, I promise.' If I only knew the answer, she thought.

'Nobody tells me *anything*.'

'Darling, that's not true. If there were something to tell – it isn't easy for us, you see . . .'

Her words trailed off lamely. He wriggled free of her arm. 'I'm going back to bed,' he said gruffly.

'Don't worry,' she told him. 'Things will work out fine. A kiss?'

He kissed her on the cheek. 'Can I go to Toby's place for the whole day on Saturday?'

'Of course.'

He disappeared, padding up the stairs on bare feet. She closed the lid of the bureau, overwhelmed by depression and a feeling of inadequacy.

Toby lived three streets away from Jake. His father was a musician, an oboist with the Royal Philharmonic Orchestra. His mother had a part-time job in an art gallery, and sculpted in a loft they had constructed without planning permission. His two older sisters treated Toby like a puppy, lavishing affection on him, or ignoring him depending on mood. The household lacked organization; it had a chaotic charm which fascinated Jake whose life seemed regulated in comparison. Meals were haphazard, they might appear at any hour or not at all, and the family had learned to forage for themselves when hungry. Flavia Madden, Toby's mother, was quite a good cook when she put her mind to it, but she was apt to get engrossed in her sculpture. She was vague to the point of amnesia: 'The house runs itself,' she would say happily to whoever cared to listen, smiling out from between curtains of untidy blond hair. There was a certain amount of truth in this, since none of the family appeared undernourished or particularly unwashed. The kitchen was the focal point of their existence, where everything from school books, discarded clothing and musical instruments got dumped alongside the crockery and jam jars like some crazy jumble sale.

'Ma says to get our own lunch,' Toby told Jake. 'There're beefburgers or baked beans. Which do you want?'

'Don't mind, you choose.' Jake stroked the tortoiseshell cat which was busy licking a butter dish on the kitchen table.

'No, you; you're the guest, I suppose.'

'OK then; baked beans.'

'You make the toast,' Toby said, finding a saucepan amongst the debris by the sink.

'Where's the toaster?'

'Underneath that anorak, over there.'

While they ate, they planned their afternoon. At the end of the street a large building, once a furniture depository and known to them as the warehouse, was being demolished. It was strictly out of bounds even to the liberated Madden family because of falling masonry, but the ground floor had been gutted, leaving a vast expanse of concrete, too tempting as a football pitch to be denied. It was Saturday, and work on the site had stopped for the weekend. They set out to walk the two hundred yards, Toby carrying the ball under one arm. Heat bounced off the pavement; the day was airless with a hint of thunder.

'D'you think the glue-sniffers will be there?' asked Jake.

The warehouse had become a draw to drifters and junkies, another reason for it being forbidden territory.

Toby shrugged. 'How do I know?'

'What'll we do if they are?'

'Go somewhere else.'

They ducked under the barriers and the warning notices which read 'Demolition in Progress. Unauthorized Entry Forbidden', and advanced cautiously across the cavernous space, peering into distant shadowy corners. The place was a shell, roofless, the walls towering upwards towards the sky. In a week they too would be gone, reduced to rubble. No-one else was there.

'OK. Goalposts,' Toby said.

They used four bricks from a pile stacked against one wall, and started to play, their voices echoing backwards and forwards, raucous as starlings. Playing one a side was strenuous work; numerous goals were scored by each of them since neither was intrepid enough to throw themselves flat on concrete to save the shot. Eventually Toby skinned his hands and elbows by mistake, and a halt was called to the game. 'Shit!' he said, examining the damage. Jake found a not over-clean handkerchief in his jeans; they mopped him up with spit, and went to sit with their backs against the wall.

'Let's do something else.'

'Don't let's do anything for a bit,' Jake said. 'It's too hot.'

'Bring any sweets?' asked Toby. 'I forgot.'

Jake rummaged in his pocket, and came up with

an Opal Fruit covered in fluff. 'There's only one. You can have it.'

'Thanks. We can share it if you like.'

'Yuck! Not after you've licked it.'

'OK, be like that.'

They ruminated in silence, broken only by the sucking sounds emanating from Toby, and the whine of a persistent bluebottle.

'How easy d'you think it'd be to fake an illness?' Jake asked out of the blue.

'What sort of illness?'

'A really worrying one where doctors are called, and parents wait anxiously to hear the results. Comforting each other,' he added.

'Not a hope,' Toby replied. 'They'd see through it. You wouldn't *look* ill for one thing.' He eyed Jake speculatively. 'What gave you a prat-like idea like that, anyway?'

'Nothing.' Jake scuffed at the floor with his trainer.

'Why ask, then?' Toby said. 'I know, it's to do with getting your pa home, isn't it? You'll have to think up something better than that. Pretending to be sick will only make them mad when they find out. Don't know why you bother, really; you see him quite often, don't you?'

'It's not the same,' Jake said. 'It's all very well for you, living with two parents.'

'I wish I didn't, sometimes,' Toby said. 'Pa's always blowing his top; not that it means much.'

'Well, *I* want Daddy back,' Jake said obstinately. 'Two parents feels right to me. It'd be better for Mum, too. She's getting to be a bit funny on her own.'

'Funny ha-ha?'

'No, funny peculiar.' He did not elaborate; bloody Niall was best left out of the conversation. 'I thought of running away, but Mum shouldn't be left. Anyway, there's nowhere to go.'

'You could come to us,' Toby offered.

'I'd be brought home again by your mother.'

'It'd be a week, probably, before she realized you were there,' Toby said, grinning. 'Or you could live rough, in a cardboard box.'

Jake imagined the discomfort. 'No, I couldn't,' he said emphatically.

Toby got to his feet and started to dribble the ball this way and that across the concrete. Jake, watching him without the energy to move, decided it was the end of the discussion. He had forgotten Toby's propensity for sticking with a problem until he had an answer, even if it wasn't the right one. After a minute or two he returned and described a semicircle with the ball round Jake's out-stretched feet.

'I know what I'd do if it was me,' he said without pausing.

'What?'

'I'd do something that got me into trouble; bad enough to shock them.'

'Like what?'

'Like nicking something from a shop; nothing important, chewing-gum or such like, and letting yourself get caught.'

'I'm not nicking anything,' Jake said, shocked himself, 'and I don't see how it would help anyway.'

'It would! It would! Specially in your case.' Toby squatted on his haunches, thrusting his face near Jake, eager to explain. 'If you do something really wrong, it puts the wind up parents. They think you're turning into a delinquent, and gang together to discipline you. Nothing makes them closer than deciding on a punishment.'

'Mine would just argue, probably,' Jake said, unconvinced.

Toby shook his head. 'Your mother would say to herself, "This is too much for me. The boy needs a father at home, I can't cope." Bet you that's what would happen.'

His voice rose in mimicry of a distraught female. Jake laughed.

'She doesn't talk like that,' he said, 'and she doesn't get really mad at me, even when I locked the cousins in the shed.'

'Oh that!' Toby dismissed the petty crime scornfully. 'It's got to be worse than that.' He rolled the ball round and round with his foot, thoughtfully.

'Well, what then?'

'I've got an idea coming to me. Hang on.'

Jake waited. Eventually Toby reached deep into his pocket, drew out a cardboard packet and opened the lid. Inside lay a number of capsules encased in what looked like glass.

'What are they?'

'You'll see,' Toby told him. 'I'll give you a demonstration, only you'd better be ready to run.'

Jake stood up. 'They're not explosives, are they?' he asked, wide-eyed.

Toby did not answer. He held one of the capsules between finger and thumb, and dropped it on the floor. 'Ready?' Then he brought down the heel of his trainer firmly and crushed the capsule into the ground. The effect was instant. An overpowering and throat-catching stench, redolent of sulphur, rotting vegetables and blocked drains rose to engulf them. Toby grabbed the ball and they ran, holding their noses, towards the street and fresh air; stopping and turning at the warehouse entrance to look back, although there was nothing to be seen.

'WOW!' Jake said. 'You can smell it from here, even. What is it?'

'A stink bomb, dumbo. Haven't you ever set one off?'

'No. Where d'you get them?'

'Joke shops.' Toby grinned. 'Come on.' He ducked under the barrier.

'Where are we going?'

'Home first, to drop the ball off, then we're going shopping. That was an *open* space,' he added as they trudged along the pavement. 'Just think how it would be in a supermarket. Brilliant!'

Jake stared at him; diabolical glee was written all over Toby's cherubic face. Jake knew that expression well.

'Is *that* your idea?' he asked, caution struggling with an excited longing to see the result.

'Can you think of a better one?' Toby said; but the question was rhetorical.

Matt found his Sunday unexpectedly disrupted. Three-quarters of his book was finished, and he had arranged to deliver it by hand to his literary agent, followed by giving Birgitta lunch. The gesture would be in the nature of a farewell to their non-affair, a thank-you and an apology in one. He felt badly about Birgitta. He had made use of her: as a stand-in stepmother and cook, and very occasionally as bed-mate. She had accepted all her roles with uncomplaining docility, and, aware that she was far more devoted to him than he to her, he had given her little in return. He was not looking forward to this assignment, but he, like Kate, needed to tidy up his life if there were to be changes. Now, owing to Kate's phone call, he had had to postpone lunch and take Jake with him to Islington to drop off the script. It was not that he minded having Jake without warning, he thought of it as a bonus; merely that Kate seemed to be making a meal out of a rather trivial misdemeanour and expected him to deliver a lecture.

She had rung him the previous evening as he was going to bed. It was several moments before he could sort out what she was saying: something about Jake causing a public disturbance in a supermarket and being brought home by the police.

'What on earth was he doing in a supermarket in the first place?' Matt asked.

'I've just told you. He went there with another boy, wretched Toby Madden of course, on purpose.'

'But what did he actually *do* to cause mayhem?'

Kate hesitated. 'They let off stink bombs. Apparently you can get the bloody things at a joke shop,' she said almost sulkily.

He had roared with laughter before he could stop himself. 'Really? I remember using those things at school. We cleared the library with them once.'

'It's not funny,' she snapped. 'They disrupted the whole place. Someone saw them, dragged them off to the manager's office, and he took it very seriously. It's a shock to have your child brought home by the police.'

'Police in the plural?' he asked. 'For one small boy?'

'Well, no. There was one constable, in fact, but I don't see that makes it any better.'

'And was Jake contrite?'

'I don't know; he was very quiet and rather pale. I started to give him quite a mild rocket, and he said he felt sick, so I left off.' She sighed. 'He used to be so easy, no problem at all. He's changed recently. I think you should talk to him, Matt. Can you have him tomorrow?'

He thought. 'I suppose so. But I'm no good at playing the heavy father, as you know.'

'Well, don't make it into a treat, either.'

'Don't expect miracles,' he said. 'I think it all stems from us, in any case. He's unsettled.'

'My fault, is what you're saying?' She sounded defensive and suddenly near tears.

'It's nobody's fault,' he said gently. 'But the sooner we come to a decision about ourselves, the better.'

Nothing was said about the supermarket episode on the drive to Islington. Jake and he talked about books, and the part that agents played in the process of getting one published; Jake holding Matt's script in its folder on his lap, gazing at it reverently. Matt's agent, Adrian Meade, worked from home, his office an Aladdin's cave of delight to Jake with its stacks of manuscripts and sophisticated word processor and shelves of books around the walls. He was allowed to choose one, and lay on the floor reading while Matt and Adrian discussed editing and other intriguing subjects, their chairs drawn up to a huge desk.

When they left, Matt drove straight to the rather expensive restaurant where he had planned to give Birgitta lunch and had not bothered to cancel the table. No doubt Kate would have put such extravagance in the category of 'spoiling'; but he was of the opinion that good cooking was a necessity, not a treat, even where ten-year-old boys were concerned. He was rewarded by Jake's unusually prodigious appetite and a willingness to talk about Saturday's crime.

'I s'pose Mum's told you what we did?' he asked through a mouthful of roast beef. 'Are you furious, because you don't seem to be?'

'Furious, no. Critical, yes,' Matt said. 'Tell me in your own words what happened.'

Jake's account was graphic to the point where Matt had difficulty in stifling laughter. The two boys had each set off a bomb in one of the queues at a check-out desk. Confusion and consternation had ensued; staff and shoppers had scattered, handkerchiefs were held to noses, a salesgirl grabbed a tin of air freshener and sprayed at random with little effect. Those shoppers who had paid for their goods escaped to the exits. Loaded baskets and trolleys were dumped anywhere as people attempted to find a stench-free zone. Two trolleys, being pushed furiously in opposite directions, collided with a crash. As an act of sabotage, the bombing was an unqualified success, but there were reprisals. A woman who had been standing behind the boys in the queue, recovered herself enough to point them out vociferously as they were edging their way cautiously towards the exit doors and freedom, and they were caught by a security guard. The supermarket manager was unrelenting: thugs started young, he claimed; they would not stop there, they would progress to shoplifting if he did not teach them a lesson. The constable, called off his beat by the local police station, gave them an amiable lecture and returned each boy to his mother with the advice to keep them off the streets in future. Jake did not mention that shoplifting had been Toby's idea in the first place.

'I suspect this was Toby's brilliant scheme, wasn't it?' Matt asked.

'Well,' Jake took his first spoonful of chocolate mousse, 'he did have the stink bombs. We *both* thought it'd be fun, though.'

'And it was, I suppose?'

'The best bit,' Jake said wistfully, 'was the trolleys in a head-on crash. I wish you could have seen it, Daddy.'

'It's not difficult to imagine, as told by you. I think you'll make a promising writer.'

'Do you?' Jake looked up, his eyes shining.

'If you stay out of a remand home,' Matt said with irony. 'Causing chaos is invariably tempting, and I can understand your giving way to it. But once is enough; after that it gets boring for everyone concerned. Mum is naturally upset. Finding you on the doorstep with the Bill in tow was alarming.'

'Yes, I know, I'm sorry.'

'So no repeats, please, and no more schemes of an antisocial nature. Stick to football or cricket or swimming; or is that a tedious suggestion?'

'We played football yesterday, but it got too hot.'

'So you thought you'd have a bit of harmless fun instead?' Matt glanced at his son over the rim of his coffee cup. 'Was "fun" the only reason for this diversion, or did it have another purpose?' he asked.

Jake's naturally pale face turned pink.

'Not really,' he answered, staring at his plate.

'Just wondered,' Matt remarked casually, signalling for the bill.

'Daddy?'

'Yes?'

'You remember when you and Mum went out together that evening? For a talk, you said.'

'I remember.'

'What did you talk about?' Jake's eyes were on Matt's face, dark and intense.

'About you, and schools, a lot of the time.'

'Oh.' Jake sounded disappointed. He fiddled with the pepper-mill dispiritedly.

'And we discussed other things,' Matt added, realizing where this interrogation was leading. 'Our lives, Mum's and mine; we were trying to plan.'

'I thought,' Jake said carefully, 'you might have decided to come home; but you haven't, have you?'

'Not yet, but I'm hoping to. Do you mind us being apart very much indeed?'

'Yes, I do,' Jake said. 'Nothing's the same without you. Even Mum's different, ever since that Niall' – the name slipped out before he could bite it back – 'it's not like a family any more,' he ended in a rush.

The mention of Niall did not go unnoticed. But it was not fair, Matt decided, to quiz Jake for more information.

'I'm not happy being away from you either,' he said, giving Jake's thin shoulder a squeeze. 'But Mum and I messed things up once, and we want to be sure it won't happen again, d'you see?'

Jake nodded.

'We're nearly there, so very nearly certain,' Matt murmured half to himself. Possibly Jake heard because his face brightened.

'It's Sports Day soon,' he said. 'The thirtieth of June. You will be there, won't you?'

'Of course I shall.'

'You weren't last year, and I won the hundred metres.'

'I was away on a trip,' Matt admitted apologetically. 'There'll be no hitches this time.'

Later, after he had taken Jake home, Niall's name returned to him accompanied by an acute stab of jealousy. Whoever he was, he was important enough in Kate's life to pose a threat, judging by Jake's bitter disapproval. The instincts of children were seldom wrong. What had become of Roly? Matt wondered. Good-hearted Roly who had seemed at one time to be acting as watchdog over Kate? On impulse he lifted the telephone receiver and dialled Roly's number.

In the days following Jake's escapade, it appeared to Kate that nothing she planned went smoothly. Niall, far from objecting to her chilling terms for the French weekend, agreed to them with unbelievable forbearance. While mistrusting his acquiescence – Niall was not a meek man – she reached the point where it seemed easier to go ahead with the ill-conceived trip and get it over and done with than to think up excuses. Immediately, she found herself caught up in a web of half-truths and deception that made her crawl with shame. Her long-standing friend Felicity was married to Edward Hurley, Second Secretary at the British Embassy in Paris, and they were brought into play as the reason for Kate's visit. Their flat was already full to capacity, which entailed her staying in an hotel, although she intended to see a lot of them: this became Kate's standard story-line, as near to the truth as she could get, for she would indeed meet up with Felicity at some point. Felicity, when telephoned, instantly guessed at duplicity. 'What's all this nonsense about hotels? You could have stayed with us. What are you up to, darling?' Kate stalled the questioning by promising an explanation when they met.

Jake was to go to her parents for the weekend, which pleased her mother Prue so much that she accepted Kate's story without query. It would do her daughter good to get a break, she commented. Her father said little, simply giving Kate a sharp glance and raising an eyebrow while remarking, 'You can't see Paris in forty-eight hours; I hope it's worth it. Who *is* Felicity, by the way?' Jake asked the same question, and a great many more besides. His eyes, wide with scepticism, told her that he did not believe her, and her guilt doubled. 'Why can't I stay with Daddy?' he demanded, the question she had anticipated and dreaded.

'He needs time to finish his book. He can't have you every weekend, darling.'

'If he was living here, I'd be here too, all the time,' he said with unanswerable logic. 'I wouldn't get in his way.'

To Isobel she told the truth; it was necessary to warn her that she would not be at work on the Friday, and she was tired of lying. Isobel remarked on Kate's apparent madness, adding that she might possibly find time to look at materials in one or two decorating establishments, and changed the subject.

Twenty-four hours before she was due to leave, when she thought she had everything arranged, Kate had a call from her mother to say her father had been admitted to hospital with a badly fractured ankle. He had fallen from a ladder while tying up a climbing rose. Prue felt that looking after Jake combined with

125

hospital visiting would be too much for her; Kate would have to make other arrangements.

'I shan't go,' Kate told her mother, regretting the time and trouble spent in organizing herself. 'I'll come down on Sunday to see Pa.'

'There's no need,' Prue said. 'I don't think they'll keep him in for long; you can visit him when he's home, later on. Can't Matt take care of Jake? He *is* his father,' she added pointedly.

'Not this weekend, he's busy. Give my love to Pa.'

Kate rang off, sought out Helga and explained that she wouldn't be going away after all. Helga waited until she had finished before saying, 'I will look after Jake. I am doing nothing serious this weekend. I would like to be with him.'

'It's very kind of you, Helga,' Kate said, 'but I couldn't leave you on your own.'

'You do not trust me? After all the time I have been with you in this house?' Helga asked in lugubrious tones.

She did not follow the normal pattern of au pairs, most of whom came to England, picked up a smattering of the language and a dubious man or two, and left after a year. She had already stayed two years, and Kate had come to rely on her, dreading the day she decided to return to her native Germany. More than just another pair of hands, Helga had become a friend, seeing Kate through the dreadful days of Matt's and her parting with a kind of brusque compassion. Statuesque but not beautiful, dour by nature, she could appear formidable to those who did not know her. Perhaps for this reason there were apparently no men in her life, although she claimed to be engaged to a tax inspector from Berlin. If it were so, she showed no burning desire to rejoin him. Exercise was her religion; every spare moment she had was spent in swimming, running or aerobics, and watching athletics on television. Above all, and most importantly from Kate's point of view, she was devoted to Jake.

'Oh Helga, it's not that,' Kate protested. 'Of course I trust you. It's the responsibility of being the sole one in charge. If something should happen . . .' she added vaguely.

'Nothing will happen.' Helga drew herself up to her full height of five foot ten as if defying fate. 'If something is wrong, then I will telephone you.'

'I can at least ask Roland if he would mind sleeping in the house so you're not alone.'

'Mr Roland is very nice, but he is a man. It would not be correct,' Helga said severely. 'I am not afraid; it isn't necessary. And I have Jake so I should not be alone.'

Kate sank onto one of the kitchen chairs. 'I wish I knew what to do,' she said wearily.

'It is decided,' Helga said. 'You must go. Jake and I will have fun together.'

Strange, Kate thought when she had given in and was packing a suitcase, how everyone seemed determined to send her on her way. How differently they would behave if they knew the whole shabby truth. She could not help a tremor of excitement as she put her passport in her handbag, the old longing for the sights and sounds of another country which had nothing to do with Niall's company. She lowered the lid of the case without fastening it, and faced up to the task of asking a favour of Roly with reluctance. Their friendship had undergone a subtle change recently. Although it continued in its familiar pattern of home suppers and dinners out, there were subjects now that they both avoided, and small tensions had crept between them as a result. It stemmed from the early days of her relationship with Niall; she was aware that Roly knew of it, and he knew that she knew. She would have to have been blind to remain unconscious of his persistent shadowing of her, and yet she never mentioned it, afraid of humiliating him.

And then, at their last meeting, he had brought Niall into the conversation; rumour had it, he said, that she was seeing a great deal of him. A blackening of Niall's character followed: his dubious reputation where women were concerned, his meanness, even his dishonesty. Roly, his bland face creased with anxiety, claimed to be issuing a warning for her sake; but Kate saw a sharpness in his eyes, made up of anger and pain which was new to her. It was not the denigration of Niall she minded, but the encroachment on her privacy. It was none of Roly's business; he had gone too far, and she told him as much with her temper barely under control. The awkward episode had been glossed over, leaving behind it an increased uneasiness. And yet, she loved and trusted Roly. There was no-one else she could think of asking to keep an eye on her household for the days she was away. Whatever happened, however distorted his emotions had made him, he would always remain in her eyes a rare family friend.

Chapter Five

In the late afternoon of the Friday of Kate's departure, Roly took Jake to the cinema. The fine weather had broken, and a light but steady rain fell from lunchtime onwards. Helga had declined to go with them; Arnold Schwarzenegger did not interest her, there would be the Wimbledon Tennis Championships on television if the rain cleared, and she would have supper waiting for them when they returned.

The film, a complicated story involving aliens, did not hold Roly's attention for long. His mind kept slipping back to earlier in the day when he had embarked on one of his fruitless and masochistic exercises. Realizing its futility but unable to prevent himself, he had cancelled all appointments for the afternoon, eaten an early sandwich at his desk and driven from his office to Heathrow. Concealment was not easy in the departure hall of Terminal 4. A crowd of school children were being organized by a teacher into an untidy queue for one of the check-in desks, and Roly had stationed himself near them, as if officially connected to the party. But they had moved slowly forwards, and he had been left, hidden behind the doubtful camouflage of a newspaper, his eyes cautiously peering over it every so often and flicking between the British Airways and the Air France counters.

Kate had appeared from nowhere, wearing a white raincoat. She put down her suitcase, glanced at her watch and stood looking around her. At a safe distance, Roly buried himself behind the full width of the *Telegraph*; minutes later, when he dared look again, she had disappeared. And then he caught sight of her, dwarfed by the male figure beside her, standing in the queue for British Airways. There was no mistaking Niall's height and mane of grey hair. Up until that moment Roly had clung to the faint hope that her improbable story was true, that the Paris-based friends actually existed. He would far rather she had been honest with him, he told himself, knowing quite well it was too much to wish for, and would have made no difference to his feelings in any case. With the now familiar sensation of sick fury in the pit of his stomach, he had turned and left the building in search of his car.

In the cinema seat beside him, there was the muted rustle of paper as Jake unwrapped a chocolate bar without taking his eyes from the screen. Arnold Schwarzenegger appeared to be running through some kind of tunnel, an athletic blonde by his side. Sound effects rose to a crescendo, denoting either imminent danger or the near conclusion of the film. Roly hoped it was the latter. He was grateful for his temporary guardianship of Jake, glad of the uncomplicated companionship of Kate's child to distract him. He wished the film would end so that they could communicate, instead of his sitting isolated in the darkness plagued by mental pictures of Kate and Niall.

Matt had telephoned him a few days previously, opening the conversation with the usual preliminaries exchanged by friends who rarely meet.

'Hi there. How are things?'

'Fine, thanks, Matt,' Roly had lied. 'And yourself?'

'Not bad, not bad. Haven't seen you around for ages. We must meet up.' A pause. 'Listen, Roly, do you mind if I ask you a rather probing question?'

'Go ahead.'

'I know you see a lot of Kate.'

(My God! Roly thought. Where was this leading?)

'You probably have an idea of who her friends are,' Matt said. 'Have you come across anyone called Neil, by any chance?'

Roly replied in relief, 'There is Niall Hunter. He spells it NIALL. May I ask what all this is about?'

'Jake mentioned him, you know the way children do,' Matt told him. 'He seems to have taken a deep dislike to him, from which I can but conclude that Kate is involved.' He hesitated. 'Whom Kate sees isn't my concern for the moment: except when it affects Jake, and then it's a different matter.'

'I see,' Roly said slowly, trying desperately to think of a way to denigrate Niall without implicating Kate. 'I'm not surprised by Jake's reactions. Niall Hunter isn't very likeable.'

'The name rings a bell. Wasn't he mixed up in an MP's divorce a year or so back?'

'Some kind of sleaze or other, certainly,' Roly agreed. He added, 'I don't believe Jake sees much of him. His antipathy is based on one meeting, as far as I know.'

'Once was enough, apparently,' Matt said.

'Look, if there's anything I can do,' Roly offered.

'No, thanks, Roly, I'm not going to drag you into my problems. You've given me a full name which is all I wanted. Although I don't know what the hell to do about it,' Matt said, more to himself than to Roly. 'Probably nothing in the end, as long as Jake's not upset. Kate is lucky to have you to keep an eye on her,' he remarked. 'You're a good mate, Roly. She's very fond of you, you know.'

'And I of her.' (You fool! I bloody love her.)

'Let's make a date to meet; it's been far too long. Do you still play tennis?'

'Occasionally, very badly.'

'Doesn't matter. How about next Tuesday evening at the Club?'

Roly could not help feeling afterwards that he could have made more of this conversation; driven Matt into a frenzy of jealousy by declaring Kate and Niall to be lovers. On second thoughts, however, Matt was not the type to seek out a rival with a horse-whip. Roly had never understood the arrangement that Matt and Kate had within the structure of their separation, which seemed to give them limitless free-dom. Neither could he understand Matt's apparent passivity over the way in which Kate was leading her life. And yet it was this same tolerance which had drawn Roly to him all those years ago at university. Matt had treated him like a serious human being, not a buffoon; virtually the only one of their crowd to laugh with him rather than at him. If he had to fall in love with someone else's wife, he wished fervently it could have been any woman other than Kate.

Helga had taken a chocolate cake from the oven when they arrived home, and was turning it out of its tin onto a wire tray.

'Black Forest Gateau. Yippee!' Jake prodded it with a finger.

Helga slapped at him with the oven gloves. 'Your hands are dirty. Go and wash.'

They ate supper round the scrubbed kitchen table, laid with a cloth in Roly's honour. Wimbledon had been rained off, Helga informed them, but she had spent the time cleaning Kate's bedroom. Jake regaled her with the full story of the film which he appeared miraculously to have understood, to make up for her boring afternoon. Later, he took Roly upstairs to his room to admire *The Diehard Chronicles*, the pages stacked as neatly as his father's script.

'I've added some stories of my own,' Jake said. 'I hope you don't mind. You haven't told me any new ones for ages.'

'I will, I promise. Anyway, I'm glad you're making them up. You're the writer; I'm just an occasional narrator.'

'I think we should have both our names on the cover when it's published,' Jake said with the supreme confidence of a novice. 'You can have joint authors, Daddy says.'

'I'd like that.' Roly wandered across the room to examine the white-painted bookshelves. 'You've cleared a shelf,' he observed.

'All the baby books,' Jake said. 'They're in that box there. I wanted to give them to a children's hospital but Mum won't let me, because of the illustrations being specially good. I want space for my script, and Daddy's book when it's finished; things like that.'

'You'll need a whole shelf if he's going to carry on writing,' Roly agreed. 'You're supposed to be getting ready for bed, aren't you?' he said, remembering his responsibilities as a temporary uncle.

Jake peeled off his T-shirt, wriggled out of his jeans and tossed them onto a chair. 'Ready,' he said.

'No pyjamas?'

'Pyjamas are for wimps,' he announced scornfully, throwing himself on top of the duvet.

'Teeth, then,' Roly told him, waiting until the cursory brushing was completed and Jake had taken a running jump into bed.

'It feels funny without Mum,' he said. 'I'm glad you're here to say good night.'

'So am I.' Roly turned to go. 'Shall I put out the light?'

'No thanks, I'm going to read.' Jake reached for a book on the bedside table. 'Roly?'

'Yes?'

'I don't think we'll have to poison bloody Niall after all.'

'*Poison* him?'

'It was your idea: don't you remember?'

'No, I don't,' Roly said, mildly horrified. 'Forget I said it.'

'Well, anyway, it doesn't matter now,' Jake said, yawning. 'I don't really mind about him any longer. Daddy will be coming home soon and everything will be all right.'

From the door Roly looked into a pair of dark eyes bright with excitement. Momentarily at a loss for words, he struggled inwardly to share in Jake's happiness. 'Really?' he managed to say at last. 'That's wonderful news.'

Helga was still in the kitchen when he went downstairs. Before saying good night to her he wandered into the empty drawing-room lit by a single table lamp. He looked around him as if seeing everything that was there for the first time; the yellow silk curtains, the sofa and armchairs with their covers patterned in blue hydrangeas, the polished dining-table and chairs up the far end of the room, the marble chimney-breast and the small carriage clock ticking away almost inaudibly in the quietness. Kate's scent seemed to linger in the air. He thought of the many evenings spent there, Jake lying on his stomach in front of the television, Kate and he, Roly, sharing the sofa, her low, bubbling laughter that was more of a giggle breaking out at one of his witticisms. And then his mental imagery changed, and his own figure was replaced by that of Matt, his arm round Kate's shoulders as she leant against him, relaxed and at peace. Roly visualized them all, a family reunited, contented and self-sufficient, within whose charmed circle there was no place for outsiders, no role for him to play. He would remain a friend, doubtless warmly welcomed as a frequent visitor, and Kate would remember him with fondness – that insipid, lukewarm emotion – and possibly gratitude; while he continued to burn with the same hopeless and unrelenting love. She would be forever removed from him, as inaccessible as a nun behind convent walls.

'You have lost something, Mr Roland?' Helga asked through the open doorway.

'Yes, I have,' he replied, deep in thought. 'That is – no, thanks, Helga. I was looking for a book I lent Kate, but I expect she's taken it with her.'

'You are looking pale,' she remarked with her usual directness as they moved to the hall. 'First you work in your office, and then go to the cinema: it's not good for you. You need fresh air.'

'You're probably right,' he agreed, attempting to smile. 'Don't forget to lock up, Helga, and give me a ring if you need me.'

It had stopped raining. The whole of his body felt heavy, weighted down by the shock of sudden comprehension. The threat of Niall had dwindled into insignificance, rendered unimportant by those few words from Jake. How, Roly asked himself, had he failed to consider the possible mending of the marriage? It had been, after all, the simplest and most likely of outcomes. He supposed his mind had blocked out automatically that which would bring about his certain downfall. He had not stood a chance with Kate; and yet, against all odds, persistent hope had never quite left him; until this moment. Jake's delight was his despair. In the privacy of his car, he leaned his forehead against the steering-wheel, while a single tear trickled slowly down either side of his face.

In the drawing-room of her flat Felicity Hurley poured coffee into two cups and handed one to Kate across the sofa table.

'I'm terribly pleased you're here,' she said, 'but I'm still in the dark about how it's come about. No Matt, a strange man – very strange by the sound of him – and that's all I know. You must fill me in; the whole saga, please, from the beginning.'

'It'll take forever if I start from the very beginning,' Kate said, taking a sip from the bone-china cup. She felt worn out, and had been thinking longingly of a large vodka and tonic, but without the courage to ask for it at eleven-thirty in the morning. 'I'll explain about this ridiculous weekend, and exactly why I've landed myself on you with my luggage sitting in your hall. You're an angel.'

Felicity brushed the remark aside. 'I haven't seen you since God knows when; I want to hear everything, but we've got all day, so start where you like.' She settled herself in her armchair, long legs crossed, and waited expectantly.

She had not changed, Kate thought. The clothes, a beautifully-cut silk shirt and dark trousers might be unmistakably French but, despite them, Felicity was as she remembered her. The same disarming toothy grin breaking frequently across a deceptively gentle face that hid a determined will; the same straight blond hair cut in a shining bob. Kate and she had worked together in the days of the interior decorating magazine, and Felicity had shot up the career ladder to be made assistant editor; only to marry Edward shortly afterwards and assume the role of a diplomat's wife. Apart from postcards and Christmas cards, communication between herself and Kate had suffered from Felicity's itinerant lifestyle. It was a pleasurable surprise to find, now that they had caught up with one another, the bond between them was still there.

Felicity's drawing-room, with the sun flooding in through tall windows, its wide expanse of pale green carpet and two large vases of white gladioli, had an Englishness about it which Kate found soothing.

'You've no idea how lovely it is to be here after the Hotel Franklin,' Kate said.

'It's *supposed* to be quite good.'

'I never want to see it again,' she stated with conviction, 'but not through any fault of the hotel. I shouldn't have decided to go there in the first place.'

This indeed had been her feeling at the start of their journey. She fully anticipated a show of resentment from Niall at her declaration of independence, now he had had time to think it over; a black mood which would probably colour the entire trip and detract from whatever pleasure there was to be had from it. In fact, he had been surprisingly amenable, planning what they should see and do, entertaining her on the flight with anecdotes from holidays he had spent in France as a penniless teenager, suggesting champagne from the drinks trolley.

'No thanks.'

'You're probably right,' he had said. 'We'll have a bottle when we arrive; it'll be better quality.'

'It's wasted on me; I don't really like it,' she replied, anxious to squash as many romantic notions as possible.

She had regretted her repressive tone; it seemed churlish in the face of his uncharacteristically boyish enthusiasm. Looking back, she realized that she should have been warned of trouble ahead for this very reason, this unexplained elation. But his solicitude had lulled her into a sense of false security, reminding her of their first evening together when he had gone out of his way to comfort her. It did not lessen her resolution to end the relationship, but it relieved the nervous tension of having to do so.

The Hotel Franklin had been decorated, rather more imaginatively than the average three-star example, in the Imperialistic colours of red, green and gold. It promised comfort which was reassuring, but it crossed Kate's mind that even a single room might be more expensive than she had bargained for. There were brochures at the reception desk where she and Niall handed over their passports, and she unobtrusively slid one into her bag. She thought longingly of a bath.

'Room thirty-eight, on the second floor,' the clerk informed Niall, handing him the key.

'Thank you. Shall we go?' Niall said to Kate.

'I'm waiting for my key. The key to my room, please,' she asked the clerk.

'I have already given it to M'sieur.'

'But I have a separate room booked,' she insisted.

The clerk consulted the bookings. 'The reservation is for one room only; a large double with bath. *Une chambre superieur*,' he added as if that in itself should satisfy her.

Kate looked at him in disbelief as the truth struck her. She turned on Niall. 'You didn't make the reservation for two rooms, did you?' she said furiously.

'Excuse us a moment,' he told the clerk, and taking her by the arm, distanced themselves from the desk. 'You surely aren't sticking to your ridiculous insistence on independence, are you?' he asked, his voice lowered.

'I wrote it down. You had it in black and white, and you agreed,' she hissed back at him.

'I didn't take it seriously. I supposed it to be a rather juvenile gesture, written in a moment of temporary disenchantment.'

'Oh, did you? Well, you were wrong: I meant every word.' She glared at him, her tone as icy as his eyes.

'I fail to understand you, Kate. What is the point of this weekend if you're going to behave like a nun?'

'I explained in the letter. I offered to back out; I gave you the choice.' She became aware of the elderly porter guarding their luggage and pretending to ignore what was obviously a row. 'I want to be my own person,' she said in a fierce whisper. 'Either I have my own room or I leave on the next plane, and I rather want to see something of Paris. Now are you going to ask at the desk or shall I?'

For a second he loomed over her in speechless frustration, then swung away abruptly to face the clerk. There was a short conversation and further consultation of the reservations ledger, and Niall returned with a second key.

'Single room with shower,' he said coldly, dropping it into her hand. 'I'm afraid it's dangerously close to mine on the same floor, but you can always lock your door,' he added with exaggerated sarcasm.

The porter, sensing action at last, picked up the suitcases and Niall followed him to the lifts without waiting for Kate who was talking to the clerk.

'I'd like a separate bill in my name for the single room, please.'

'And the name is?'

'Protheroe, as in my passport.'

'Very well, Madame.'

'Thank you.'

A look of resigned bewilderment crossed his face, barely masked by the one of bland official courtesy. The English were all deranged, it stated clearly.

Only the creaking of the lift broke the silence as they rose to the second floor and were led along the corridor by the porter. They paused at Niall's room while the door was unlocked for him.

'We'd better meet downstairs in an hour's time,' he said, avoiding her eyes. 'We have to eat'; and he disappeared into his bedroom, while Kate was escorted to hers.

Felicity broke into Kate's discourse at this point to say, 'Weren't you rather asking for trouble? No man would put up with that kind of arrangement, surely?'

'That's why I wrote to him; I never expected him to. I imagined the whole thing would be cancelled.'

'And when it wasn't, why didn't you cry off yourself?'

Kate said, 'For two reasons, both of them selfish. I had a sneaking longing to catch a glimpse of Paris, which I last saw eighteen years ago. And more importantly, I wanted to see you.'

'You could have done both without Niall in tow,' Felicity refilled their coffee cups, 'and without the aggro.'

Kate sighed. 'It's too late to tell me that,' she said. 'Quite simply, the opportunity arose and I took it. The tickets were there, the hotel was there, and I thought I could handle the rest of it. The letter made it clear enough my feelings had changed; Niall appeared to understand and then reneged. I suppose it was naïve of me', she added, 'to have expected otherwise.'

'So what's new?' Felicity said cheerfully. 'You were always prone to getting yourself into impossible situations, I seem to remember.'

'I never looked at anyone but Matt in those days,' Kate protested.

'Maybe not, but many looked at *you*, and you could never be unkind to them, with disastrous consequences. Leaving that aside, why didn't you come to me yesterday evening when you knew the difficulties?'

'Because,' Kate told her, 'for a short while, a truce was called. It only lasted until the middle of dinner, but by that time it was too late for alternative plans.'

The single room had been small but newly decorated in shades of green and pink, and the bed when tested was comfortable. She ordered a bottle of mineral water by telephone, unpacked, took a shower and brooded over the evening ahead. There were several hours yet to be got through in an atmosphere that promised to be awkward. She cursed herself for a fool, and thought involuntarily of Matt and how different Paris would seem had he been there; an unwise speculation since it made her want to cry. She opened the window wide and leaned her arms on the sill, fighting off depression and breathing in the subtly foreign smell of the city. It was then that the telephone had rung, making her leap across the room anticipating some awful disaster at home. Niall was on the other end of the line, however, saying, 'I appear to have the duty-free Scotch. We might have a drink here, don't you think?' He sounded normal.

'Why not?' she said.

'Come along when you're ready.'

She started to look for something to wear, cautiously relieved by his gesture of goodwill. Perhaps, after all, it would be possible to spend the evening in reasonable harmony, providing they could avoid controversial subjects. Her reaction to his change of mood was a sense of guilt that this whole weekend was her fault, that she had behaved badly. She knew that if she did not stop herself, she would start to remember the better aspects of Niall and forgive the worst, in her mistaken desire for a peaceful settlement.

The room which had been destined for both of them and was now his alone, had all the space and comfort promised by the reception clerk. It even boasted a small sofa into which she sank while Niall poured their drinks. The décor followed the pattern of her own room with a similar striped wallpaper, dark red in this case, and unusually good prints on the walls.

'Having a look at what you're missing?' he asked,

handing her a glass; but it was said without animosity.

'There's nothing wrong with my room,' she replied equably.

'I suppose I should offer to change places with you. I will, if you like.'

'I'm quite happy where I am, thank you. Why are you being so nice all of a sudden?' she asked.

He shrugged. 'Because there's no point in open warfare. Bearing grudges is so tiring; you have to keep reminding yourself of their existence.' He swallowed the remainder of his drink and moved to refill the glass. 'I can't fathom the workings of your mind, Kate, but perhaps you'll enlighten me over dinner.'

She avoided a direct answer by asking, 'Where are we going?'

'There's a place in Montmartre; a restaurant I thought you'd like. I've been there once or twice in the last year or so, and it's become rather a favourite of mine.'

He was hinting at weekends spent with other women, she thought, and doubtless she was supposed to respond by asking questions. Unable to raise the interest to do so, she confined herself to a vague smile. Perhaps, at the very beginning of the relationship, she had cared enough to be moved to jealousy, but it had been short-lived; and now, in its dreary conclusion, her only emotion was regret. 'It sounds great,' she said brightly of the proposed restaurant.

She would have liked to have walked part of the way, mingled with the crowds on the busy streets and boulevards, stopping perhaps for a drink at one of the brasseries. But Niall was anxious not to lose his reservation at the Relais de Montmartre, and hailed a taxi, and she had to content herself with gazing from its windows. It was a warm evening, after a recent shower of rain, and the last rays of the sun filtered through the chestnut trees in their full summer foliage. The taxi ride, taken at unnerving speed, became a confused blur of street life, jostling traffic, the shrill whistles and gesticulating arms of police on point duty and the blare of horns. It was all as she remembered, only rather more so. Even the restaurant itself, when they had been settled at a corner table, had a feeling of *déjà vu*, although she had never been there before. With her mind preoccupied by the ambience, her fellow diners and choosing what she was going to eat, she had temporarily forgotten that there were difficulties attached to the evening. Niall, however, did not allow this relaxed state to continue for long; he had the restless air of a man who had decided on a certain line of debate and wanted to get on with it. Although nothing, she thought in retrospect, could have prepared her for what he had to say.

'This is delicious,' she commented halfway through her first course of aubergine mousse.

'The cooking's good,' he agreed impatiently. 'May we talk about us, Kate? Or about you, principally, since you're the one with the change of attitude. Perhaps you could explain it.'

She lifted her eyes to meet his briefly, then studied her plate again. 'I rather thought explanations could wait until tomorrow. They're complicated.'

'I fail to see why,' he said. 'My question is perfectly simple: what has made you suddenly put our friendship on a different basis? What could be more straightforward than that?'

'It's the answer that's tricky,' she replied, 'because there are several reasons, not just one.'

'One would be better than nothing. At least I wouldn't be completely in the dark.' He leaned towards her, lowering his voice. 'We arrange a weekend break and twenty-four hours later I get a letter from you which reads more like a legal

143

document than a loving communication. Surely I deserve some sort of clarification?' he said, resorting to sarcasm. 'After all, I was under the impression, up until that moment, that we were fast becoming an item. At least we were lovers, "were" being the operative word.'

Kate swallowed the last forkful of mousse before answering. She put her head on one side thoughtfully, and said, 'I can't be part of an item while I'm still married. It's a ridiculous expression anyway. And "lovers" is a misnomer when applied to us. We slept together occasionally, that's all.'

'You're splitting hairs,' he said, his eyes arctic with anger.

She shook her head. ' "Lovers" denotes "love", which didn't exist between us; just a certain amount of old-fashioned lust.'

'Just because it wasn't mentioned,' he retorted defensively. 'It's not a word to be bandied about lightly—'

'Come off it, Niall. At least I'm trying to be honest.' She waited while a waiter poured their wine and removed the used plates. 'It wasn't a sudden change of attitude on my part. I'd realized for some time I wasn't happy with something that wasn't meant to last. I haven't tried an affair before; I'm obviously not very good at it.'

She smiled tentatively, wondering whether she had overplayed the deprecation. She knew his moods by heart, watched the present one switch subtly from irritation to a knowing condescension. He eyed her over the rim of his wineglass.

'The trouble with you, Kate darling, is your insecurity,' he said kindly. 'This entire hiccup stems from a lack of self-confidence. D'you know that?'

She felt indignation rise in her, opened her mouth to argue hotly, but he held up a hand.

'Hear me out,' he went on. 'It's partly my fault. I

could, and should have done more about it, given you a sense of stability; which brings me to a proposition I was going to make you in any case. It's time we put ourselves on a different footing, but together, not apart. I think I should move in with you. How do you feel about that?' he asked as if it were a foregone conclusion.

She looked at him in disbelief. 'Shattered,' she said weakly. It seemed inconceivable that he could have so hopelessly misread her message.

'On a part-time basis, perhaps,' he elaborated. 'I'd return to my flat at weekends; that would give us both space. We could see how it worked out. It wouldn't do that boy of yours any harm to have a little male discipline, either.'

Kate spoke through lips stiff with resentment. 'He has a perfectly good father, thank you.'

He ignored the remark, continuing relentlessly, 'I don't on the whole agree with cohabitation: it requires a hell of a lot of tolerance, but I think it would probably suit you. I'm willing to give it a whirl if you are—'

'Shut up, Niall!'

Her voice, louder than she intended, seemed to reverberate round the restaurant. Heads at other tables turned in curiosity. Niall's flow halted in midstream and he gazed at her in silent astonishment.

'I'm sorry,' she said, 'but I have to make you understand. I can't go on seeing you, at least, not on the same basis. The affair, if that's what it is, is over for me. I've been trying to find a nice way to tell you; I thought my letter would make it obvious, but it didn't, so I see I'll have to spell it out. I don't suppose you'll be heartbroken,' she added in a rush. 'We neither of us pretended it was ideal: I don't know which of us irritated the other most, in fact. But it still isn't easy to say, and I'd like us to stay friends, if possible.'

Flushed from her declaration and slightly shaky, she drank half her wine to steady herself. When she dared look, he was studying his fingernails intently and his facial muscles had tautened. He was, she realized, extremely angry.

'I can't think why your decision should surprise me,' he said with cold sarcasm. 'A relationship needs maturity from both parties if it's going to succeed, not a constant demand for reassurance. It's a game for grown-ups.'

She felt the adrenalin return to her system at his disparaging pronouncement. 'Funny, I never thought of it as a game. How stupid of me to imagine simple things such as common interests and possibly love were needed,' she answered.

He ignored her, saying, 'It's taught me a lesson, not to get entangled with women who have low self-esteem, husbands in the background and badly brought-up children. There's no room in their cluttered lives for emotional commitment.'

She stared at him, suppressing an almost uncontrollable impulse to fling a glass of wine in his face. 'Really? Well, I've got news for you. There's no room in this woman's life for patronizing, egotistical, self-satisfied, devious men,' she said, amazing herself by her own calm. 'You're a bully, Niall, a bully and a shit.'

The arrival of the second course brought an uneasy hiatus in hostilities, while plates of *coq au vin* were placed before them, fragrant and unwanted. Despite their verbal exchange having been conducted in muted voices, she was aware of diners on either side listening in with interest. There was no mistaking a row in any language. Niall topped up her glass with exaggerated courtesy.

'After that last observation of yours, I fully expected you to walk out on me,' he said. 'It was melodramatic enough.'

'I wouldn't have given you the satisfaction of calling me childish,' she replied, picking up her knife and fork. 'Besides, I was taught it was a crime to waste good food.'

She took a mouthful of chicken and chewed determinedly to prove her point, and they ate for a moment in uneasy silence. Without looking at her, he said at last, 'We had better decide what to do about the rest of this redundant weekend.'

'I've already decided,' she said. 'I'll stay with Felicity for tomorrow night. You needn't even see me in the morning; I'll leave the hotel quite early.'

'Why shouldn't I wish to see you?' he asked bitterly. 'I'm not a complete monster. You're the one who wants out.'

He pushed his plate away and drew out a packet of small cigars. Watching him as he lit one, noting a barely perceptible despondency behind the coolness of the pale blue eyes, she felt an unexpected pang of contrition. He was not solely to blame for the failure of their liaison; she had played her part, both in its conception and its collapse.

'I'm sorry about the weekend,' she said. 'It was a mistake, and all my fault. What will you do until Sunday?' she asked hesitantly.

He shrugged. 'See friends, take in a gallery. Killing time won't be a problem.' He signalled for the bill. 'One thing I'd like to get straight: am I to take it you no longer want us to meet in any capacity, once we're home?'

She thought of Matt, and the tidying-up of her life which was not proving as simple as she had imagined. There must be no loose ends. 'Not for a week or two,' she told him. 'I'd like time to myself'; and then recalled using much the same phrase in answer to Matt.

He shrugged. 'It's up to you. I shan't contact you. You know where I am.'

There had been the final parting, fraught with awkwardness on her part as they paused by the door of his room.

'I'll see you on the plane,' he said. 'That is, unless you want to change your ticket to another flight.'

'Of course not.'

'Kate—'

'Yes?'

'I suppose you wouldn't spend the night with me: only as a swan song, of course?'

'No, thank you, Niall.' She looked at him, his jacket draped over one shoulder, his features impassive. The shaming fact was, she would have found it only too easy to accept, now that she had cut herself free.

'No,' he said with irony, 'you're probably right.' He unlocked his door. 'Enjoy tomorrow. Good night, Kate.'

Alone in her room, the strain of the evening took her unawares with an attack of the depression which accompanied all endings, even those that were self-induced.

'D'you know, I'm inclined to feel sorry for him,' Felicity remarked when Kate had completed the story.

'There's no need,' she said. 'He doesn't love me and he's a born survivor. I doubt if I've done more than bruise his ego; I've an idea that women don't do that to him very often.'

'What a cynic you've become.' Felicity collected their coffee cups, piled them on the tray and carried it through to a streamlined kitchen with Kate in her wake. 'I bet you haven't heard the last of him. He'll persevere.'

'It's finished. It's over.' Kate ran her hand over

a pristine pale green work surface. 'What a lovely flat this is. I'll wash the cups.'

'Marie will do it when she comes.' Felicity guided Kate out of the kitchen. 'I'll show you your bedroom, and then we're going to plan the day. We've got to go to a reception this evening, but the rest of the time is ours. There's a lot of news still to catch up on,' she said. 'I haven't heard about Jake yet.'

'I've brought some photos.'

'I'm a rotten godmother. I haven't seen him since he was a baby.'

'He's exactly like Matt, dark and skinny.'

Felicity said, 'And what about Matt? You've hardly mentioned him. Where does *he* fit in to the scheme of things?'

'Matt,' Kate replied with conviction, 'is coming home. We're giving ourselves a second chance.'

Jake woke on the Saturday night and peered blearily at the luminous clock by the bedside. It read 3.20 a.m. A sound had disturbed him, one which was out of keeping with the normal infinitesimal creaks of the house. Or perhaps it was part of the dream he had been having. He lay very still and listened. In the silence that followed, the sound of his breathing seemed particularly loud. His eyelids drooped, he was floating halfway to sleep; and then the noise came again: the soft slither of a drawer being opened, it was difficult to say from where. Jake switched on the lamp and swung his legs out of bed. He was not immediately frightened; the most likely explanation was that Helga, unable to sleep, had decided to write an English essay for her language school, and was creeping around downstairs in search of paper. Wide awake himself by now, he padded on bare feet across his bedroom and out onto the landing, to lean over the banister rail and stare down at the hall.

Two things struck him as odd. For one, the hall was in darkness, apart from the pool of light from the street lamp shining through the fan-shaped glass above the front door. If it were Helga down there, she would surely have turned on the light to see her way downstairs. Secondly, the window beside the stairs, normally firmly locked by night, was open with the net curtains stirring in its draught. Jake came two stairs lower and crouched, his ears straining to catch the least sound. As his eyes grew used to the semi-darkness, he could make out that the door to the drawing-room facing him was ajar and also unlit, but then the most usual place for Helga to be was the kitchen, which was out of sight at the end of the hall. Intuition, a feeling of wrongness, stopped him from switching on a light and going to find her. There were no obvious noises; he sensed rather than heard the presence and the movement of someone on the other side of the drawing-room door. His spine tingled from fear and excitement; he gripped the banister struts, wondering what to do next, unable to move. Then a weak beam of light appeared momentarily in the gap of open doorway and swung away: the beam from a torch. Burglars. He let go of the banister and crept back to the landing, his heart thudding. The excitement had evaporated; he was just plain scared. Where was Helga?

Treading softly, careful to avoid creaking floorboards, he made his way up the short flight of stairs to her room at the top of the house. He went in darkness, not daring to turn on a light in case it was seen from below. The door was wide open, and the bed empty, the duvet thrown back and the pillow dented where her head had been. Jake's fear threatened to become panic; there was only one place she could be and that was in one of the rooms on the ground floor. Was she hiding there? Or had they, horror of horrors, done something awful to her? Slowly he returned to the landing, trying to think logically. He knew what he ought to do: leave the intruders alone, don't try to be a hero, they may be armed; that was the police advice on television crime programmes. They also said to contact the police if possible, but if he rang 999 from the extension in Kate's bedroom, it would make a clicking sound on the telephone in the drawing-room. Whoever-it-was would know there was someone upstairs and might come to find him. His skin prickled at the thought. Suddenly he didn't want to be alone any more: he needed help. Creeping to his mother's bedroom, he lifted the receiver carefully and punched in the number. It seemed hours before a woman answered and asked which service he required, and when he finally gave his message, he had to repeat it because his voice came out in a croak.

He stayed in Kate's room, sitting on the side of the bed, comforted by the faint aroma of her scent, listening for dreaded footsteps on the stairs. The police would come, quite soon probably, and he would have to let them in, forcing himself to go to the front door since Helga was missing; he hadn't thought of that. He wished he had something to arm himself with and could only think of his cricket bat. It wouldn't be much use against a knife or a gun, but it would make him feel better to hold it in his hands. He moved softly to his own room and over to the cupboard; the door squawked as he opened it like it always did. He grasped at the bat and held his breath, his fingers tightening round the familiar handle. There was sudden movement downstairs, a sense of activity, the sounds quite audible now: the squeak of rubber soles on the parquet floor in the hall, the crash and tinkle of breaking glass or china, the swift tread of feet on the stairs that he had been waiting for. He froze where he stood, the cricket bat clutched in both hands, his heart beating so hard it felt as if it would burst out of his chest. And then he heard the bang of a window being pushed open to its limits, and the scrabble of hands and feet inside the sill, and a muffled curse. They were leaving: something must have disturbed them. On legs made shaky from relief, he went cautiously to the door and peered out, in time to see a pair of gloved hands gripping the sill of the stairs window. He had a brief blurred glimpse of a face before the hands loosened their hold and disappeared. There was the thud of someone landing on a shed roof, and a car in the street revved into life and roared away; then silence. Jake sat down at the top of the stairs and waited.

When the police arrived, he let them in with the cricket bat still in his hands. There were three of them, two men and a WPC and the hall seemed all at once crowded with people asking questions.

'They've gone,' Jake said, pointing up at the window, trying to stop shivering. 'About five minutes ago. Please can you find Helga? She's somewhere in the house and she may be hurt.' He appealed to the WPC who had a kind face.

'Is Helga looking after you?'

'Yes, and she's not in her room.'

The elder of the two men gave brief instructions for the policewoman to stay with Jake while they searched.

'I haven't dared look for her,' he admitted, ashamed of himself.

'Don't worry. She'll be fine,' the WPC said encouragingly. 'You're suffering from shock. We'll get you a hot drink when we've found her.'

It did not take them long; Helga was discovered tied to a chair in the kitchen by a length of cord. She had been gagged with the wide sticky tape commonly used for wrapping parcels, and her wrists and ankles were bound with insulating tape. Jake and the

WPC were allowed in when she had been released, unharmed apart from red marks on her skin where the tape had inflamed it. She hugged Jake in an untypical show of emotional relief.

'Thank God you are all right. I was so worried about you.'

'Me too,' he said. 'What were you doing? I thought you might be dead,' he added accusingly.

'I heard a noise and came downstairs, very quietly without light to look.' Her eyes sparked with anger. 'I am proficient in judo, I was not afraid. But they came from behind, by surprise, and pushed me into the kitchen. The bastards!' she said, rubbing her wrist. 'I could do nothing. There were two of them.'

'You shouldn't attempt to have a go,' the elder of the two men told her. 'You had the lad here to think of.'

'So what was I expected to do? Wait while we are murdered in our beds?' Helga said scornfully.

'The boy did right to call us,' he answered passively.

Helga, having displayed remarkable calmness, suddenly turned pale and groped for a chair.

'It's the shock,' the WPC said sympathetically. 'I'll make tea. All right if I use these mugs?'

The men disappeared to examine the window and the drawing-room.

'I think you were really brave,' Jake told Helga comfortingly, horrified to see her on the verge of tears; Helga of all people.

'There we are,' said the policewoman, putting mugs on the table in front of them. 'Plenty of sugar in those, that's what's needed.'

'There's brandy in the cupboard,' Jake suggested.

'Better not. Tea's best.'

After a few sips the colour slowly returned to Helga's face, and Jake found he had stopped shaking. She wrapped her towelling dressing-gown round her more firmly as if to pull herself together, saying, 'The officer is right, of course. I should not have come downstairs, it was a risk.'

The WPC nodded. 'It's not worth it.'

Some of the old sparkle showed in Helga's eyes. 'I did not want them to get away with Kate's good things. Poor Kate, it will be a bad homecoming for her.'

The two men came back to the kitchen after their investigation, more tea was poured, and more questions were asked and answered in something of a social atmosphere. A whole pane of glass had been removed from the window and the lock broken; the drawing-room apparently was surprisingly in order. A silver salt cellar had been dropped on the carpet and a porcelain figurine smashed in the hall as the burglars had made their sudden getaway. They were obviously professionals, according to the detective sergeant, whose rank had been divulged at Jake's request. The television and video were untouched; they had been selective about what they took, which looked to be smaller items of value.

'Impossible to say how much has gone until Mrs Protheroe gets back,' he said. 'We'll send someone round to see her. It'll help if some of the stuff were marked for identification. There'll be a forensics officer round tomorrow, for fingerprints and so on; don't touch the room until then.'

'They wore gloves,' Jake told him. 'I saw one of them climbing out of the window.'

'It doesn't surprise me.' The detective sergeant turned to Helga. 'Did you get a good look at your assailants?' he asked. 'Can you give a description of them?'

She did her best, but since they were wearing Balaclava helmets which obscured their faces, and identical dark jerseys and jeans, there was not much to describe. One was black, the other white, one tall, one short; as for voices, they had hardly spoken apart from warning her to shut up. Little as there was to go on, the information was duly noted down.

Before they left the police gave the house a thorough search to make sure it was as secure as possible, and supplied Helga with telephone numbers of locksmiths and glaziers to repair the window without delay. The Chelsea police were alerted to keep an eye on the house for what was left of the night, and Helga was offered counselling which she declined with vigour, seeing its necessity as a sign of poor moral fibre. It was five o'clock by the time she and Jake found themselves alone, and the misty beginnings of a fine June morning showed through the kitchen window. They looked at each other, their faces pallid from exhaustion, neither of them wanting to make the first move towards their solitary beds.

'I'm hungry,' Jake said.

Helga looked immensely relieved. 'So, why don't we have breakfast? We will sleep afterwards. I will make scrambled eggs.'

He laid the table and made toast while she cooked, and they ate it accompanied by large cups of milky coffee, in the companionable atmosphere of a shared traumatic experience.

'It's the feeling that they've been here that's so creepy,' he said. 'Touching things, poking about in drawers and cupboards. Mum will flip. Ought we to warn her so she can come home earlier?'

'We will telephone her,' Helga agreed, 'later, when she is awake. And now we must sleep for a while. Come, I will wash up afterwards.'

Daylight was coming through the curtains in his bedroom, dispelling fears.

'Don't go downstairs again without me,' he warned Helga as he climbed into bed, yawning.

'I won't, I promise.'

'You know something?' he said. 'We should have let Roly stay the night.'

'The burglars would still have broken in, even with Mr Roland here.'

'I suppose so.' Jake's eyelids were heavy with tiredness. 'But he would have made me feel safer. He's that kind of person.'

Kate was standing in her drawing-room later on Sunday afternoon, making a list of the things that had been stolen. The forensics officer had arrived and gone, pessimistic about the results of her tests; endorsing the view that the thieves had been professionals, leaving the minimum of evidence. The collection of porcelain, most of it inherited, one or two pieces discovered by Kate in country antique shops, was missing in its entirety. The group of Dresden shepherdesses, shattered in the get-away, was past mending, and the glass-fronted mahogany cabinet which had housed the familiar well-loved pieces stood with its lock broken and the doors open. Gone too were the snuff boxes and the carriage clock. From the corner cupboard where she kept the few bits of silver she and Matt possessed, the burglars had taken a Georgian milk jug which she had always meant to have specially insured and had forgotten. The room had a sad, depleted air with its empty shelves and unaccustomed spaces on tables and mantelpiece. She had tried telling herself more than once that she was lucky they had not been the type of intruder to leave an obscene mess behind them, but it was small consolation. Fighting depression, she continued to write everything down methodically, determined to get the job behind her as quickly as possible.

Upstairs, her suitcase was sitting in her bedroom where she had dumped it, still packed. She had managed to catch an earlier flight that brought her home by midday, fraught with guilt at having left

Helga and Jake alone in the first place, made worse somehow by the fact that she had enjoyed herself for the latter part of her stay. She felt, illogically probably, that the burglary was just retribution for what had started out as an underhand weekend. The journey home had given her ample time to dwell on what might have happened; Helga on the telephone had sounded composed, but Jake was full of her ordeal, giving away every detail. The whole saga from beginning to end was laid before Kate during a snack lunch of salad and cheese, leaving her more in shock than either of the other two appeared to be. It was as well that the afternoon was taken up with an interview by the police, workmen repairing the window, and the search for insurance documents which had been wrongly filed. Helga had gone to the gymnasium for a workout and Jake, protesting, had been persuaded to rest on his bed, and had fallen asleep immediately. Kate's instinct, looking in on him, was never to let him out of her sight again.

The list took over an hour to complete, and it was six o'clock before she decided there was no more to add to it. She sank onto the sofa wearily, and wondered whether the drawing-room would seem more normal after a good clean. At present it felt to her defiled by the fingering of alien hands. There was one more obligatory task to be dealt with: a telephone call to Matt. Naturally he must be told about the burglary, and her absence could not be kept a secret. In any case, the time for secrets was over if they were to start again, with one exception: the part that Niall had played in the weekend. No-one, even Matt for all his tolerance, would accept the true explanation; she could imagine how it would sound, a confused tale of hotel bookings and wrong decisions, and final ultimatums. That it had been her way of tying up loose ends, however ineptly, would seem like an unbelievably lame excuse for a last sexual romp.

But Niall was no longer a part of her life; searching her conscience, she decided that nothing would be gained by a confession, and a great deal might be lost. Nevertheless, the subterfuge made her uneasy, and she remained where she was sitting, postponing the call to Matt until she had had time to unwind.

The beneficial effects of Paris in Felicity's company, doing only the things she wanted to do without having to consider anyone else, had already worn off. She recalled the one day she had had with pleasure; Felicity had made suggestions rather than taking over, and Kate had fallen in with them willingly. They ate lunch out of doors at a café off the beaten track; a prolonged lunch with a bottle of wine during which they talked shamelessly about themselves. 'Shopping or culture?' Felicity enquired when they had finished. Kate had not wanted to shop: 'I daren't,' she said. 'I'm broke, and anyway, I'll never look chic like you do.' They had gone instead to the Musée Marmottan and wandered round the Monet paintings until their feet began to hurt. The afternoon had ended in the comparative cool of the Jardin des Tuileries, where they bought ice-creams and sat on a bench in the shade watching the children playing.

'I'm glad you and Matt are getting back together again,' Felicity said. 'You essentially belong together, out of all the couples I know.'

'It isn't absolutely certain,' Kate said. 'I have to make sure he hasn't changed his mind. As for belonging, I would have thought that could be said of you and Edward rather than us.'

'I nearly left him once,' Felicity remarked calmly as if commenting on the weather.

Kate stared at her in disbelief. '*Edward?*'

'He had an affair with his secretary,' Felicity said, licking carefully round her ice-cream cone.

'What happened?'

'I threatened to leave, and he finished it. It didn't last long.' She smiled her deceptively gentle smile.

Kate pictured Edward, bespectacled, amiable, intelligent and besotted, so she had always thought, with Felicity. 'Are you both all right now?' she asked.

'All right, yes; but not the same,' Felicity replied. 'It's not something you forget. We're quite happy in a different sort of way. At least you haven't had to contend with unfaithfulness,' she added, 'and don't go confessing to Matt about your own, even though you did have a pact to lead your own lives. He may suspect, but he doesn't have to know: there's a big difference between the two.'

Kate had carried Felicity's home-spun advice back with her, remembering it now as she lifted the receiver to telephone Matt. He answered after the first ring as if expecting the call.

'We've been burgled,' she told him immediately.

'Oh God! When?'

'Last night.' She took a deep breath. 'I was away for the weekend, I'm afraid. Jake and Helga were in the house.'

'God almighty! Are they OK?'

'They seem fine.'

'You shouldn't have left them there alone,' he accused her. 'Why didn't you tell me? I would have had Jake.'

He was saying all the things she had expected him to say. 'I did think of it, but I knew you were busy with the book,' she said. 'I'm full of remorse, so don't rub it in.'

'Have they taken much? Is the house a shambles?'

'All the porcelain's gone,' she told him. 'The room isn't too bad. Matt, I can't find the insurance papers. I was sure they were in the file.'

'I took them. Don't you remember? I wanted to check on the premium. I did tell you.'

'You didn't.'

'I did. You didn't listen.'

'Oh well.' She felt suddenly exhausted. 'As long as I know where they are. I'm sick of being separated,' she said vehemently.

'I suppose husbands do have their uses,' he remarked with a touch of bitterness; adding with more warmth, 'Shall I come round and lend moral support?'

'Yes. No. I don't know. There's nothing to be done; the police have been. Come tomorrow evening; I'll be less tired.'

'If you're sure,' he said. 'I'll ring the insurance people in the morning.' He paused. 'Where were you for the weekend?'

'Paris, staying with Felicity and Edward.'

He made no comment.

'Matt?'

'Yes?'

'You haven't changed your mind about us, have you?'

'No,' he said quietly. 'But I'm still waiting for you to make up yours. I'll see you tomorrow.'

Jake wandered into the room as she replaced the receiver, bug-eyed from recent sleep. 'Was that Roly on the phone?' he asked.

'No, it was Daddy. He's coming over tomorrow.'

'Great.' He lolled against her in one of his rare moods for a cuddle. 'Aren't you going to call Roly? He rang this morning before you got home, and he's really worried about not being here last night.'

Poor Roly, always the last to be remembered. She gave Jake a hug. 'That's ridiculous,' she said. 'I'll ask him to supper, put his mind at rest. If only,' she added with a sigh, 'he didn't feel so wholly committed to us.'

Chapter Six

Sports Day was nearing its end. From where he sat cross-legged on the grass, Jake could make out his mother and father on the other side of the field in the front row of parents seated in upright deck-chairs. More often than not at this event there was a forest of umbrellas sprouting above the parents' heads, but today was one of the hottest of the year and sun-hats were in evidence. Kate was wearing the floppy straw hat she took on holiday, not the sort which Jake found embarrassing, he was relieved to see. Matt had a rather battered panama, but it wouldn't have mattered what he wore: Jake was too pleased to have him there to mind. The last of the high jumping was being fought out; after that there would be the hundred metres in which he would compete, followed by the mothers' race, and finally the fathers'. The day always finished with tea served from a tent at the far end of the ground, sandwiches and home-made cakes handed round by the boys, flushed and damp from their exertions. It was the best part of the afternoon.

Toby lay on his stomach beside Jake, scratching at a mosquito bite. 'Is that your father over there?' he asked.

'You *know* it is.'

'Haven't seen him for ages, I've forgotten what

he looks like. Has he come back to live with you, then?'

'Not yet, but he's going to,' Jake said with confidence.

'Bet it's because of the stink bomb jape. Told you so; he's frightened you're turning into a yobbo,' Toby said grinning.

'Oh ha-ha! Very funny,' Jake replied. 'He's coming home because he wants to; nothing to do with me, clever dick. Where are your parents, anyway? I can't see them.'

'Ma's always late for everything,' Toby said placidly. 'She'll probably turn up for the tea if she remembers.'

A master using a megaphone was ordering all boys who were competing in the hundred metres to line up. Jake scrambled to his feet.

'See you later.'

'Bet you come last,' Toby said cheerfully.

'Piss off!' Jake told him, equally amicably. 'Pity you're too fat to run.'

Amongst the spectators, Kate touched Matt's arm. 'Jake's big moment,' she murmured.

'Seriously big,' he agreed, with a smile.

She found herself comparing the day to the same event of the previous year, when she had attended alone and it had rained. Every mother on that occasion seemed to be paired off; not a single parent amongst them except for herself. She had seen the years ahead stretching out in front of her, punctuated by solitary attendances at similar events, with something like despair. Now, gently frying in the sun, she experienced a sudden rush of happiness, and an overpowering need to communicate it to Matt. 'On your marks, get set, go!' came the megaphone command from a distance, and the white-clad line of boys hurled itself forward.

Later, when the afternoon was over and they joined

162

the families straggling away from the sports ground in search of their cars, her feeling of contentment persisted. Jake put a warm hand into hers.

'I could have won if I hadn't slipped,' he said.

'You came second,' Kate pointed out, 'which is a great deal better than being an "also ran" in the mothers' race like I was.'

'Daddy was first in the fathers', anyway.'

'He's brilliant,' Kate said.

'A star,' Matt agreed immodestly. 'It was that burst of speed at the end that clinched it. Personally, I think we all deserve a reward in the form of dinner out.'

'Then we must include Roly,' Kate told him. 'I've already asked him to supper. You don't mind, do you?' she added.

'Why should I? He's an old mate, Roly.'

'It's just that I've neglected him recently,' she added.

The real purpose in her inviting Roly on this particular evening, she left unmentioned. Although she had grown used to his habit of following her, it remained a worry, pointing to the fact that his love for her had become obsessional. Whether he deluded himself that she was unaware of his persistent watching and waiting, or whether it was part of his weird plan to be recognized, she could not be sure. The last time she had seen him had been at the airport, ineffectually hiding behind a newspaper like some amateur private eye. Alternating between irritation and pity for his irrational behaviour, remembering her father's words of warning and realizing the blame lay partly with her, she had chosen to ignore it. But one thing was certain; it could not be allowed to continue indefinitely. She would of course tell him about herself and Matt getting back together again, choose a moment when they were alone.

Her hope was that when she was irrevocably out of reach in a restored marriage, his fixation would automatically peter out. Meanwhile, this evening he would have the chance to see them together as a complete family; a gentle intimation of the way things would be from now on.

'You're frowning,' Matt said. 'What's on your mind?'

'I was thinking what a pity it was that there's no girl in Roly's life.'

'I'm fairly sure there is, but she's unavailable.' He glanced at her. 'Am I right?'

She flushed. 'Possibly, but how do you know?'

'Guesswork.'

'What's "unavailable"?' Jake asked.

'Not within reach, already booked, engaged, married,' his father told him. 'Like we are.' He took Kate's arm. 'At least, I hope we are, aren't we?'

'Yes,' she said, looking him in the eye. 'Definitely.'

'Then,' he said in a voice no-one else could hear, 'it's about time we did something positive about it.'

Matt woke as dawn was showing through a gap in the curtains, lightening the darkness of the room to shadowy grey. Disorientated, it took him several seconds to realize where he was, to locate the window and the shapes of furniture grown unfamiliar to him. Then he saw Kate's head on the pillow beside him, strands of dark brown hair spread randomly, and his memory cleared.

It had been a strange night, reminiscent of the earliest ones they had spent together before they had grown used to each other. They had made love, slept, woken, talked and repeated the pattern until morning, restless with the newness of it all. In the beginning there had naturally been no past; that was the difference which, oddly enough, had brought none of the difficulties he had expected. Whenever he had thought about this moment, he had foreseen an insurmountable awkwardness, caution inhibiting every word and move. It had not happened like that; it was as if the lacerations and the separation of the last eighteen months had been overridden, and he had merely returned from one of his working trips. He was not going to delude himself that their problems no longer existed, solved by a miraculously happy few hours in bed. Nothing between them must ever be taken for granted again. He reminded himself of these facts in an effort to keep a sense of balance; but he could not help feeling light-headed with relief that the worst part, the closing of a divide, was behind them.

Its success, he realized, lay partly in the unexpected. He had not planned to stay; it was Jake who had been the instigator, with a child's unerring knack of simplifying a quandary. After dinner at the nearest Chinese restaurant, they had returned to Denbigh Street with Roly, and Kate had made coffee since he seemed reluctant to leave. It was late by the time he finally rose to go, and they waved him off from the open doorway, Jake half-asleep but determined to keep going.

'I suppose I'd better be on my way,' Matt had said as they cleared the coffee mugs. 'I'm whacked, I don't know about you. If I don't leave now, I'll fall asleep on the sofa.'

Jake lolled against the kitchen door. 'Why don't you stay the night?' he asked. 'You don't have to go, do you?'

'Perhaps you ought to do that,' Kate had said, her face hidden over the sink. 'You're probably over the limit anyway. We had two bottles of wine.'

'I haven't got a toothbrush.'

'There's a spare one in the bathroom cupboard.'

'Please stay,' Jake said, through a huge yawn.

'Jake,' Kate told him. 'Bed. We'll be up to say good night in five minutes, so no dawdling.'

'Is Daddy going to—'

'Yes, he is,' she said firmly.

Left alone, she and Matt had faced each other across the kitchen. 'Are you sure that's all right by you?' he asked tentatively.

'Positive,' she said.

'I'll sleep in the spare room if you'd rather.'

'I think it's a rotten idea.'

'Thank God we agree,' he had said, taking her by the hand and pulling her gently towards him.

He was wide awake now; turning his head, he willed Kate to wake also, anxious for her company. Her eyes opened with startling suddenness, then closed again. 'What's the time?' she mumbled into the pillow.

He peered at his watch on the bedside table. 'Five-thirty.'

'Too early,' she groaned. 'Why did you wake me up?'

'I didn't.'

'You were staring at me, I felt it.'

He leaned over and kissed her nose, the only visible part of her.

'Hell,' she said, rolling over on her back. 'Now I'm completely awake.'

'I'll go and make some tea.'

When he returned with the two mugs on a tray, she was sitting up in bed brushing her hair.

'I hope we're not going to make a habit of these broken nights,' she said. 'I can't stand the pace.' She looked and sounded remarkably peaceful for one disturbed.

'Don't grumble.' He handed her a mug and climbed into bed. 'The steady grind of everyday life will take over only too quickly.'

'We talked a lot,' she commented. 'I can't remember a word we said, can you?'

'It was all about us, what we'd done and were going to do. Lovely, inconsequential stuff.'

'No serious issues like money and insurance and education?' she asked, sipping her tea.

'Not a word. They weren't mentioned.'

'It was fun,' she said. 'Perhaps we should be inconsequential more often. You know something? I was dreading this part of your ever coming back. I imagined us arranging a day and a time for you to arrive, and standing around in the bedroom not knowing how to handle the situation; terrified of doing or saying the wrong thing.'

'Like booking into a hotel for a dirty weekend for the first time in your life.'

She did not answer.

'We needn't have worried,' he added.

'No, we needn't have worried,' she said.

He took her mug and put it with his own on the bedside table. 'I'm going to be serious for a moment,' he told her, tucking a wing of hair behind her ear to get a clear view of her face. 'Are you sure about my coming home? You haven't yet told me in so many words.'

She pulled his arm round her and lay with her head in the crook of his shoulder. 'I'm quite, quite sure,' she said.

'It won't always be easy. I don't plan to travel so much, but there will be times—'

'I know that; I'm still certain. I've been certain for some time.'

'All this "tidying-up" of your life,' he asked, 'was Paris a part of it?'

'Paris,' she replied, 'was rather a muddle. It was meant to be a final sweep of the broom, but as it happened, it wasn't really necessary to go there at all. I went out of self-indulgence because

I wanted to see Felicity, and get away for a couple of nights.'

'I see,' he said. 'I thought – well, never mind what I thought. It doesn't matter now. Are we going to get another hour's sleep?'

'I'm not in the mood; my mind's too full of what's happening to us. How soon can you move back?'

'I'll have to arrange about the flat; I'm supposed to give a month's notice, but I'll get on to the letting agents on Monday. It'll take me about a week to sort things out, I should think.'

'A whole week?'

'It'll go quite quickly,' he said, putting his other arm round her, 'and I'll be here constantly. We'll have a celebratory dinner; somewhere outrageously expensive.'

'When shall we tell Jake?'

'At breakfast.'

'He'll be over the moon. It's what he's wanted ever since you left. All his worrying about me will be over.'

'Has he been worried?' he asked.

'It's simple psychology,' she said. 'One parent leaves home and the other one becomes vulnerable. He was frightened I'd disappear, whisked away by some villain.'

'I don't imagine Roly fitted the part?'

She smiled. 'Roly's been a great stand-by,' she said. 'I really believe Jake loves him.'

Matt said thoughtfully, 'I don't think he's going to be overjoyed by our news, poor man.'

'I'm not sure. The inevitable is probably easier to settle for than the undefined, which is how my status has been without you: fuzzy round the edges. Very confusing for everyone,' she added, hoisting herself into a sitting position against the pillows. 'Now I'm about to be a proper wife again, Roly will transfer his worship to someone else, I hope.'

168

'I wonder. I don't share your confidence; I have an idea he doesn't switch affections easily.'

'Oh dear,' she sighed. 'You've made me feel responsible for him. I seem to get my life in a muddle, or so Felicity says.'

'From now on you won't get the chance,' he said. 'I shan't let you; I don't fancy disentangling you from predicaments.'

'Chauvinist!' she replied.

He swung his legs out of bed and walked to the window, pulling back the curtains to let in the first hazy morning sun.

'It's a beautiful day,' he announced.

'Of course it's beautiful,' she said. 'It wouldn't make any difference if it was raining.'

In the corner of the Teddy Bear Club in Shepherds Market, Roly sat with a double brandy on the table before him. He could not have borne to go straight home after leaving Kate and Matt. The sight of them as they called out their good nights, etched against the lighted doorway, had caused him such infinite pain that it was all he could do to keep the careless smile on his face as he lifted his hand in a final salute. Any doubts which he might have clung to regarding Jake's prediction of their reconciliation, were dispelled during the course of the evening. They had been hospitality itself, drawing him in to share the conviviality of a family dinner with descriptions of Sports Day, encouraging him in his talent for funny stories. He had done his best, made Trojan efforts to produce the humour that was expected of him and to present the bland, slightly barmy façade which most people supposed to be normal. But the strain had been almost unbearable, conscious as he was of an undercurrent of excitement running between them. They might have been two people on the verge of becoming lovers rather than a couple who had decided to shelve their differences after eleven years of marriage. There was no mention of their plans for the immediate future; the brief glances that passed between them, despite being kept to the minimum out of politeness, said it all. Their attempts to hide their elation for Roly's sake made him feel more alone than if they had openly admitted it; while Jake's eyes, wide with happiness, only served to underline his terrible sense of loss. He had difficulty in eating much from the numerous dishes set in front of him; the food, good as it was, stuck in his gullet and had to be washed down with frequent libations of wine, so that he was not entirely sober by the end of the meal. It was not for this reason that he had accepted Kate's offer for coffee at Denbigh Street, however. He desperately hoped to see Matt leave the house for his flat at the same time as himself, in order that he, Roly, did not actually have to witness his reinstatement as a husband. It was an infantile wish and a forlorn hope: Matt stayed on, very much a part of the family group waving their farewells from the top step. The front door had closed before Roly pulled away from the kerb in his car, shutting them off from the outside world; in his misery, it felt to him like a rejection, brutal as a slap in the face.

He had driven the short distance to his home with caution, aware of being well over the alcohol limit. The little mews house which ordinarily he found welcoming, faced him with the cold blank stare of closed windows. He had garaged the car and taken a taxi to Shepherds Market and the refuge of the Teddy Bear Club where, in the shabby red plush atmosphere of an old theatre, one could find solitude or companionship depending on mood; no-one bothered one either way. Several of the girls who frequented the club between assignments he knew well enough to chat to, and he would listen in fascination to their accounts, sometimes grotesque and occasionally funny, of the way in which they earned their substantial living. He found them relaxing company and suspected they felt the same about him, since he seldom demanded anything of them. But this evening he avoided their eyes, his feelings too raw and vulnerable to find their anecdotes even faintly amusing. He finished his brandy and ordered another, unable to think of any option open to him other than drinking himself into a stupor.

After half an hour or so, he realized the intake of alcohol was not having the desired effect. His mind remained clear while a wall of resentment and anger built up steadily inside him. These symptoms were not unfamiliar although they did not manifest themselves often. He recognized them from way back, when the jibes and the teasing at school had driven him close to the edge; a kind of obstinacy had occasionally come to his rescue, a refusal to be used as the whipping-boy without a fight. There was little similarity between those instances of childhood cruelty and the situation in which he now found himself; and yet there *was* a common thread. In either case he was the loser. For a whole year he had devoted himself to Kate, propped up her morale, watched her go through the throes of an affair, without ever quite losing the conviction that his tenacity would pay off; one day she would come to love him. Even now he believed it to be possible. The intervention of Matt, who had left her to fend for herself in the first place, seemed grossly unjust. What had he done to deserve her, beyond seeing she did not starve, presumably?

Roly pulled out a handkerchief and mopped his forehead. The atmosphere in the club was unusually warm; perhaps the air-conditioning was on the blink. A girl took away his two empty glasses and brought him a third brandy at his request. He hardly noticed these ministrations, his thoughts entirely taken up with Kate. It did not strike him as peculiar that, against all odds, she remained the pivot of his existence; he had never tried to analyse his feelings for her. The fact that she was who she was, and irreplaceable, and he had by some miracle met her, was enough. He knew with complete certainty there would never be anyone else whom he could love. She was the be-all and end-all of his life; without her, there was no point in continuing. The thought shot into his mind unbidden, closely followed by a stubborn refusal to entertain it. To give up now was unthinkable: in any case, he doubted very much that he would be able to, so much a part of him had she become.

He started on his brandy, drinking more slowly now, sipping at it pensively while the first inklings of a plan began to formulate in his brain. The fact that his intentions were dishonourable if not downright vindictive, never entered his head. He looked upon Kate's marriage to Matt as a proven disaster, and their reunion a dreadful mistake which it was his duty to disrupt if possible. Separately, they were both lovely people; he liked Matt, he was a great friend and Roly wished him no harm. It was simply that together Kate and Matt were the wrong mix. It had not worked first time round; a second attempt was folly. Better to nip it in the bud while it was in its infancy; kinder in the long run than letting it become another failure. A questioning pang of guilt stabbed Roly as he pictured Jake's face, with its shining expectancy extinguished by disappointment. He smothered the thought quickly; Jake was too young to realize the complications of adult relationships. Having justified any action he might take to his own satisfaction, he sat on for some time, planning a campaign of disillusionment; eyes must be opened, secrets carefully leaked.

Eventually, he drew out from an inside pocket a small address book and thumbed through it until he found what he wanted. With a decisive air he swallowed the last of his brandy, went to the pay phone in the hall and dialled a number. It rang for some time before a voice answered, curt and foggy with sleep.

'Yes?'

'Niall, Roly speaking.'

'Roly! What the hell sort of a time do you call this?'

'I've no idea. Sorry, have I woken you?'

'You sodding well have, you nerd. You're drunk.' There was a noise of Niall shifting himself against the pillows. 'What do you want, for God's sake?'

'I'm sober as the proverbial judge,' Roly said. 'It's about Kate.'

There was a pause, then Niall's voice, cold and distant. 'What about Kate?'

'I've got some news that might interest you, but I'd rather not discuss it over the phone. I thought we might meet.'

'My interest in Kate is limited,' Niall replied, yawning. 'Your *news*, as you call it, had better be good.'

'I believe it's worth listening to, from your point of view.'

'Curiouser and curiouser,' quoted Niall sarcastically. 'And what might my "point of view" be, I wonder?' Then, obviously bored with the conversation he added, 'Midday at the Pembridge Club, tomorrow, Sunday. I'll be swimming.'

He rang off without so much as a good night. Roly lifted his shoulders in a shrug and remained unperturbed. If Niall was as uninterested as he pretended, he would not have agreed to a meeting. The preliminary tactics of Roly's plan had been successfully completed. He went back to the bar to pay his bill, called a cheerful goodbye to the cluster of girls and left the Teddy Bear feeling not unlike a general who had missed his vocation.

On Sunday, Kate visited her parents for the first time since her father's accident. Jake was spending the day with Toby, under strict instructions to get up to nothing more subversive than cricket or football; although Kate doubted that she need worry. He was a changed child in the light of Matt's imminent return.

She was glad to be driving down alone. The news of the reconciliation was bound to be received with mixed feelings. Her father would be unequivocally pleased for her, but her mother, her hopes for a new son-in-law destroyed, was unlikely to show the same enthusiasm. Kate knew exactly what her reaction would be, could hear her grudging acceptance of the inevitable – 'Well, darling, I only hope you both know what you're doing' – the sighs and the snide remarks about Matt's shortcomings. All these were easier to deal with by herself. She wondered sometimes what had happened to put the acidity into her mother's soul, and came to the conclusion it was probably congenital. It was hard to imagine her father ruffling the smooth waters of their comparatively uneventful marriage. In Kate's eyes he made a delightful husband, handling his prickly wife with humorous equanimity; but then, one never knew what went on below the surface of people's lives, particularly those of one's parents.

George Brownlow, his foot in plaster, hobbled from the garden to greet Kate as her car came to rest on the gravel drive.

'You're pretty nippy on those crutches,' she said, kissing him. He looked thinner and therefore older, despite a face tanned by the spell of good weather.

'I've got the hang of the bloody things now,' he told her. 'I kept overbalancing at first.'

'Poor Pa. That'll teach you to climb ladders.'

'Steps, not a ladder; I'm not completely decrepit. At least, I wasn't until this happened.'

'You'll soon mend', Kate said, 'knowing you. Where's Mum?'

'Shelling peas over there by the cedar tree. Shall we join her?'

'I've got some good news for you,' she said. 'Wonderful news from my point of view, that is. Mum isn't going to be overjoyed, though.'

George said drily, as they progressed slowly across the daisy-strewn lawn, 'It isn't difficult to guess, in that case. You and Matt are making a fresh start.'

'Right.'

He halted, balanced on one crutch and squeezed her hand. 'I'm so glad. Be happy this time, dearest Kate.' He looked into her face, his blue eyes creased up against the sun. 'Be happy some of the time,' he corrected. '"Always" is asking too much; a mistake most of us make until we've learnt better.'

Kate smiled. 'I've learnt it, I promise.' Glancing across to where her mother was sitting, she added, 'I actually dread what Mum's going to say; it'll put a blight on the day. I suppose you couldn't tell her, Pa, after I've left?'

'And bring down a whole heap of recriminations on my head? No, thank you. She probably won't be as difficult as you think.'

And pigs might fly, Kate thought as she sat on the grass beside her mother's deck-chair and talked. Prue was silent for several seconds, but her lips compressed into a thin line and the shelled peas rattled into the colander on her lap at an increased speed.

'I wish you'd say something,' Kate said.

'There's nothing much *to* say. You've made up

your minds and that's that. Who am I to comment?' The first of the predictable sighs escaped, a barely audible comment in itself.

'I hoped you'd be pleased for us,' Kate replied, stifling her irritation. 'But I suppose that's too much to ask: your blessing.'

Prue put down the colander on the grass carefully. 'No need to sound bitter, Kate. All I want is your happiness. If patching up your marriage is your way of achieving it, then so be it; but you shouldn't blame me for having my doubts.'

'What is it you've got against Matt?' Kate asked, plucking daisies furiously. 'You've never liked him, have you, right from the beginning.'

'Now you're being childish, darling,' Prue answered calmly. 'I'd probably have liked him very much if he hadn't chosen to marry you,' she said with unexpected honesty. 'As it is, I think he's behaved in a cavalier fashion, doing exactly what he wants to do and dashing all over the world, leaving you to cope with Jake. No wonder you fell apart; you were seldom together.' She smoothed her cotton skirt over her knees, avoiding Kate's eyes. 'It's no surprise you haven't had a second baby. There hasn't been time.'

Goaded by the accuracy of her mother's assessment, Kate leapt to Matt's defence. ' "Dashing around" is part of his *job*, Mum. I settled for that when I married him. Anyway,' she added, 'he's going to do less of it now he's started to write.'

'It's a great pity,' Prue said with another sigh, 'that he can't find a more remunerative job, in my opinion. It's well known that writing is a precarious way of making a living.' She glanced at her watch. 'Time I began the lunch. And I expect you'd like a drink.'

She picked up the colander and set off across the

lawn with Kate trailing in her wake feeling like a sulky child. Her mother had had that effect on her ever since she could remember. Charlie was the favourite, always had been.

'If writing is what he wants to do,' she retorted to her mother's back, 'then he should bloody well do it. We'll manage; we always have.'

Prue did not answer, following her principle that difficult offspring were best ignored. She walked with firm, youthful strides, but her bare legs, stick-thin below the floral skirt, were pale and laced with blue veins. Catching sight of this sign of age and vulnerability, Kate felt a wrench of the heart and her frustration fade as a consequence. It was easy to forget her mother was no longer young.

By tacit agreement, the subject of Matt was shelved if not dropped. She helped Prue prepare the roast lamb, potatoes and two kinds of vegetables in an atmosphere of amity aided by frequent swigs of gin and tonic. They prattled about non-controversial things such as the state of George's ankle, the mess the Government was making of the Health Service and the difficulties of finding help in the garden. The issue of Kate's marriage would not go away, Kate knew this. Her mother would continue to regard Matt with mistrust; all that could be hoped for was a lessening of her obvious disapproval.

'I should have made a smaller size,' Prue observed towards the end of lunch, when Kate had left half her treacle sponge.

'It's wonderful, Mum, I'm just not used to puddings.'

'What a pity we haven't got Jake with us,' her mother said. 'Children are so rewarding when it comes to puddings. Roly is the only adult I know who does justice to them. I hope you'll still bring him down here when you and Matt – well, when you're settled again.'

177

'Of course. He's Matt's friend as well as mine,' Kate said pointedly. She caught her father looking at her, his expression quizzical, and sensed the colour rise in her face. He still had the power to disconcert her.

'Please take care,' she told him affectionately before she left. 'Don't do anything remotely dangerous.'

He smiled at her. 'It's hardly possible to play silly buggers with this leg.'

They stood waving in the drive, framed in the overhead mirror of the car as she slowly drew away, and put her hand out of the window in farewell. She felt that uncomfortable mixture of sadness and relief, of nostalgia and escapism, that always attacked her on these occasions.

Roly paid for two glasses of fresh orange juice at the swimming-pool bar and carried them to where Niall was seated, wrapped in a towelling robe, at one of the small tables. Niall nodded his thanks, took a sip and glanced at his watch.

'This will have to be brief, I'm afraid,' he said. 'I've got a lunch date.'

'It won't take long,' Roly replied. 'In short, Kate has been enquiring after you. I thought you might like to know.'

'Are we talking about Kate Protheroe?' Niall raised a sceptical eyebrow.

'Well, yes, I thought you and she—'

'You thought we were what?'

'That you and she were seeing something of each other.'

'Oh, you did, did you?' Niall sounded amused.

'Word gets around,' Roly said vaguely, aware of steering a tortuous course between lies and reality.

'Doesn't it just?' Niall said, drinking half his juice and setting the glass down. 'Oh well, it's no secret.

To bring you up to date, however, we are no longer in communication. Her idea, not mine; she's a trifle neurotic, I've come to the conclusion. I'm surprised she's making enquiries through you, though. I'd have expected the direct approach if she wanted to get in touch with me.'

'She didn't confide in me,' Roly said, 'but I got the distinct impression she would like to call you, but hadn't got the courage. It was only an impression, of course; her questions were rather oblique.'

'What did she say?'

'I can't remember exactly; asked if I'd seen you lately and how you were and so on. It wasn't a long conversation. She sounded almost regretful,' Roly added, 'or perhaps wistful is a better word.'

Niall digested the information for a moment. 'Is that all? It's not much to go on,' he remarked.

'I remember she said something about it being a pity when one lost touch with friends,' Roly said.

'She knows where to find me,' Niall said shortly.

Roly leaned forward in his chair, his round face puckered in an earnest frown. 'Kate's reserved,' he said. 'I'm very fond of her; she hasn't had an easy time. I believe she'd really appreciate a call, particularly if you've had a falling-out.'

Niall ran a hand through his hair. 'I'll think about it,' he answered. He looked at Roly with a faint smile. 'You're a funny sod, you know, Roly, like some old agony aunt, sorting out other people's lives. What motivates you, I wonder?'

'I don't make a habit of it,' Roly said with hauteur. 'This is only on behalf of Kate.'

'The trouble with Kate is, she's dominated by family, engrossed in that unpleasant small boy of hers,' Niall commented. 'The little bastard emptied a bottle of wine over me; I've made a point of avoiding him since. Still,' he took another look at his watch, 'no harm in calling her, I suppose.' Pushing his chair back, he added, 'I'll have to leave, I'm afraid. Thanks for the cosy little chat.' The sceptical eyebrow shot up once more. 'See you later.'

After he had gone, Roly sat on in contemplation. He was not deceived by the nonchalance of Niall's manner; he had swallowed the bait, of that Roly was certain. Some of the pleasure had been taken out of his accomplished mission, however, by belated feelings of disloyalty. Who would have thought he would be forced to collaborate with the enemy? He tried to reassure himself that it would not be for long, that Niall wouldn't get far with Kate, now he was past history in her life; an innocuous lunch, maybe, for old times' sake, was all Roly needed for his purposes. His dislike of Niall turned to near hatred when he thought of the words he had used to describe Jake, and with a stab of conscience, Roly regretted the course on which he had set himself. But then he recalled Kate standing in her lighted doorway with Matt's arm round her shoulders, and he pictured the bleakness of his own future on the outside looking in, and the moment of doubt passed. He had started and he would finish.

He tried not to think about Jake too often: dwelling on him would bring about a complete collapse of resolve.

Isobel took the news of Kate's reconciled marriage with her usual friendly cynicism.

'I'm delighted for you,' she said, 'if that's what you want. Though how the hell you've managed to iron out all those tedious problems of yours, God only knows.'

'We've dealt with the important ones,' Kate answered cheerfully, 'which is what matters. My mother's already casting gloom and despondency over our future: don't you start, please.'

'I'm not. I stand in awe of your courage, that's all.' Isobel surveyed Kate's glowing face. 'You look so ridiculously happy, I should think it's bound to work. What does Jake feel about the plan?'

'Ridiculously happy, like me.' Kate finished tidying patterns into their correct positions on the rails. 'Would you do me a great favour, Izzy?'

'That depends.'

'I don't want Niall Hunter as my client any longer, for various reasons. His curtains and covers will be ready next week. Would you be a friend and take him off my hands, please? I'll be forever grateful.'

Isobel said ironically, 'I'm sure you will. How many more erstwhile lovers of yours can I expect to be handed over to me?'

Kate turned pink. 'None, I promise. Please say "yes".'

'All right,' Isobel sighed. 'Just this once, mind.'

'Thank you. How did you know about him being . . .?'

'You're transparent, darling. It was obvious what had happened, equally obvious it wasn't doing you any good.'

'Oh,' Kate said feebly. 'You're right, of course, it wasn't, and I'd rather not see him again.'

'Coffee break,' Isobel announced briskly, changing the subject. 'It should be champagne to celebrate your new-born bliss; I think there's a bottle tucked away downstairs somewhere.'

'Champagne does funny things to me; I get legless on one glass. You must come and celebrate with us, Izzy, when Matt is home,' Kate said gratefully. Matt, who professed to being terrified of Isobel, would grumble, but Kate meant to keep her word.

When she arrived home that day, there was a message from Niall on the answerphone, as if he had been conjured up by telepathy. The sound of his disembodied voice came as a shock; she had not

181

expected to hear it again after their ragged parting in Paris. What he had to say was short and to the point, and did not concern his soft furnishings as might have been supposed. 'Kate, hi. I've missed you. Will you have lunch with me? If you don't answer, I'll call you back.' She felt there was an element of menace in the last sentence, but that was ridiculous. What harm could he do her? Switching the machine off, she went to make tea, deciding as she drank it that the matter was quite easily settled. She would ring him and explain about Matt, forestalling any badgering on the phone he might have planned. There could be no arguing with the fact of a returning husband; how wonderful it was not to have to invent excuses, to have the ultimate one to hand.

Jake arrived home from school with Helga at that moment and Kate postponed any telephoning until later. School holidays began the following week, and he was full of end-of-term ebullience, flushed and dishevelled from a paper-darts match with Toby on the bus.

'They were *terrible*,' Helga said, trying to sound severe. 'I thought we would be ordered to leave.'

'I don't see why,' Jake argued grinning. 'We were only throwing paper around. The old man called us "yobbos", and we weren't anywhere near him.'

'It sounds as if he were right.' Kate reached for two extra mugs. 'You were being boring, which is nearly as bad.'

'I'm starving. Can I go and buy a "Big Mac"?'

'No, you can't. You'll have a sandwich and lump it,' Kate told him.

'I'll make it! I'll make it!'

'*May* I make it,' she corrected. 'Anything to keep you occupied. And wash your hands first.'

'And pick up your things from the floor,' Helga ordered.

He sighed exaggeratedly. 'Nag, nag, nag!' he grumbled under his breath while reluctantly obeying. 'S'like prison.'

'I doubt it,' Kate said. 'There are chocolate brownies in the tin: you wouldn't get those behind bars.'

She was feeling in an indulgent mood; Jake's onrush of exuberance was due as much to Matt's awaited homecoming as to eight weeks of freedom. She recognized the symptoms, for she too was on a high.

She phoned Niall at six o'clock when Jake was supposedly doing his homework, and found that she had forgotten the number, so completely had she discarded him from her mind. The phone rang twice only before he answered, as though anticipating her call.

'Kate, it's good to hear you,' he said in the voice that she had once found attractive and now did nothing for her at all. 'How are you, and what are you up to?'

'I'm marvellously well,' she replied; and then, realizing her enthusiastic tone might be attributed to his getting in touch, added, 'We've been particularly busy at the shop, I like that; no time to be bored. And you?'

'Fine. A lot of summer parties to organize; busy-busy, like you.' A short pause; the niceties now out of the way. 'You've been on my mind, Kate. Paris was a fiasco; nobody's fault, but our parting was unnecessarily hostile, it seemed to me. And then, when you weren't on the flight home, I took it I really had been blacklisted.'

'I had to take the early flight. There was a burglary while I was away.'

'Really? Sorry to hear that. Did much get taken? Shit! That's sad.' Another hesitation, during which she could hear him lighting one of his small cigars.

'It's nice to know you weren't avoiding me, though. How about lunch? I'd like us to remain friends.'

'Sorry, Niall. I don't think it's a very good idea.'

'A peaceful, innocuous lunch with no strings?'

'Things have changed for me; I do have strings attached.' She took a deep breath and told him joyously, 'Matt and I are getting together again.'

'Really?' he commented. 'Well, well. It doesn't surprise me; in fact, it accounts for a lot of enigmas. All the same, it surely doesn't rule out lunch with an old friend.'

'Yes, it does,' she said firmly. 'It might worry Matt.'

'I've never known a husband object to *lunch*. In that case, why tell him?'

'We're making a fresh start; going behind his back is hardly the right way to set about it.'

'It sounds,' he remarked with a touch of sarcasm, 'as if you look forward to being well and truly shackled by marriage. Begin as you mean to go on, Kate. Or are you frightened of him?'

'Frightened of Matt?' She laughed, genuinely astonished. 'You must be joking.'

'Then you are scared of *me*,' he said, 'or the effect I have on you.'

'Don't flatter yourself.'

'If we sit yards apart and discuss politics and religion, will you lunch with me? Please, Kate.'

She hesitated, wondering whether she was in fact making too much of an issue out of an hour or so over a meal. He pounced on her wavering.

'I shall merely go on calling you until you agree,' he told her, 'which will be boring for both of us.'

'It's already becoming so,' she said with a sigh. 'All right, Niall. I'll meet you this once since it's not worth arguing about. But don't expect me to make a habit of it.'

'I don't expect a thing except your company,' he

said with deceptive meekness. 'When shall we make it?'

'It'll have to be this week. Friday, perhaps.'

'Fine, Friday it is. I'll book a table somewhere. You can meet me there; I don't want to embarrass you by collecting you in full view of the neighbours.'

She ignored this final caustic comment, said good-bye and put down the receiver. Her mind turned immediately to plans for Matt's return; the small room he and she once shared as an office must be sorted, her things cleared and tidied to make space for his. The date with Niall meant nothing to her; it was so unimportant in her present blissful scheme of things that she even neglected to put it in her diary. A certain surprise that he had not apparently found someone else to manipulate was quickly forgotten, and the lunch date also remained forgotten until he rang to let her know which res-taurant. She did not purposely keep it from Matt but by that time it hardly seemed worth telling him, the matter seemed so trivial.

Matt telephoned Kate as she was going to bed. It had become a ritual, this late-night communication.

'I've arranged to vacate the flat on Tuesday of next week,' he told her. 'They've found another tenant.'

'Wonderful! Only eight days to go and you'll be home.' She added tentatively, 'You're not beginning to regret it, are you, darling?'

'How did you guess?' he teased her. 'I'm planning to leave my clothes on a beach and do a runner.'

'Don't! It's too serious for joking.'

'I love you,' he said. 'And you? Are you having second thoughts?'

'You know I'm not. I just have that awful feeling children get before some gorgeous treat, that some-thing will happen to prevent it.'

'*Nothing* will happen. You're still on for Wednesday?' Wednesday evening had been set aside for their celebratory dinner.

'Yes, but I've had to do a bit of rearranging,' she said. 'Helga's boyfriend is in London for a few days and she wants to show him the sights. I've asked Roly to babysit.'

'Should we make use of him like that?' Matt said.

'He loves it; it makes him feel wanted, and it's a popular move with Jake.'

'I'm not sure your psychology's right,' Matt insisted. 'Haven't you seen his expression when he forgets to guard it? One doesn't lose a passion for someone overnight. I almost feel as if I should stay at home while he takes you out, just to give him a few hours of happiness before it disappears for good.'

'You don't mean it?' Kate cried.

'Not the last comment,' Matt said. 'I'm not that altruistic.'

When his final good nights had been said to Jake, Roly settled himself in an armchair in the drawing-room and switched on the television at low volume. Jake's company had been enjoyable enough to distract him, so that the ever-present yearning for the impossible was almost forgotten for an hour or so. They had filled their evening with a variety of pursuits, including a rather rudimentary attempt at chess and a less demanding game of draughts. As usual when they went upstairs to Jake's bedroom, the latest addition to *The Diehard Chronicles* had to be read and approved of, and another story dragged out of Roly.

'You don't need my ideas any more,' he said. 'You're the brains behind the project.'

'We're joint authors,' Jake reminded him; and

then, snuggling into his duvet and reverting to babyhood, 'I love being told stories.'

'Does Captain Diehard have a wife?' he asked when Roly had finished. 'He must have because he's got two sons. So what's she doing while they're whizzing around the galaxies having adventures?'

'She stays behind and waits for them to come home. Then she cooks huge meals and washes their clothes,' Roly said for want of a less sexist answer.

'Boring! Why doesn't she go with them?'

'Too dangerous,' Roly shook his head solemnly.

'They have girls on space missions,' Jake pointed out.

'Why don't you write her into your next chapter?'

'Brilliant! I will. Otherwise,' Jake said through a muffled yawn, 'she'll get fed up with being alone and push off somewhere. 'Night, Roly.'

It struck Roly as he went downstairs that Jake's insight into neglected women stemmed from anxiety for Kate in her late solitude; an anxiety put to rest now by her revived marriage. A wave of guilt threatened to engulf Roly; he fought to block it while his eyes stared at the flickering television screen unseeingly. It was becoming a familiar one, this battle between loyalty and affection for Jake and desire for Kate. Irrational and obsessive, the latter won on this occasion, as it always did to his shame. On the screen, one man was beating another to a pulp in a dark alley. Roly switched off the set and turned his mind to tactics.

His plan was far from complete; he needed more evidence; solid evidence of Niall's involvement with Kate. Something in writing would be ideal but almost too much to hope for; he doubted that letters had been a part of their relationship. All the same, he would never get the same opportunity to find out, with the house to himself apart from Jake. It was worth looking: he had nothing to lose. The obvious place was Kate's elegant walnut bureau standing in an alcove near the window. He rose from the armchair and moved across the room, automatically assuming the stealth of burglars and shamefully aware of being no better than they. Carefully he lowered the bureau's lid, pulling out the rests to support it and switching on the desk lamp. Three separate piles of papers lay below the pigeon-holes; a quick survey showed them to consist of bills, receipts and bulkiest of all, a pending stack. His attention turned to the pigeon-holes, a row of three either side of a small cupboard door. This, he imagined, was the most likely place for correspondence to be stored, and judging by the dog-eared corners of envelopes poking out, Kate, like a lot of women, was a hoarder of letters. He sighed, daunted by where to start searching and the unlikelihood of her having kept any incriminating note from Niall. It was ridiculous to suppose she would be so careless.

Simply because it was the easiest place to start looking, he unlocked the door to the miniature cupboard, having first removed the papers in front of it with care. Inside were half-a-dozen envelopes in newer condition than the others. He laid them on the desk, glancing at the handwriting on each one before pulling out the contents and reading the signatures. Four were from women, the fifth, on blue writing-paper with his address in white, was from Niall. Disconcerted at his luck, Roly sat down on an upright chair to decipher the sprawling, rather feminine writing. It did not take long; there was only one side of a page and in no way could it be termed a love-letter.

> My dear Kate,
> Have received your letter, and I accept the strange rules you insist on for the coming weekend. I don't profess to understand, but

*if that is the only way I can get you to spend
the weekend with me, then so be it. I
daresay we shall enjoy bits of Paris, but not,
sadly, in the manner I had envisaged.*

*The plane leaves at 4.30 p.m. I imagine it
would suit you for us to meet at Heathrow at
3.30, close to the check-in desk on Friday 23rd.
If I don't hear from you, I'll take it you'll be
there.*

Love, Niall.

Brief and to the point with no more warmth to
it than a business communication. Roly folded the
single sheet and pushed it back in its envelope. From
his point of view, it served its purpose marvellously
well, including as it did dates and locations. He
slipped it into his trouser pocket, conscious that
what he was doing was tantamount to stealing but
unable to contain his delight at the success of his
plans so far. Besides, the letter would remain within
the family; it was merely being transferred from wife
to husband which hardly amounted to theft, so he
managed to persuade himself.

He tidied the desk and softly closed the lid, wondering as he did so what had possessed Kate to
keep such a damning piece of evidence. It could
only be supposed that she had forgotten to throw
it away; she was unlikely to have hung on to a
cold-blooded note for sentimental reasons, to be
read and reread. He blessed her silently for her help,
crossed to the tray of drinks left ready for him and
poured himself a whisky, finding a slight tremor in
his hands from sheer excitement. He was just too late
to catch sight of Jake's departing figure as he left the
open doorway where he had been stationed for the
last few minutes, watching.

*　　*　　*

Jake, sleepless from another warm and humid night, had crept downstairs with the intention of persuading Roly to allow him ten minutes of telly-viewing. But the television was switched off and Roly was by the open bureau, reading what could only be one of Kate's letters. Instinct stopped Jake from interrupting him; he stayed motionless in the doorway and watched while Roly stuffed an envelope into his pocket. When he turned away from the desk, Jake turned too and bolted upstairs on bare and soundless feet, to lie more wide awake than ever on top of the duvet.

He was confused. Roly was the best, second only to Matt, and yet reading other people's letters was wrong. Reading them and then nicking them was a double wrong. There had to be a reason for this un-Roly-like behaviour but, hard as he tried, Jake could not think of one. There was probably a perfectly simple explanation which, if only he knew what it was, would seem obvious and laughable. Tossing and turning and trying to find a cool bit of pillow under his head, he wished he had not been a witness to Roly's actions. It left him with the awful decision of whether or not to tell his mother.

He was still awake when his parents came home; he heard the front door open and close and the muted laughter in the hall. When Kate crept into his room, he pretended to be asleep in case his secret came tumbling out without his meaning it to.

Chapter Seven

Two incidents occurred to disturb Matt's Friday morning. The second of these, a call from his literary agent Adrian, to say that the book had been accepted by a reputable publisher offering a fair advance, came too late to cancel out the sheer nastiness of the first. He was left pulverized by conflicting emotions.

The letter had arrived by post; a typed address on a manila envelope with nothing to distinguish it from business mail other than a first-class stamp. He had opened it at breakfast while counting the number of mornings he would be eating stale croissants alone before returning to Kate. His immediate reaction to the single handwritten sheet of writing-paper was that one of her letters had somehow been misdirected to him. After he had read it with Niall's flamboyant signature at the bottom, and reread it noting the dates, he sat staring into space trying to make sense of it. The letter had presumably been in her possession before being posted to his address, but by whom? Someone wished them harm, and yet he could not for the life of him think why unless it were Niall himself in a fit of jealousy. Nor was the letter particularly explicit; it was about as passionate as a laundry list. Not until he had looked at it a third time did he realize that it was the dates that were all-important, corresponding with Kate's weekend in Paris, some three weeks previously. He moved abruptly, pushing his chair back with a harsh grating on the kitchen floor, and carried plate and cup to the sink. A sick, hollow feeling of helplessness invaded the pit of his stomach while he fought to remain logical and to get his thoughts in order.

It came as no surprise to him that Kate had had an affair with Niall Hunter. He suspected as much after Jake had expressed his violent dislike of the man and Roly had shown embarrassment when questioned. That fact no longer worried him; he and Kate had agreed to lead separate lives, after all. But he had imagined that what she termed as the 'tidying up' of her life included the riddance of lovers, and now he was far from sure she had done so. Her Paris weekend was recent, only a few weeks back, and she had lied to him, pretended to have been staying with Felicity. There was no need for that; he would have understood. Possibly she had been planning to use the trip to end the affair, but her lying hurt him all the same. There had never been mistrust between them before, however bad the conflicts. He left the breakfast things unwashed and went to dress and shave, going through the process mechanically, desperately trying to persuade himself that the situation wasn't as grim as it looked.

His mind kept returning to the question of who had posted the letter, and the motive behind it. It seemed initially to be such a pointless act; and yet not so trivial on further reflection. If the intention was to cause trouble between himself and Kate, then it had already gone some way to succeeding. It was not only a question of motive but also of opportunity and here identity became an enigma. Presuming the letter was in Kate's desk at the time it was taken, the number of people with access and the maliciousness needed was practically nil. The more he thought about it, the more Niall appeared to be the only possibility, and that meant – his hand holding the razor gave a jerk – he must have been in the house quite recently: not ousted, but still a part of Kate's life. Persistent as nagging toothache, the idea infiltrated Matt's thinking and stuck there, refusing to be dismissed. His reflection stared back at him from the bathroom mirror, specks of blood on the chin where he had nicked himself. It seemed to him that his face had aged and grown thinner in the space of minutes, the eyes shadowed from frowning. Searching the cabinet fruitlessly for cotton wool, he doctored his cuts with bits of tissue which gave him a bizarre appearance, entirely in keeping with a cuckold, he decided with some bitterness.

While he dressed, pulling on jeans and shirt distractedly, his feelings fluctuated wildly. One moment the fact of Kate having an ongoing affair appeared impossible considering the strength of their revived happiness. No-one could simulate such whole-hearted fervour for their commitment as she had shown, least of all Kate. A quick temper she might have, and a propensity for thinking she was in the right, but she was guileless: or so he had always thought. And here his spirits took a downward plunge, and he became full of doubts. He imagined he knew her inside out; but did one ever know another human being that well? Wasn't there always a side to them, however close they were, that remained hidden? The suspicion frightened him; he wished fervently that he had never been forced to read the bloody letter, that he had been allowed to continue in blissful ignorance. He was inclined to pretend it had not happened, to treat it as a vindictive joke and return home on Tuesday as planned; but he knew he could not do that, could not go back without talking to her first. When the telephone rang, he answered it with trepidation, half-expecting to hear Kate's voice and not knowing what the hell to say to her. It was Adrian, jubilant at being the bearer of good news.

Matt tried to convey gratitude and to match his agent's enthusiasm. It was all there, the excitement and the pride and the amazement at being published, but buried now under a blanket of worry. He felt mostly bemused and sounded it, a reaction which did not escape Adrian's notice.

'You are all right, aren't you? Not ill or anything?' he asked, puzzled.

'Good Lord, no,' Matt replied with false heartiness.

'Fine, fine. Only you don't sound your usual self. I hope you're as pleased as I am.'

'I'm over the moon.' Matt searched for the right words.

'The advance may not be quite what you were hoping for—'

'I wasn't hoping for anything.'

'—but don't be disappointed. It's a great deal more than the normal offer for a first book.'

'Adrian, it's wonderful. I'm enormously chuffed and terribly grateful for all your efforts.'

'You'll like the publishers; they're a friendly crowd, and they have an impressive list of authors. We'll arrange for you to meet them as soon as possible. They're full of enthusiasm for the photographs, by the way.'

'Great. What happens now?' asked Matt, attempting to appear eager.

'Contracts are drawn up, and when we've approved them, you sign. After that's completed, you'll receive the first half of your advance. Then there are designs for the cover to be discussed, a short autobiography from yourself, an author photograph and so on. There's a lot that goes on. I'd like to see you soonish, Matt, to put you in the picture. Are you free for lunch today, by any chance?'

'Today's difficult, I'm afraid.' Then, because the

explanation did not seem enough in itself, he added, 'There's some family business I have to see to, but I'm here all weekend.'

'We might meet tomorrow, open a bottle to celebrate.'

'Sounds lovely.'

'*Something's* wrong, isn't it?' Adrian said. 'I can tell by your voice.'

'A slight crisis, that's all,' Matt answered him. If only it *were* all.

'Want to confide? There's a sympathetic ear waiting if you do: discretion guaranteed.'

'Thanks, Adrian, but I'll get it sorted.'

'Mind you do. And take heart; think of your name on the shelves of the bookshops, writ large. I'll call you later.'

He rang off, and the silence of the flat closed round Matt with only the hum of the distant traffic to break it. There had been a moment when he was tempted to tell Adrian the whole story in a couple of succinct sentences, but he had stopped himself. Adrian was a good friend, but not one of longstanding, and Matt rather doubted the sworn discretion. It had made him realize, however, that he needed someone to use as a confidante before he talked to Kate. He could not, he felt, spend another minute with his brain going round in circles while he stared out of the window at the green of Battersea Park. Later, in about an hour, he was due at the offices of the Sunday newspaper where he was still employed part time. That at least would fill a portion of the morning. Meanwhile, he would telephone Roly, the obvious, indeed the sole person he could turn to. Roly, who could be depended on to view a critical problem with his logical accountant's mind, who possibly knew something that Matt didn't, and might just be able to prove him wrong about Kate. He lifted the receiver and dialled Roly's number.

*   *   *

Roly had been putting a lot of thought into his planning in the past week. The coming weekend was crucial; that was when the results of his efforts should come to a head and show themselves to be successful or a complete fiasco. Timing was everything.

The gathering of necessary information had had to be carried out with subtlety so as not to arouse suspicion. He had dropped in on Kate one evening and tackled her while they had a drink in the garden. 'So Tuesday is D-Day,' he had remarked. 'The return to the married status. Would you find time to have lunch with an old friend before you become unavailable?'

She had looked at him fondly. 'Silly old Roly,' she said, laughing. 'Matt won't mind me seeing you, darling. As a matter of fact, I'm lunching with Niall on Friday and I don't suppose he'd mind that either.'

'He doesn't know?'

'No, but only because it's not worth mentioning,' she had said. 'We're very sure of each other now, Matt and I.'

He had not expected to discover what he needed to know with such ease. Second on his list was Niall, whom he contacted by telephone ostensibly to arrange the catering for his firm's anniversary drinks party. After that matter was settled, Niall brought up the subject of Kate without any nudging from Roly.

'By the way,' Niall said, 'I've a bone to pick with you. Why didn't you tell me Kate is having another shot at wedded bliss? Her husband is moving back.'

'Really?' Roly said. 'It's news to me. Mind you, it's always been a strong possibility. I suppose,' he added, 'this means further communication with her is at an end as far as you're concerned?'

'What a quaint old-fashioned notion,' Niall remarked. 'We're lunching; although I can see there's no future in it. She took some persuading. It's hardly worth the expenditure, but I do enjoy seeing her: she's so decorative.'

'Taking her somewhere nice?' Roly asked.

'Haven't decided. The Waterside Café probably. One can eat out of doors if the weather holds, which will suit her.'

Roly had enjoyed this talk with Niall, took a great deal of pleasure in using him to his advantage. There was no such satisfaction to be gained from disrupting Kate's and Matt's future. It was something that he had to do, that was all, a necessary if painful duty. He sincerely believed that if it worked out as he intended, it would be the best not only for himself but for all of them. His conscience which had plagued him at the start no longer bothered him; he had gone too far for that and his concentration was centred on the next move.

He was not surprised when the call from Matt was put through to his office. He had posted Niall's letter to arrive on Friday morning in the hopes there would be an immediate reaction from Matt; but he was modestly pleased that the plan was falling so neatly into place. Curiously, he was not prepared for the barely controlled note of desperation in Matt's voice, and for a dangerous moment felt his resolve waver.

'Listen, Roly, I need advice,' Matt said without preamble. 'Can you by any chance meet me later this morning? I can't discuss it on the phone.'

'Professional advice?' Roly asked.

'No, that of a friend.'

'Can't you tell me anything?'

'I've had a shock concerning – look, will you give me an hour? I'm worried out of my skull.'

'Of course, Friday's seldom busy. How about the Royal Court Hotel, Sloane Square, in the bar at twelve o'clock? You sound dreadful,' Roly added sympathetically.

'Thanks, Roly. I'll be there. You're a mate.'

Matt was already in the bar when Roly arrived, sitting at a table with a drink in front of him. His face, without colour at the best of times, looked a shade paler, and there were two small scabs on his chin where he had cut himself shaving. He rose, clasped Roly's hand briefly and went to fetch him a half-pint of bitter. When they were settled in their seats, he took the envelope from his pocket, drew out the letter and handed it across the table.

'It came with this morning's mail,' was all he said.

Roly read it, taking his time, and reread it as if trying to make sense of it. 'I don't understand,' he said at last. 'Who sent it?'

'Search me. Niall-bloody-Hunter seems the only likely shit.'

'But what is the purpose?'

'Don't you see? Someone is trying to tell me that Kate's embroiled in an affair. The dates of the Paris weekend prove it.'

'I'm sure, even if she has been in the past, it's over now,' Roly said seriously. 'For God's sake, Matt, it's obvious she can't think of anyone but you. I've seen you together, remember.'

Matt glanced at him, a flicker of hope in his eyes, then stared down into his glass. 'I wish I could believe you. But explain this. How did the letter disappear from her keeping and into my hands? It had to be Niall, which points to one fact only: he was in the house recently.' He gave a noise halfway between a groan and a sigh. 'I don't care what's happened in the past; it's the here and now that matters. If she's having an ongoing thing with him, I'll – I'll – ' he searched for words – 'I don't know what the hell I'll do,' he finished, and swallowed the last of his drink in one abrupt, despairing gesture.

'You really shouldn't leap to conclusions,' Roly

urged him gently. 'You have to talk to her, hear what she has to say. There's probably some perfectly simple explanation to all this.'

'Has she', Matt asked, 'said anything about this little bastard to you; mentioned him lately?'

Roly shook his head. 'No,' he lied, 'but then she'd hardly confide in me. I'm pretty certain Jake would have said something if Niall had been around; children make good watchdogs.'

Matt seemed to brighten. 'That's true,' he said. 'Although if it wasn't Niall, who was it? I can't think of anyone else vindictive enough to try to split us up, let alone have access to the letter.'

'Oh, I think it was Niall,' Roly said. 'He probably took the letter weeks ago with a view to using it later. Jealousy is a powerful emotion,' he added half to himself.

'Roly, you've done me good. Let's have another drink.'

'Lunch is what you need.' He glanced at his watch. 'I've got a table booked at the Waterside; I was taking a client but he cried off.'

'I don't feel like eating.'

'You will when you get there,' Roly said persuasively. 'A short stroll down to the river first, perhaps.'

'All right, if you twist my arm,' Matt agreed. 'I haven't brought my car; didn't trust myself not to over-drink.' When they were in the street he said restlessly, 'I wish I didn't have to wait until this evening to speak to her, I'd like to have it over and done with.'

'It soon will be,' Roly replied softly.

The Waterside Café was set back from the stretch of river immediately below Putney Bridge. A lawn ran down to the water's edge and there were trees at either side screening off two ugly blocks of mansion flats. It was a popular place to eat in summer, its plate-glass windows running the length of the restaurant and overlooking the terrace where one could lunch outside. At one of the terrace tables shaded by an umbrella, Kate and Niall were halfway through their meal, carrying on the rather desultory conversation of two people whose attitudes had changed towards one another. She felt, and looked, serene, tranquil in the knowledge of her new security where no-one could reach her. He, aware of her remoteness, was thinking how this rendezvous was a waste of time and money, but on the whole worth it for her decorative quality. On this day and in this light, she was beautiful.

'You look like a sleek little cat that has just demolished a bowl of cream,' he remarked.

'If that's supposed to be a compliment,' she said amicably, 'it might have been better put. It makes me sound self-satisfied.'

'Perhaps you are.'

'No,' she answered, 'not that, just gloriously happy. It's an amazing feeling; I've realized suddenly how seldom it happens, that unadulterated happiness.'

'And this is all due to the loss of your freedom and being shackled once again to one man?' he asked ironically.

'Not *any* man; only Matt.'

'He must have exceptional qualities.'

'He loves me,' she said simply, 'and I him.'

'So do I love you.'

'Oh Niall,' she said, laughing, 'that's the biggest whopper I've heard for ages.'

'I've only just discovered it,' he said, and catching her eye, laughed too.

'You treated me as if you were Svengali, trying to mould me into someone I wasn't.'

'Well,' he commented with a sigh, 'I made a mistake. I've lost you now.'

'It would have happened whatever you'd done.'

'Shall I see you again?'

'I think not,' she said. 'Or not for some time, at least, when I'm sure Matt wouldn't mind.'

'How bleak,' he said, 'like the end of most affairs.'

She leant back in her chair and smiled at him. 'It's been a very nice ending,' she told him. 'Much more peaceful than that dreadful dinner in France. You should try settling down, Niall; I recommend it with all my heart.' She looked at her watch. 'And now I must dash back to work or Isobel will fire me.'

But he was not listening; his attention had wandered to somewhere in the middle distance over her shoulder. 'There's a man staring at you,' he said, 'from the end of the terrace.'

When she turned in her chair, there was no-one there.

Matt made his way to Denbigh Street that evening with the sickening sense of someone going to his own execution. The pain and anger that had followed the dreadful moment of catching sight of Kate at the restaurant had burnt itself out, and he was left with a kind of despairing resignation. It was better to know now that she was capable of betrayal, he had made himself believe, than to find out after they had begun a new life. Driving slowly through the rush-hour traffic, he willed himself to behave reasonably, to listen to what she had to say without rushing headlong into blistering accusations. He hated rows, had always been the one to back out of them at all costs. But then this nightmare had never arisen before and he could not trust his self-control. He kept reliving the sight of her beneath the umbrella, her dark shining head turned towards the man she was with. She had been laughing, although

Matt was too far away to hear, and the laughter had seemed to mock him personally.

Roly, who had been checking on their table reservation, had joined him by the terrace, taken in the situation at a glance and guided him forcibly into the restaurant, murmuring reassuringly. But Matt had marched straight through without speaking, and out of the front entrance to stand on the pavement in the heat of the afternoon sun.

'Did you *know* about this?' he asked furiously when Roly, hot and flustered, caught up with him. 'Did you know she'd be here?'

'My dear boy, how could I?' Roly thrust his face earnestly towards Matt. 'I swear to God – half London eats here in the summer.' He put a hand on Matt's arm. 'Don't take it to heart,' he said. 'Lunch with a friend means nothing. Wives lunch with male friends every day of the week. You really mustn't damn Kate out of hand for that.'

'Even when the friend in question is Niall Hunter, and his fucking letter is burning a hole in my pocket?' Matt said with quiet venom. 'It *was* Niall, I presume?'

Roly nodded reluctantly.

'I can't take any more,' Matt said. 'I'm going home.'

'You shouldn't be alone,' Roly protested. 'We'll go somewhere and talk this through. You need to eat.'

'Wrong. I need to talk to Kate. Sorry, Roly, if I seem an ungrateful sod.'

'I'll drive you.'

But Matt had already hailed a passing taxi and dived into its stuffy depths to be borne out of view. He realized Roly had not deserved to get the brunt of his angst, but he had been unable to prevent it.

He could not remember a day seeming so interminably long, and it was far from being at an end. In the afternoon he had been unable to settle to anything. He sat down and banged out the first page of the novel he intended to write, two dozen lines of sound and fury which had no bearing on the plot he had in mind, but relieved his tension. He telephoned Kate at the shop at three-thirty when he could not wait any longer, and the warmth of her voice as she answered him grated on his nerves like a lie. It was only afterwards that he felt intense relief that she was not in bed with her lunch companion. Her warmth had changed to bewilderment, but he had refused an explanation, merely saying he had to see her and he did not want Jake there: would she please arrange for him to be elsewhere. He had put down the receiver before he could hear her reaction.

The house was silent as he let himself in. He had imagined her coming forward to meet him the moment she heard the key in the lock, but there was no sign of her. He peered into all the rooms before he finally found her sitting in the garden and sewing buttons on one of Jake's shirts.

'Hi.' She looked calm and unwelcoming, and did not get up to kiss him. 'Do you want a drink?' she asked, severing the thread with her teeth.

He felt almost foolish. 'Yes, but indoors if you don't mind. I don't want our conversation echoing round the neighbours.'

'If you like.' She gathered up her sewing and they moved into the house, passing through the room that had been their shared office. He noticed her things had been tidied and his desk made ready for him.

'You weren't very nice on the phone,' she said in the kitchen as she poured whisky into tumblers.

'I don't feel "nice",' he replied unprepared for her surprising coolness. 'Where's Jake?'

'At Toby's. Helga's at one of her classes. Where shall we sit, kitchen or drawing-room?'

'Doesn't matter; drawing-room, I should think,' he said, impatient with the delaying tactics.

203

'What *is* all this about?' she asked, planting herself in a corner of the sofa.

He drew the letter from his pocket and slapped it down beside her without speaking. She picked it up and glanced at the writing, then up at him with a puzzled frown.

'I don't understand,' she said. 'How do you come to have this?'

'It arrived in the post, sender unknown, having presumably been nicked from your possession.'

'But why? And how? There doesn't seem to be a point. It's all dates and things; not very interesting.'

He wondered if she were being purposely obtuse. 'The dates *are* to the point,' he said. 'They underline the fact that you went away with this effing man Niall for the weekend. I presume it was he who thought up the delightful idea of informing me, since I can't think of anyone else.'

She flushed, a swift rising tide of colour that swept up her face from neck to forehead. 'It wasn't like that,' she said, not looking at him. 'The weekend, I mean. I had already ended our – oh, our relationship for want of another word – before this letter was written.'

'Are you saying,' he asked, 'that you didn't go away with him?'

'We travelled together, and stayed one night in the same hotel, in separate rooms. Then I moved to Felicity's flat.'

'Why did you lead me to believe you were with Felicity the entire time?'

She looked at him standing whitefaced by the fireplace. 'Would you have believed me if I'd told you the truth as I've just explained it? Do you believe me now?'

'Frankly, no.'

The colour receded from her face as quickly as it had come. 'You must have known there was someone

204

I'd been seeing,' she said with sudden defiance. 'I don't imagine you were living like a saint. That was our agreement. Why are you tearing your hair out about something that finished weeks ago, all because of an unimportant letter?' She screwed the writing-paper into a ball and threw it at the waste-paper basket. 'I don't know why I ever kept the bloody thing: I just forgot to bin it, I suppose.'

'As a memento, perhaps,' he replied unpleasantly.

'Oh, for God's sake, Matt—'

He pushed himself away from the mantelpiece and began pacing restlessly backwards and forwards.

'I wish you'd sit down.'

Coming to a halt in front of her, he said, 'If I thought it had finished, I wouldn't be here now, not knowing what to do.' His voice was not his; it grated with the effort of keeping it under control.

She lifted her hands and dropped them in a gesture of defeat. 'Matt, I've told you it's over. What's got into you?'

'The letter was stolen from you, from this room, from your desk presumably. Wasn't it?'

'Yes, I suppose so.'

'Can you think of anyone other than your *friend* who had a reason for taking it and posting it to me?'

'No,' she answered, 'but then, I can't think of anyone who would want to ruin our marriage. Because that's what this is about, isn't it, and they seem to be doing a pretty good job of it.'

'Someone does. It wasn't taken by Helga or Jake. Who else but Niall?'

'He can't have,' she said wearily. 'He hasn't been here for ages.'

'So, you're not seeing him any more?'

'No.'

'I suppose lunches don't count?' he remarked, sarcasm hiding an awful sense of being about to lose her. 'And cosy dinners as well, leading to the inevitable?'

She jumped to her feet, her temper in shreds. 'How dare you spy on me! You're paranoid!' she spat at him.

'You lied to me.'

'No, I did not. When you asked if I was seeing him, you meant sleeping with him, didn't you? Didn't you?'

She glared at him, anger puckering her face like the onset of tears.

'That's what I want to know,' he said almost sulkily. 'Are you?'

'What's the use of denying it? You won't believe anything I say.' She turned away abruptly and went to stare sightlessly out of the window. 'Three hours ago I was gloriously happy and said so; those were my words – "gloriously happy". And why? Because you were coming home, simple as that. I might have known a feeling like that wouldn't last.' She swivelled round to face him. 'You're hell-bent on destroying us, all because of a grimy little prank which isn't worth a second thought. I thought we were so certain of each other. Now I don't give much for our chances.'

He felt overwhelmingly tired all of a sudden, his own anger draining away as hers took over. This was the way it had always been between them. 'You can't blame me for wanting some sort of re-assurance,' he said, staring at his shoes. 'It seems you don't want to give it to me.'

'What do you expect?' she replied. 'A signed denial? You came marching in accusing me of being a liar and a cheat and refusing to accept the truth, or even to listen. Quite frankly, Matt, I've had enough: from now on you can stuff it.'

'Why,' he asked quietly, 'can you never, ever see a point of view other than your own?'

But she ignored the remark, too incensed to notice. Retrieving her untouched drink from the table where she had left it, she said with bitterness, 'There are enough people to corroborate what I've told you, that Niall hasn't been to this house for weeks. Question Helga, or Jake if you feel like stooping that low. And why not phone Felicity while you're about it, to confirm my alibi with her? There's no need to take my word as gospel.'

Silence fell abruptly, unnerving in its suddenness. She held the glass shakily while she drank. He stood watching her, knowing he had mismanaged everything and wondering in panic how to redress the damage. The right move, he realized, would be to put his arms round her, apologize, and stay the night, and the whole wretched business would be cleared up by morning. For some reason he did not do it; a lingering, nagging shred of doubt, childish self-pity for the terrible day he had had to endure, preventing him. Before he had time to speak, she said in a tight little voice, 'I think it would be best if you left now.'

He looked at her in disbelief. 'I was hoping we could talk reasonably if we've both calmed down.'

'There's nothing more to say, is there?'

'If I say I'm truly sorry for getting it wrong and making you miserable, would that help?'

'Not really.' She stared intently at her glass. 'Because you wouldn't mean it. You don't believe you've got it wrong, do you? It's written all over your face. And I'm more angry than miserable.'

'Well, I've managed to make *myself* miserable,' he said. 'It was simply shock; I acted automatically without thinking. Please try to understand; it's because I love you so much that it mattered.'

He went to her and tried to hold her by the arms, but she shook him off, spilling some of her whisky down his shirt-front.

'You've a funny way of showing it,' she said. 'You don't trust me, and that's something I can't live with; I'm sorry, but I can't.'

It was a moment before he realized the full implication of her words; even then he had difficulty in believing it.

'Are you saying you don't want me back?' he asked incredulously.

She nodded. 'Not until I've proved I haven't lied. I don't imagine *you* want to share a bed with a wife you presume to be bonking someone else, do you?'

'For Christ's sake, Kate, that's not what I think any longer,' he protested. He felt helpless, unable to reach her, their future slipping rapidly away. 'The flat's been re-let as from next week. Where am I supposed to go next Tuesday if not home?' he added, clutching foolishly at practicalities in his desperation.

He anticipated her reply before she spoke. 'That's your problem,' she said. 'You're the one who's lost faith. Try Roly; he's got a spare bed, I'm sure he'll take pity on you.' She turned towards the door abruptly. 'I've got to get supper ready.'

'Is that all you can say? "I've got to get supper ready." ' A resurgence of his original anger flowed in to combat the panic that threatened him. 'You're acting like a first-class bitch.'

'You've got yourself to blame for that: you've made me into one.' She hovered by the door, her chin thrust forward in grim refusal to give way. Her eyes, however, were glassy with tears as she glared at him, and he felt his heart leap in hope. 'Please go, Matt. I don't want Jake coming home to find me howling.'

'All right, if that's what you want.' He moved slowly past her into the hall, sensing her draw back from him as if he were a stranger. 'You might at least give me an idea of how long my banishment is to last before I leave,' he said. 'We won't achieve anything without communication. You're not slapping an embargo on my phoning you, are you?'

'If you've got something constructive to say, I'll listen; otherwise I'd rather be left alone. I intend to find whoever hates me enough to mess up my life. I wonder you don't do the same if you care about what happens to us.'

'Of course I bloody care.' On impulse he added, 'Kate, let me stay. This can all be sorted out between us if we try.'

'Sorry, it's too late for that.' She faced him, her shoulders hunched as though cold, reminding him of a small abandoned cat. 'Go on, Matt, please leave.'

Tears trickled slowly down her face as he opened the front door and let himself into the dusty evening sunlight. He could not bear to look back.

In the shade of an oak tree in Richmond Park, Jake bit into a baguette of ham and lettuce and chewed without appetite. Beside him his father had not started to eat. He had lit a cigarette and was smoking it propped on one elbow; to keep away the midges, he said, but Jake guessed that was just an excuse. Smoking calmed the nerves, so people claimed, and Matt was not a smoker as a rule. The picnic followed a swim at Roehampton. Jake had watched his father thrashing up and down the pool relentlessly as if determined to exhaust himself which he had probably succeeded in doing since there were dark rings under his eyes, and he was unusually quiet. Jake hoped this untalkative mood would not last: he badly needed things explained to him.

Something terrible had happened. The week, which should have been the best, what with the start of the holidays and Matt coming home for good, had gone wrong. There had been a row; his mother called it an argument, but it must have been worse than that for Matt to stay away. Kate wouldn't say much about it, only that she and Daddy needed time to sort something out. She pretended to be cheerful but the lines of her face were drawn downwards when they were used to curve upwards, and twice Jake could see she had been crying. Today she had gone to see her parents and Matt had collected him after she had left, just like he had done all through the separation. Disappointment weighed heavily on Jake. He resented the unfair adult practice of not telling children what was going on; being uncertain was a kind of torture. He had his own theories on the subject, but they were vague ones and he had to have more information in order to test them. Ever present at the back of his mind was the memory of Roly searching Kate's desk. Had he pocketed an envelope, or had Jake just imagined it, late at night and half-asleep? He hadn't told anyone what he had seen; instinctively he felt Roly wouldn't like his actions known. Now, in the light of what had happened to his parents, he wasn't sure he had been right in keeping Roly's secret. It might have an importance hitherto unguessed at.

The bread was like sawdust in his mouth. 'Got any Coke, Daddy?' he asked.

Matt heaved himself upright and produced a tin from a plastic carrier. 'Sorry. I was miles away. Not a very good companion today, am I?'

Jake released the metal tag on the Coke tin and his worries in one go. 'Why have you and Mum been fighting, Daddy?'

Matt ran a hand through his hair.

'It's a complicated story to explain,' he said evasively.

'Why does everyone keep things from me? I'm ten: that's old enough to understand. Children have rights,' Jake pointed out, 'and I want to know what's going to happen.'

His father looked at him thoughtfully, two sets of dark eyes taking stock of each other. 'I agree,' he said. 'You deserve an explanation. Here goes. Evidence fell into my hands about Mum which made me accuse her of something: falsely, I believe. We both got very upset and she decided we weren't ready to be together again. That's the gist of it.'

'That's stupid.' Jake scuffed at the mossy turf with his shoe. 'Mum's unhappy, and you look as if you are. Why can't you make it up like Toby and I do when we row?'

'My sentiments entirely,' Matt said. 'But I've hurt Mum badly. She needs time to recover, and she's got a bee in her bonnet about discovering the trouble-maker.'

'Troublemaker?'

'Whoever sent me the evidence stole it from Mum, presumably with the intention of causing mayhem. He succeeded.'

The memory of Roly at Kate's desk sprang into Jake's mind with awful precision. 'It was a letter, wasn't it?' he said.

'What makes you say that?' Matt asked, eyeing him sharply.

'Nothing,' Jake mumbled, reddening up. 'I've been reading a thriller about poison-pen letters, that's all. What was in it?' he added to draw his father away from awkward questions.

'Oh no! I'm not telling you that,' Matt said firmly. 'Parents are allowed their rights and their secrets as well as children.' He peered into the carrier bags. 'You haven't eaten much,' he remarked.

'Neither have you,' Jake said.

'I guess neither of us feels hungry. What would you like to do now? Another swim? A knock-up on the Battersea tennis courts?'

'I've got a headache,' Jake said. 'I'd like to go back to your place and watch a video.'

'OK,' Matt agreed. 'We'll pick one up on the way.' He wondered if Jake were sickening for something; he looked rather flushed.

One of the best things about fathers, Jake considered, was that they didn't make a fuss over things like being indoors on a fine day. It wasn't just his head that ached. He felt bowed down by the quandary of whether or not to keep the secret of Roly to himself; the awesome responsibility of divided loyalties. He needed to lose himself in some silly movie until he could be on his own to think.

'Has it helped at all, what I've told you?' Matt asked when they were in the car.

'Sort of. But you still haven't said when you'll be coming home.' Jake blinked fiercely, wobbly at the thought that it might be never. 'Can't you make it up with Mum? Say sorry, or something; that usually works with her.'

'I've tried that,' Matt said. 'I'm afraid it's going to take more than an apology.'

Jake stared gloomily out of the window in silence. Matt put a hand over one of his and gave it a squeeze. 'Don't worry, it's going to be all right,' he reassured him. 'For one thing, I've only got the flat for another two weeks. They've allowed me to stay on the extra time purely because the next tenant isn't ready to move in.' He glanced at Jake with a smile. 'I'll have to come home after that, or sleep on the streets.'

Jake cheered up at the idea. 'Mum wouldn't let you do that,' he said. 'Sleep in a cardboard box, I mean.'

In her present frame of mind, Matt reflected, anything was possible.

'She'll be much happier once this mystery is cleared up,' he said. 'The worst aspect from her point of view is the fact that someone has it in for her, and I sympathize. It's intolerable to feel hated.'

Jake did not answer. He was thinking about Roly;

how from the first moment Jake had met him, he had made him feel safe and secure. Most importantly, Roly had seemed to watch over Kate like a friendly guard dog. No harm would come to her while Roly was there, Jake had been convinced. Could he have been so terribly wrong? His heart, or perhaps it was his stomach, lurched inside him at the idea of Roly's possible wickedness, and the realization that he couldn't stay silent any longer.

Kate drove home from her parents feeling drained. If there had been a way to avoid telling them of the recent breakdown of the marriage, she would have taken it. But they had to know from her before some busybody like her sister-in-law advised them of the fact.

Her mother had received the news character-istically, with ill-concealed pleasure at being proved correct in her assessment of Matt.

'Well, darling, it's no use pretending I'm surprised. You know my views on the subject: I won't bother to repeat them,' she said; which was tantamount to 'I told you so'.

Kate, her nerves on edge, decided to do battle with Prue where ordinarily she would have allowed the familiar phrases to go over her head. 'Ma, tell me, have you ever been in love?'

'Of course, I married your father. What an odd question,' her mother replied without pausing in her task of chopping carrots.

Kate persisted. 'I mean, truly, deeply, hopelessly in love, so that to be parted is like being only a quarter alive.'

She picked up a carrot slice, bit it and waited for Prue's patient little sigh. It came on cue.

'I'm afraid you're confusing sexual attraction with real love which is based on mutual respect, loyalty

213

and kindness,' Prue recited calmly. 'One lasts, the other doesn't. It's a mistake most young people seem to make these days: a pity, in my opinion.'

'Oh, bollocks!' Kate snapped, reverting to adolescence, and strode away to the garden to find her father, who was deadheading the roses.

He stopped snipping when she approached and went to pour them gin and tonics which they carried to deck-chairs in the shade of the cedar tree. The plaster was gone from his injured ankle now, and he was walking with the aid of a stick and a barely perceptible limp. Kate took a sip of her drink and said, 'I've just been rude to Ma. I'll have to apologize, I suppose, or the atmosphere at lunch will be absolutely arctic.'

Her father raised his eyebrows and smiled. 'I take it she was proffering unwanted advice?'

'I couldn't listen to her homespun philosophizing; I'm not in the mood. I didn't give her any details of what happened between myself and Matt; she thinks badly enough of him without encouragement.'

'There's no necessity to tell either of us,' George Brownlow said. 'It's your life.'

But her father's reticence invited confidences, and Kate disclosed the whole story, crying at the end of it as she had guessed she would, gaining relief in the flood of hot tears held back so far for Jake's sake. She left out nothing, and wondered whether the uncommendable account of Niall would stretch her father's amazing tolerance beyond its limits. To her surprise he reached for his glass and asked, 'So, you've had a right old barney. Do you want me to comment, or merely make sympathetic noises?'

'I'd like a chunk of your wisdom,' she said, extracting a wad of tissues from her bag and blowing her nose.

'Nice of you to credit me with any; your mother doesn't. Well, for a start, although I can understand how all this came about, it seems a trivial affair, hardly worth the breaking-off of relations.'

'*Trivial?*' she said, astonished. 'When I've been called a liar, and more or less accused of being a tart.'

'Aren't you exaggerating slightly?' her father suggested mildly.

'Well, perhaps not a tart exactly,' she muttered. 'But it was what he was thinking.'

He laughed. 'Come on; you can't know that for sure.'

'He didn't believe a thing I said. You've no idea how that hurts.'

'Haven't I?' he replied ironically.

They were silent for a moment; then he leant forward in his deck-chair and became altogether more alert. 'From what you tell me, he admitted he'd made a mistake,' he said. 'Isn't that so?'

'He didn't mean it. He was just saying it because he thought he'd gone too far.'

'And he apologized,' her father continued. 'You should always accept an apology.'

She shredded a tissue between her fingers without meeting his eyes.

'All right,' he said. 'You've managed to wound each other. That fact accepted, what do you propose to do about it? Throw away the chance of a lifetime's happiness out of pique?'

She raised her eyes and gave him a watery smile. 'Tough question, Pa,' she said. 'I don't know.'

'Yes, you do,' he insisted. 'You're simply being obstinate. I can always tell by your jaw advancing several inches.' Taking a gulp of his drink, he added, 'What's the worst aspect of this unhappy little saga, in your view?'

She paused before answering. 'Strangely enough, it's the fact that someone begrudges us our marriage. I find that frightening; the sheer maliciousness of it.'

'Now that I do understand,' he said. 'Very well then, why don't you turn your stubbornness into determination and do some positive detection? The list of suspects can't amount to many.'

'So few I've failed to think of any,' she replied. 'And yet somehow the wretched letter found its way from my desk to Matt's flat.'

Her father asked inconsequentially, 'How's Roly these days? I haven't heard you mention him lately.'

She looked at him, puzzled by the question. 'He's the same as ever, solid and reliable. Why have you changed the subject?'

'I haven't. I think Roly may well have a bearing on it.'

'You don't mean – you can't mean – Roly, of all people?' she said, inarticulate with disbelief. 'No, no, it's not possible,' she added, half to herself. 'He's a friend to both of us, an old and trusted family friend. There isn't a shred of malice in Roly, I swear.'

George lay back in his chair and gazed at the sky thoughtfully. 'You were never much of a judge of character, dear girl. Do you remember a conversation we had in the autumn on the same topic?'

She frowned, recalling a bonfire, the pungent smell of burning leaves, Pa's dissertation on jealousy and revenge. 'I remember,' she said. 'You issued a warning about men and unrequited love.' She shook her head. 'I still can't believe it of Roly.'

'The nicest of men can turn obsessional,' he answered. 'Think about it. And now I reckon it's time for lunch.'

Kate had made her apologies to her mother in the kitchen where she was taking a leg of lamb from the oven, and Prue had unexpectedly put down the baking tin and given way to tears. Kate put her arms round her mother and hugged her, feeling vulnerability in the thin frame grown, quite suddenly it seemed, much older. The relapse was short-lived, and lunch proceeded in a relaxed manner, considering the circumstances. She did not stay for tea, making Jake her excuse.

'Take care of yourself,' Prue said through the open window of the car. 'You're looking peaky. You need some fresh air. Come to us for a week and bring Jake.' Kate recognized it as a peace offering. She thought sadly of the half-formed plans she and Matt had made for a Tuscan holiday that might never come to fruition.

'Thank you, Ma,' she said. 'We'd like that.'

'Keep me posted,' said her father, raising his stick in salute.

She knew what he meant. His words kept bothering her throughout the homeward drive, refusing to leave her in peace; while in between her mind searched feverishly amongst recollections of Roly for clues. By the time she was in central London she had run through the length of their friendship without arriving at a conclusion. Certainly he must have developed a fixation for her; there had been all those night vigils, following her by car and hiding ineptly in the shadows. But unnerving as that was, it did not amount to more than eccentricity and, in any case, it had ceased since he knew Matt was returning. Try as she might, she was unable to equate the Roly she knew with the necessary vindictiveness. All the same, once the idea of him as villain had been planted in her brain, she could not entirely dispel it, and she had asked him to supper. In her present state of anxiety, the prospect dismayed her.

Roly poured himself a nightcap on arriving home after dinner with Kate, to counteract a certain sense of unease. There had been an atmosphere, of what he could not quite place but which was in itself uneasy; a feeling of things not being as they once were. Of course, Kate was understandably subdued; it wasn't surprising considering the rift with Matt, and the mood, if one could call it that, seemed to have rubbed off on Jake. Roly regretted upsetting Jake most of all; he wished very much he could have sat down with him and explained what he had done and why he had had to do it.

He had been looking forward to the evening intensely. It was like the old days, the days before Kate and Matt made the disastrous decision to get back together again. It would not have worked, witness how easy it had been to part them. Roly was frankly amazed at his success, and not a little proud of his planning ability. It filled him with a new-found confidence; he felt as though anything were possible having achieved his aim. Even Kate appeared less remote and inaccessible. It would take time and patience, but he could wait, he was used to waiting. It had been necessary to take a grip on himself as he was getting ready to spend the evening with her, to tone down his elation and prepare to sympathize, to put himself back in the role of infallible prop. He took care with his dressing, knowing quite well it would not make the slightest difference; in five minutes he would be a crumpled mess. It no longer worried him; it was personality that counted rather than appearance.

He drank his nightcap slowly in contemplation. What was it about the evening that had seemed out of place? He had been welcomed with the usual warmth. Kate was making mayonnaise when he arrived, carrying a bottle of Chablis and a bunch of white gladioli. She stopped her beating to give him a brief hug and kiss.

'How lovely,' she said, peering at the flowers. 'My favourites. I'll arrange them in a minute when

I've finished this; I'm trying to stop it curdling. We're having a cold meal, I'm afraid. I've spent the day with Ma and Pa so I didn't have time to cook, and Helga's not here.'

She was prattling, he thought, making conversation. 'I like cold,' he said. 'Much nicer on a warm night.'

'Help yourself to a drink,' she said.

'How about you?'

'I've already got one, thanks: I started shamefully early.' She smiled over-brightly. 'A tiring drive is my excuse. So what's your news?'

'Very little,' he replied, adding water and ice to a whisky. 'Kate, I just want to say how sorry I am that you and Matt are having – problems. If you want to talk about it—'

'I'd rather not, Roly.' She had resumed her beating and kept her eyes fixed on the pudding bowl. 'It's something only he and I can work out; I'd like to forget about it for the time being.'

'I understand,' he said; but he could not help feeling slightly disappointed. Hearing a full description of the causes behind the rift would have been gratifying, like holding up a mirror to his cleverness.

'Would you give Jake a shout?' she asked. 'We're ready to eat'; then, seeing him eye his drink, she added, 'sorry, forgetting my manners. You'd like time to finish that, wouldn't you?'

'Not to worry; I'll finish it at the table.'

'I don't want to hurry you, but to be honest, I'd like an early night,' she confessed, leaning her weight against the worktop and smiling another brilliant smile of apology. She did in fact look transparent with tiredness, and his heart turned over with love for her.

That was how the evening had been: a little rushed and jerky. He was uncomfortably conscious that there would be relief all round if he left promptly after supper, although perhaps he was being ultra-sensitive. Jake worried him the most; normally he would pepper mealtimes with non-stop questions, his eyes on Roly, egging him on in his repertoire of stupid jokes. Tonight he appeared withdrawn, answering when spoken to and otherwise silent. Once Roly caught him staring at him, and the look in Jake's eyes was bewilderingly intense, as if he were trying to read Roly's mind. The one or two jokes he attempted raised polite and short-lived laughter and that was all, and he found himself drifting into the mundane small talk employed at dinner parties in desperation.

'Have you heard from the insurance company since the burglary?' he asked Kate.

She shook her head. 'They take their time. We're under-insured, of course, so I don't expect more than half the value of what was taken.'

'The police may trace some of the porcelain,' he said. 'It occasionally happens.'

'True,' she agreed; and then she made an odd comment. 'Something else went missing from the house,' she said, 'but that has been found. Things turn up in the strangest places.'

He looked at her, startled, but her eyes above her raised wineglass were noncommittal.

'How are *The Diehard Chronicles* coming along?' he asked Jake at the end of supper.

'I haven't written much,' Jake said evasively. 'I've been given a holiday project to do.'

'Why don't you show Roly while I clear away?' Kate suggested. 'It's an essay on the Arthurian legends, isn't it?'

'I haven't done much of that either.'

'Then maybe Roly can give you some ideas,' Kate said firmly. 'Off you go.'

Jake looked mutinous. 'I feel sick,' he muttered.

'Why don't you go to bed, and I'll put my

head round the door to say good night?' Roly said tactfully.

When he went upstairs five minutes later, Jake was lying on his back staring at the ceiling.

'How are you feeling?' Roly asked.

'The same.'

'I'm going now. Wish you better.'

'Yeah, OK. Thanks.' As Roly withdrew he called him back. 'Roly, is it ever right to grass on a friend?' Jake asked, his eyes large and dark in a pale face.

'Grass on him?'

'You know, tell on him when he's done something bad?'

Roly thought. 'If you think it's the right thing to do, then it probably is.'

'But how do you *know*?'

'Instinct,' Roly replied. 'A man's gotta do what a man's gotta do,' he added jokingly.

'That doesn't mean anything,' Jake said in a tired voice.

'Trouble at school?' queried Roly.

'Sort of.' Jake closed his eyes. ''Night, Roly.'

There was no doubt that Jake's troubles stemmed from those of Kate and Matt. In the seclusion of his sitting-room, Roly's conscience caught up with him in a moment of unremitting remorse; then ebbed again as he reminded himself of the whole purpose of his actions. But it had been a disturbing evening altogether, and a great deal of his earlier ebullience had left him. He swallowed the last of his nightcap, heaved himself out of the sofa and made his way to bed, where sleep evaded him. After an hour of restless turning from one side to the other, he gave in and took a sleeping-pill.

Kate was covering the remains of the potato salad with cling film when Jake appeared in the kitchen doorway. 'Still feeling sick?' she asked. 'I'll get you something from the medicine cupboard in a moment.'

He looked like she felt: drawn and washed-out.

'There's something I have to tell you,' he said.

'Can't it wait until morning?'

'It's important,' he told her. 'If I don't say it now I shan't get to sleep.'

She sighed. 'Come on, then,' she said, holding her arms out to him. 'Let's sit down.'

He talked and she listened; it did not take long.

'Roly's my friend,' he said miserably after he had finished. 'He'll never speak to me again.' His eyes filled with tears.

Kate hugged him to her. 'Of course he will,' she reassured him. 'There's no need for him to know.' Then she led him upstairs to bed. 'Thank you for telling me,' she said, kissing him. 'And don't worry. It was the right thing to do.'

Five minutes later when she looked in at him, he was asleep. She went to her bedroom and without bothering to check the time, lifted the telephone receiver and dialled Matt's number.

Chapter Eight

The sitting-room was spread with holiday brochures; they lay in untidy piles on every available piece of furniture. Matt and Kate sat on the sofa, their heads bent over the glossy photographs depicting impossibly blue skies and sun-drenched vistas, trying to find somewhere suitable within their price range. From time to time Jake would stop whacking a tennis ball in the garden and join them to lie full length on his stomach at their feet. Matt had been installed at home for five days now, and Jake had shadowed him, Kate noticed, hardly daring to let him out of his sight in case he disappeared.

There was no evidence to show that Matt intended to do so. His belongings were everywhere; half-unpacked suitcases in the bedroom, office equipment in the downstairs office. Her clothes were squeezed to one side of the cupboard to make room for his, and she kept tripping over his discarded shoes. She had almost, not quite, forgotten his untidiness and loved its inconvenience as a sign of permanence. In a few months' time it might well become an irritation: for the moment she was, in her own words, gloriously happy. She had not expected the barrier between them to be so easily demolished; it had seemed to her to be almost insurmountable. There had been rows before, but never one with such a core of bitterness.

When she phoned Matt it was with caution, prepared for possibly days of negotiation while they tried to forget the things they had said to each other in anger. Perhaps the shock of Jake's revelation about Roly and the letter had much to do with it. Matt had insisted on coming round that very night, brushing aside her protests and arriving in the record-breaking time of ten minutes. They had stood looking at each other in the kitchen without speaking.

'You shouldn't drive so fast,' she said foolishly when the silence became unbearable.

She had thought they would begin to discuss Roly, but he had stepped forward and wrapped her in a suffocating embrace. 'I'm sorry, I'm sorry, I'm sorry,' he repeated, burying his face in her hair. She had no idea how long they stood like that. She could not have escaped if she had wanted to and, in any case, to be nearly crushed to death seemed infinitely wonderful.

Eventually she murmured, 'The corner of the table's digging into my back.' And he withdrew reluctantly, and she collapsed onto a chair. He squatted at her feet and took her hands in his. 'Darling, darling Kate,' he had said.

They had made mugs of coffee and taken them to the sitting-room, and talked in muted voices so as not to waken Jake. There they agreed to put the recent trauma behind them instead of raking over the accusations and the insults.

'I hate post-mortems,' she said, lying stretched out on the sofa with her head in his lap. 'That day was dreadful enough without reliving it.'

'It won't happen again; we won't let it.' He bent over to kiss her. 'I'm coming home for good,' he said, 'if I may.'

'I'll be furious if you don't.'

After a while he asked, 'Why did knowing about Roly make you change your mind? I'm curious.'

'Promise you won't be cross?'

'Promise.'

'I thought it was very likely that *you* had found the letter in my desk, that no-one had posted it to you,' she admitted.

'Yes, I see,' he said slowly.

'Who would have thought it of Roly?'

'Who indeed? What are we going to do about him?'

'Nothing at all tonight; I'm too tired even to discuss him.' She struggled upright. 'You are going back to your flat, and everything is going to be shelved until tomorrow.'

'Can't I stay?'

'No,' she said firmly. 'I'm superstitious; look what happened last time. When you next move in, it's for keeps, bag and baggage, and I'll come and help you pack up just to make sure.'

She kept her word, and two days later the move was achieved, using both cars loaded to the roofs. They were busy arranging his things in the house in Denbigh Street, and it was forty-eight hours before they found the chance to sit down and address the subject of Roly. The weather had broken and Helga and Jake had gone to the cinema. Matt and Kate spent the afternoon trying to find space for his books, and subsided eventually onto the sofa in relief. Roly's enormities remained almost impossible to believe.

'I suppose Jake couldn't have made it up?' Matt suggested.

'Of course not,' Kate replied indignantly, defending her ewe lamb. 'He loves Roly; next to you, he considers him the best thing since sliced bread. Besides, what earthly reason would he have had?'

The answer was obviously none. It was not difficult to understand how Roly had accomplished his objective. Once they started to retrace events relating to the letter, a number of incidents sprang to mind that had seemed quite unremarkable at the time; conversations with both of them that led directly to the fateful lunch with Niall, the manipulation of Matt to ensure he witnessed it, and the arrival of Niall's letter, timed to cause the maximum psychological damage. As they compared notes, the pieces of the puzzle slotted together to form a clear picture of what was apparently a carefully structured plot. There was no disputing Roly's involvement.

'He must be sick,' Matt said. 'There's no other explanation.'

Kate sighed. 'It's my fault to a great extent; I've been careless about his feelings right from the start. He showed signs of becoming obsessed a long time ago, but I didn't take it seriously.'

She told Matt about the constant watch kept on her, the parked car waiting in the shadows.

'Kate, you should have let me know,' he said reproachfully.

'There was nothing you could have done about it.'

'I could have talked to him, shamed him out of it before it escalated into something worse.'

'Shame is the last emotion he needs,' she said sadly. 'Poor Roly; I suspect he's been going through hell.'

Matt was less magnanimous. 'And put us through it in the process,' he said. 'If we all behaved the way he has in the face of unrequited love, life would be chaotic.'

'It's no use viewing his behaviour logically,' she pointed out, 'when there's no logic attached to it.'

'No, I suppose you're right. I can't get over it,' he said. 'Roly is the least likely person I would have expected to go off the rails. He's always seemed the epitome of sanity: stalwart, kind and rather phlegmatic.'

'Kind and stalwart, yes,' she answered. 'Phlegmatic, no: that's the mistake I made.' She added,

'We have to decide what to do about him.'

'Well, one thing's for sure, we can't just leave this unmentioned,' he said. 'I'll have to go and have it out with him.'

'No, please, Matt.'

'Darling, he must be issued with a warning.' He put a hand over one of hers. 'He may try to prise us apart again. Heaven knows what he might not think up.'

'He'll only deny it. We have no proof of what he's done.'

'Jake is a witness.'

'I won't have Jake dragged into it,' she said determinedly.

'Then what do you suggest?'

'I'll go to see Roly,' she said. 'I shan't accuse him to his face, but he'll be in no doubt that I know after I've talked to him.' She looked down at their hands clasped together. 'I'm still fond of him; I don't want to humiliate him and I'd like it if he remained a friend.'

'Is that possible, or, more to the point, wise?' Matt asked.

'He won't harm us again,' she said. 'I'm certain of that. As for the possibility, I can but try.'

Roly completed his shaving, splashed the residue of soap from his face and patted it dry with a towel. Then he moved from bathroom to bedroom and dressed himself for work in striped shirt, tie and light-weight suit, the last creased from several wearings, and brushed his fine brown hair into a semblance of order. He did not like looking at his reflection in the mirror, could not meet his own eyes. They accused him of failure and a whole lot of things he wished to forget. It occurred to him without emotion that he would not have to face himself for very much longer.

Since Kate had come to talk to him, he had performed this early-morning ritual mechanically, his mind frozen into blank despair, and continued through the day in the same series of automatic moves. Only in his office was he forced to think positively, and even there the work was so familiar to him it made few demands on his intellect. Some days before she had telephoned and asked herself for a drink, and his heart had raced at the unprecedented suggestion. He had not known whether it boded good or ill as far as he was concerned, but went on hoping, right up until the moment she told him that she and Matt were reconciled. She sat in one of his armchairs nursing her drink, her pale linen skirt riding up her legs, and he was reminded vividly of the evening that her brother Charlie had brought her to the house. A terrible pang of longing shot through him just as it had done on that first occasion; except that then there had been real hope, and now only a sense of utter loss which threatened to overwhelm him. He turned away and busied himself by the drinks tray. From somewhere, and with a superhuman effort of will, he found the strength to articulate the appropriate congratulatory words. Even to his ears they rang false.

He asked her whether she had discovered who had taken the letter. 'We have a fairly good idea,' she told him, 'but we've decided not to pursue the matter. Someone was playing silly buggers, but we're together, which is what counts.' Her eyes as she glanced at him were without guile or accusation; but in that moment of eye contact, he knew that she knew. The realization capped his misery; forever more she would think badly of him. He did not even have left the consolation of a loyal reputation. She had not stayed long, giving as her excuse that, now there was a man to cater for, more demands were being made on her time. Before she left she emphasized her determination that the marriage second time round should be permanent; her voice gentle but firm. 'You are our dearest friend,' she had said, laying a hand briefly on his arm, 'and I hope you always will be. Come and see us often, Roly.' Her kindness and understanding had been unbearable; he would have preferred to have had furious recriminations flung at him, been the recipient of her temper. As it was, the plans which he had laid so carefully, the dreams he had dreamt, had been dismissed as not worth a second thought; the schemes of a deluded fool. He watched her drive away from his front door, and it seemed to him that she took with her his sole reason for living.

It was not until a few days later that it occurred to him to do something about it. The grief of bereavement – for that was how he viewed his loss – had given way to depression, deep and immovable. Unable to sleep, he went to his doctor and asked for a renewal on his prescription for pills, pleading pressure of work as the cause. The doctor complied reluctantly, and Roly had placed the month's supply by his bedside, wondering as he did so how many of them it would take to kill oneself. He had never contemplated suicide before; even after it first became apparent that Kate did not love him. He realized now that he had not quite believed her; only recently had hope completely deserted him. When he looked into the future, all he could see was a dark nothingness. Death, surely, would not be very different, but without the desolation. He had no religious qualms to prevent him; he had not been a churchgoer since his grandmother had marched him to matins each Sunday. Unscrewing the bottle, he poured a small amount of pretty turquoise-and-black capsules onto the bedcover, and gazed down at them, trying to judge the number needed and imagining the release they would bring.

There was nothing to stop him carrying out his objective that very evening; lying down with a bottle of Scotch at his side to help the process and waiting for oblivion. But his orderly mind intervened; his suicide had to be planned if it were to succeed. There was an obligatory last visit to his mother to be got through, and the timing of his death carefully chosen. The daily came on Tuesdays and Fridays. It was important to leave the maximum number of days between taking the pills and the likelihood of his being found. The ignominy of waking up resuscitated in a hospital bed did not bear thinking about. And now the day had arrived: Friday; with the whole of the weekend ahead of him to lie inert and undisturbed. This, the final scheme of his life, must not fail; there had been too many failures, and he liked to think of Kate weeping at his funeral.

On the fourth day of their holiday, Kate and Matt were sitting in the taverna overlooking the sea, watching Jake have his first lesson in water-skiing. Behind them olive groves swept down to the coast from the foothills of the mountain. They had found the two-bedroomed flat in an advertisement and taken it on the spur of the moment. Surprisingly, it lived up to its description of comfort and close proximity to the clear waters of the Aegean, and they had already settled into the mindless contentment induced by sun and no commitment for two whole weeks.

Out to sea, Jake was travelling unsteadily behind the motor boat with his bum sticking out.

'He's getting the hang of it,' Matt observed. 'Are you going to have a go?'

'I've never tried and I'm not starting now,' Kate replied lazily. 'You'd laugh at me.'

'I would not. You won't say no to a glass of wine?'

'Mineral water, please.'

'Really?' he said. 'You are feeling all right, aren't you?'

'I'm fine.'

When he returned with their drinks, she said, 'I've got something to tell you.'

'Good or bad?' he asked, sipping his wine.

'Good; at least I think so. I'm not sure what your reaction will be. I'm pregnant.'

'Heavens above.' He stared at her, glass poised in mid-air. 'But we've only been together for – what is it? – under a month.'

'Our one-night stand; don't you remember?'

'Oh,' he said. 'I thought you were on the pill.'

'I forgot about it,' she said happily, 'on that particular occasion.'

'Are you certain about this?'

'I haven't had it confirmed, but I know. You don't sound very pleased,' she said in a disappointed voice.

'It's come as something of a shock,' he admitted; then, seeing her expression, he got up from his chair and wrapped his arms round her. 'Now it's begun to sink in,' he said, 'I'm delighted.'

'Truly?'

'Truly.' He kissed her. 'A baby. I can't believe it.'

'It'll alter our lives,' she warned.

'I know that; we've already had one.'

'It'll mean moving. The house isn't big enough with two children.'

'I suppose not. I wonder what Jake will think about it.'

'It'll be a novelty,' she said with confidence, 'like getting a puppy.'

They sat for a moment in silence. Jake was coming into shore, wobbling but upright. No newcomer, they thought in unison, could ever take his place.

'I don't think Roly should be given the news,' she said. 'Not until it becomes obvious.'

'That won't be for months. It's unlikely he'll get to know before that, anyway. He hasn't been near us since you spoke to him.'

'I can't help worrying about him,' she said. 'I believe he's desperately unhappy.'

'Listen, darling,' Matt told her firmly, 'we can't go pussyfooting around trying to spare his feelings for ever.' He took one of her hands and squeezed it. 'You've got plenty of things to worry about other than Roly's welfare.'

When Roly arrived home, he treated the evening like any other; taking a shower, putting on a dressing-gown over his pants, listening to the messages on his answerphone, pouring himself a modest drink. If he were to be honest, he was in danger of losing his nerve. Within an hour or so of taking his own life, he felt the prospect grow more intimidating by the minute. It was not death itself that he feared so much as possibly bungling the job, making himself painfully and irreversibly ill, giving himself brain damage. He was not sure of the consequences of overdosing, had not paid attention to what he had read or heard on the subject, therefore any number of horrors came to mind. It was understandable that the majority of suicides were unpremeditated, carried out the moment life became intolerable. He forced himself to count out thirty sleeping-pills and put them in an envelope before descending to the sitting-room. Taking the bottle of whisky from the drinks tray, he placed it on the sofa table with the envelope beside it and fetched a jug of water. He did not like neat whisky, and as a condemned man he was allowed to pander to his tastes. Sitting himself on the sofa with the accoutrements of death in front of him, it struck him how innocuous they looked, as if he were merely preparing for a cosy evening watching television. There was still time to change his mind. To counteract the insidious idea, he found it necessary to keep Kate constantly in the forefront of his mind, to remind him of the source of his despair. To his surprise, thoughts of her were now interspersed with spurts of quite considerable anger that she should have driven him this far.

He shook two pills from the envelope and swallowed them with a draught of whisky, and contemplated the twenty-eight he had left. In order to do the job efficiently, they must be taken swiftly before drowsiness overcame him. His fingers fumbled in the envelope for the next batch, clumsy from apprehension and a sudden fear of the unknown. And then, a shattering noise in the stillness, the doorbell rang. With glass and pills poised in mid-air, Roly froze. He had not foreseen interruptions; friends did not call unannounced, they telephoned. It was most likely to be charity collectors or a door-to-door salesman. He lowered the glass and the pills carefully to the table and waited hopefully for the person to go away. The bell gave another peal, with a finger pressed against it for a length of time. He heard the flap of the letter-box as if someone was peering in. Bloody cheek, he muttered to himself. A voice called him by name, a male voice which he knew but could not place.

'Roly! Are you there? It's Charlie.'

Charlie Brownlow, on this night of all nights; Roly stayed where he was, on the off-chance that he would give up and leave him alone.

'Roly, I know you're there. Stop buggering about and let me in. This is a crisis.'

With a curious mixture of resignation and relief, Roly realized that this, after all, was not destined to be his last night on earth. He picked up the envelope, stuffed it into his dressing-gown pocket and went to open the front door.

'Thank God.' Charlie brushed past him and into the sitting-room and flung himself into an armchair. For one whose appearance was normally impeccable, he looked decidedly dishevelled; the knot in his tie was loosened, his jacket collar turned half inside out and his sleek blond hair ruffled. 'I thought you'd never answer. Guessed you were in: your car's in the garage,' he said.

'I'd decided to ignore the bell,' Roly replied. 'I'm feeling anti-social, as a matter of fact. Would you like a drink now you're here?'

'Yes, please. Whisky on the rocks. Apologies for landing myself on you, Roly, but I'm in deep trouble.'

'What sort of trouble?' Roly asked, settling for the inevitable.

'Stella's thrown me out.'

The statement was dramatic enough to hold even Roly's attention. He poured whisky onto the ice-cubes, handed Charlie the glass and sat down on the sofa.

'Good Lord! Why?'

'I've been having an affair for some time. Stella found a letter which I left lying around like a complete nerd, and that was that – out on my ear. I was allowed to pack a bag and told to get lost.' Charlie swallowed half his drink in one gulp. 'She wouldn't listen to reason.'

'I suppose that was to be expected,' Roly remarked, 'under the circumstances. She'll probably calm down after a day or two.'

'She's suing for divorce,' Charlie said gloomily. 'May I have a refill on this?'

'Help yourself.' Roly envisaged having to listen to the entire story and wondered how to shorten the ordeal.

'Where's the whisky?' Charlie asked from across the room. 'Oh, I see, in front of you.' He filled his glass and returned to his chair. 'Looks as if you were settling in for the evening before I cocked it up,' he observed.

'I was planning on an early night,' Roly said pointedly. 'I still am.'

'I was going to beg a bed off you, if that's all right. You don't have to worry about me, retire when you want to. I'll be fine.' Charlie gave a sigh and buried a disconsolate face in his tumbler.

'Of course, stay by all means,' Roly was shamed into saying.

'Thanks,' Charlie said. 'Can you bear with me for a short while? I badly need a sympathetic ear.'

Roly waved a hand wearily in assent, and Charlie unfolded his story from beginning to end. He was far too engrossed in his dilemma to make it brief, although it did not appear to differ in description from a hundred other accounts of marital infidelity. He had become involved with his secretary, a replacement for the one who had left the firm to get married. Discreet lunches and dinners had escalated into entire nights in secluded hotels, and even the occasional weekend. The affair had continued for nine months without Stella having a ghost of a suspicion. It had, in fact, so Charlie claimed, added extra zest to their sex life which had grown somewhat stale. And then had come the letter from his mistress, altering the date of one of their arranged meetings and going on to include intimate details of their relationship. Stella had discovered it in the inside pocket of his jacket when about to take his suit to the cleaners and, in Charlie's words, all hell had broken loose. He had tried to tell her the affair was over, that it meant nothing to him and Stella meant everything, but she was too incensed to listen.

Charlie had filled his glass twice during the course of his account and was now far from sober.

'But the affair isn't over, is it?' Roly asked.

'I fully mean it to be from now on,' Charlie said, squinting owlishly at him.

'You don't want to marry whoever-it-is?'

'Good God, no. I can't imagine being married to anyone but Stella. The thought of losing her, and the children . . .' Charlie's eyes grew misty at the idea. 'The trouble is,' he said, 'Miranda's fallen in love with me, or so she says. I never intended it to be more than a light-hearted fling. After all, how many men remain faithful to their wives for the whole of their married life? I think,' he reached unerringly for his drink, 'she *does* expect me to get a divorce and marry her. I wish she'd never written that bloody letter. What makes women put their feelings on paper? Letters are an abomination, don't you agree?'

'Yes, indeed I do,' Roly replied with heart-felt sincerity.

He had not drunk as much as Charlie, but his eyes had grown heavy and he felt overpoweringly sleepy. The two pills he had swallowed were beginning to take effect.

'The thing is, what the hell am I going to do next?' Charlie was saying. 'Here I am, homeless, with two women threatening to destroy me.'

'I don't see what you can do except try to placate Stella,' Roly said. Charlie's casual attitude towards his lover mystified him. He could not help feeling that Charlie deserved to suffer to some extent; he would be the one to avoid heartache out of the three of them. 'I don't know why you took the risks,' he added, 'if you don't love, er, Miranda.'

'Have you never been tempted by a nubile fig-ure and a pair of legs?' Charlie eyed him blurrily. 'She was, and is, irresistibly beddable. But then, I wouldn't expect you to understand, Roly old mate. My guess is, women haven't played much of a part in your life; you can take them or leave them. Am I right?'

Roly was gripped by a sudden spasm of fury at Charlie's words. Patronizing, denigrating, they questioned his maleness. What did Charlie know about the real thing, the consummate passion that governed one's whole being? In that instant he felt something akin to hatred. He wanted to blister Charlie with words of his own, but sedation had slowed up his thought processes.

'My feelings aren't confined to my trousers, as yours appear to be,' was all he could manage to utter. 'I haven't eaten,' he muttered, heaving himself off the sofa. 'I'm going to cut sandwiches.'

From the open door of the kitchen he heard Charlie blundering about knocking into furniture, and when he returned with two ham doorsteps, Charlie was peering into the recesses of the sideboard. 'We've run out of whisky,' he told Roly glumly.

'You've had enough.' Roly held out the plate. 'Blotting-paper,' he said, 'then bed.'

'You're probably right. Got the feeling I've upset you,' Charlie said indistinctly through a mouthful. His inebriation was getting to the maudlin stage. 'Wouldn't want to do that. You're one of the best; I love you, you know that? So does Kate.'

Roly stayed silent.

'Sorry for interrupting your early night.'

'My suicide,' Roly said.

'What?'

'I said, you interrupted my suicide.'

'Thought that's what you said. You have some weird jokes.' Charlie rose unsteadily to his feet. 'Must have a pee,' he said, finding his way across the room with exaggerated caution.

Roly finished his sandwich and lay back with his eyes closed. Dimly he was aware of Charlie returning and opened his mouth to speak. 'Your sister is my undoing,' he wanted to say, but the words came out in a mumble. The next moment he was asleep.

In the week following their return from Greece, Kate's anxiety over Roly still weighed on her mind. There had been no communication from him for nearly a month.

'I really think we must ask him round,' she told Matt. 'He's probably too ashamed to get in touch with us.'

'I'm not surprised,' Matt said, who was finding it harder than Kate to forgive. 'Personally I rather dread sitting over supper with him, trying to pretend that nothing outrageous ever happened.'

'You could at least make the effort,' she said.

In the end, it was Jake who suggested an answer to the problem. For his eleventh birthday, he had been allowed to choose his form of celebration and had settled for the theatre, an evening performance of a musical and supper in a restaurant afterwards.

'I expect you'd like to bring Toby, wouldn't you?' Kate enquired at breakfast as they were planning the day.

'Can I ask Roly?' he said. 'I haven't seen him for ages.'

'That', Kate answered, 'is a very good idea. You can ring him up; he'd like that.' With luck, she decided, there would be enough jollity attached to the evening's entertainment to ease any awkward atmosphere.

And so Jake telephoned and left a message on Roly's answerphone, feeling slightly relieved that Roly was not there to take the call. Although Kate had reassured him time and again that he had done the right thing in telling her about Roly's theft, it still worried him that he had grassed on a friend. He hated the thought that Roly might suspect it was him and never want to speak to him again. Kate had not told him what had been said when she went to talk to Roly, but whatever it was, he had not appeared since. Jake wished, not for the first time, that children were not kept in the dark about important issues. He waited in a certain amount of nervousness for Roly's answer to the invitation.

Roly made no more attempts on his own life. After his one and only plan to do so had been aborted by Charlie's appearance, he had woken the next morning with aching limbs and thumping head on the sofa. Opposite him, Charlie was slumped in an armchair, snoring. By the time he had dosed himself with aspirin, showered and generally pulled himself together, half the day had gone by, and the rest of it was spent in organizing Charlie. Roly made it clear to him, when he was in a state to listen, that Charlie could stay one more night while he found alternative accommodation, but that was the limit to Roly's hospitality. He did not care if he were thought to be mean; there was enough confusion in his life without having to sort out Charlie's problems. On the Sunday, Charlie departed for a hotel, and Roly, with the house to himself once again, found the compulsion to commit suicide had left him.

He did not at once comprehend the reason for this change of heart, and imagined it was man's innate instinct for self-preservation which had intervened. It was not until several days had gone by that he realized his feelings for Kate had suffered a metamorphosis. He came to recognize the fact by chance; while sitting at his desk in the office, he had been extracting a credit card from his wallet and accidentally pulled out a snapshot of her at the same time. It had been taken in the garden of her parents' house in early spring, and all the things he loved most about her seemed to be embodied in her sunlit, laughing face. He stared down at it as it lay before him on the desk, and saw only mockery in the wide grin and dancing eyes where previously he had read fondness. She was laughing at him, not with him; everything he had had to suffer in the past year, pain of rejection, false hopes, shame, were due to her. She had left him without even the will to live; but he no longer wanted to kill himself, sheer fury had seen to that. He picked up her photograph and tore it into pieces, dropping them in the waste-paper basket. When his secretary entered the room minutes later, she found him at his desk with his head buried in his hands. Just a bad headache, he told her in answer to her solicitous enquiries. After she had gone, he rescued the four bits of snapshot and slipped them back in his wallet; even now, when he thought his love for Kate had turned sour, he found he could not bear to let her go.

He did not know what to do about Jake's message on the answerphone. The attack of anger that had seized him in his office had not lasted, but the sudden violence of it made him uneasy. A kind of bitter resentment against Kate had taken its place, gnawing at him like an ulcer. He longed to be able to put her out of his mind as one longs for an end to pain, but she remained there persistently as ever. He was not sure he could stand another evening seeing her within the smug, secure confines of her family after all that had happened; and yet, it was difficult to refuse Jake. He had sounded so endearingly anxious that Roly should come to his birthday celebration; his message had run off the tape in his enthusiastic explanation of what they had planned. In the face of such uncomplicated warmth, Roly telephoned him and accepted the invitation.

Jake had chosen to go to *Cats*, which everyone else had seen but was prepared to see again, and Roly bought him the CD of the music for his present. He met them at the theatre on a sultry August evening typical of the month. Thunderstorms were forecast and he could feel himself sweating into his shirt; although this might have been due to nerves as much as to the weather. It would be their first meeting since he had tried to mess up their lives, and he did not know what reception to expect. He need not have worried; they were already waiting for him in the crowded foyer, Matt, Kate, Jake and his friend Toby, and they greeted him affectionately as though they had seen him only the previous day, without a trace of awkwardness. To his surprise, it was Jake who appeared temporarily at a loss for words, staring at him solemnly; but Roly shook his hand and said 'Hi, man!' which had become their own particular form of greeting, and the moment passed. Over drinks in the stalls bar before the performance, the conversation was mostly of their holiday and kind enquiries as to when he was planning his own. Next time, they told him, he should go with them; Greece was to be recommended. Kate was wearing a white sleeveless dress that showed off her tanned arms and face. Her eyes, when they rested on him, were calm and friendly as if she were anxious to welcome him back into the fold; but he avoided their pale attraction and concentrated on Jake.

'I've got your present,' Roly told him, slapping his jacket pocket. 'The one you asked for.'

'Great! Thanks, Roly. Can I open it now?'

'Wait until dinner. The third bell's gone,' Matt said; and they moved away to find their seats.

The first part of Roly's ordeal was over. He found himself regarding the evening as a series of hurdles waiting to be negotiated, instead of a straightforward gathering of friends. Jake was seated beside him with

Toby on his other side, and Kate was far removed from them at the end of the row. Roly, relieved by the distance between them, prepared to give himself up to being entertained, to relax at least until the interval. He did not succeed. He could not rid himself of a mounting apprehension, a feeling that something disastrous and beyond his control was about to occur. It was illogical, but none the less intense, and he felt his hands grow damp with anxiety as he watched the whirling, leaping dancers with their painted cats' faces that reminded him of Kate. Unable to forget her, the spectacle before him took on the macabre aspect of a carnival, where, behind their masks, the revellers were not as they seemed. He saw her face amongst them, mocking as her photograph had mocked him before he destroyed it, and felt himself in the grip of the same cold rage.

The interval brought relief. In the packed bar, he managed, with the help of a double whisky, to join in the animated discussion of the performance and the enthusiasm of the two boys. The respite came to an end; they drifted back to their seats, where they changed places for the second half of the show, and Roly was placed next to Kate. His body grew taut with nervous tension as her thigh inadvertently brushed his. He recalled with sudden vividness the very first evening they had met, and the excitement he had felt then at her close proximity and the smell of her scent; shockingly different to the effect it was having on him now. Appalled by the violence it aroused in him, he sat rigid in his seat, hands clasped with the nails digging into his palms.

She touched his arm, leant towards him. 'Are you feeling all right?' she whispered. 'You're very pale.'

He forced himself to glance at her. 'A little queasy. Don't worry, I'll be fine.'

It seemed as if the musical would never draw to

a close. A trembling had seized him, uncontrollable as his feelings. There was nothing he could do but sit pinned to his seat like a prisoner until the finale released him. If Kate noticed, she gave no sign; during the last song she leaned forwards with a pair of theatre binoculars to get a better view. Out of the corner of his eyes Roly watched her against his will, saw her smooth brown arms raised and the silhouette of her hair piled up on the crown of her head. Her neck, stretched upwards, was like the stem of a flower, and so slender he could have circled it with one hand. And all at once he had an unbearable urge to do so, to feel the softness of her skin beneath his hold and to squeeze and squeeze until her eyes bulged and her body went limp. The sweat was coursing in rivulets down his forehead as the performance came to an end; he sat gripping the red plush arms of his seat, incapable of joining in the thunderous applause and the cries of 'Encore', terrified of this nightmare fantasy becoming fact. The cast were giving a repeat rendering of one of the show's most popular songs; all at once he knew he had to escape before claustrophobia caused him to black out. Rising shakily to his feet, he mumbled an excuse into Kate's ear and stumbled his way clumsily down the row to the aisle and freedom.

They caught up with him in the foyer, standing by the open doors through which the audience was pouring into the night. He made a more or less coherent apology for upsetting the evening – something he had eaten – and declined Matt's offer to see him home. He would be perfectly all right on his own, he said; all he needed was a good night's rest. Their concerned faces peered through the window of his taxi, Jake's eyes wide with bewilderment, before he was borne away. In the back seat, he huddled, shivering from the aftermath of his experience, and tried to make his mind a blank; at some point he would try to find a logical explanation, but not tonight, he was too confused. In his heart he knew there was no logic to be found in emotional impulses; that what he had felt for Kate was pure hatred, an emotion that up until the present he had never known, and that he could have sworn was alien to his nature. Nothing made sense any longer; his life seemed to be disintegrating round him and above all, he was scared beyond measure.

Towards the end of September, Kate had a postcard from Roly of a Florentine church. She carried it to the kitchen with the rest of the mail and read it out loud to Matt over breakfast. It ran along the lines of most holiday cards, eulogizing the unchanging fascination of the city, describing the weather and the hotel where he was staying and sending his love to the family. Only the last two lines were interesting: 'Met a soul mate on flight out, a widow. Have joined up for various expeditions.'

'Thank God, it sounds as if he's made a complete recovery,' Kate said.

'It seems rather quick considering his state of mind,' Matt replied sceptically.

'He's been in the hands of one of the best doctors in London.' Kate refused to be deflated. 'Oh, I'm so relived. I've felt so guilty about him.'

'Come off it. You can hardly be blamed for his mental breakdown. Obsessional behaviour is a medical condition; there's a term for it: some syndrome or other.'

'Poor Roly, he must have been through hell.' She glanced down at the card. 'What do you think about the widow?' she asked.

'As long as she's plain and doesn't resemble you in any way,' he answered, 'she'll probably be good for him.'

'I wonder if he's home by now,' she said. 'If so, we should get in touch, ask him to supper.'

'Kate, I'm not sure that's wise just yet.'

'Just ourselves, nothing that would put a strain on him.'

'Darling, how do you know what is or is not a strain on him?' Matt pointed out. 'I think we should leave it a while longer.'

She sighed. 'We've got everything, he's got nothing,' she said. 'I do so want him to be happy.'

It was true that their life together seemed as near perfect as it was ever likely to be. Jake had returned to school with a new contentment and his future education settled; he was to go on to St Paul's, Matt had finally agreed to accept the grandparents' offer of financial help. 'We really do *need* help with two children to consider,' Kate had insisted. Jake was to sit for a scholarship, but it would not be disastrous if he failed it. And there was a baby on the way, a fact which Matt was beginning to view with pride. He would pat Kate's stomach every so often in the hopes of feeling tangible evidence of the new life inside her. The only interruption in the even tenor of their lives was the marital upheaval of Charlie and Stella into which they had been drawn as unwilling counsellors; alternately dealing with Stella's tearful bitterness and Charlie's self-pitying gloom. Matt and Kate found even this unwelcome diversion a minor irritation: it was someone else's problem, a very different matter from one's own.

After the night of Roly's panic attack at the theatre, they had agreed between them that he was in serious need of professional treatment, and Matt was the one who persuaded him to seek it. Kate had felt she was the last person to advise Roly; she was, after all, largely responsible for his collapse. Neither of them knew what happened to him in the weeks that followed his first appointment with the psychoanalyst. He had not telephoned or written, and the card from abroad was the first communication they had received since then. Once or twice Kate had rung him, but only got the answerphone. She did not tell Matt about these calls; since they had been together, he had become protective of her, perhaps because of her pregnancy, and did not want her worried on Roly's account. He did not realize she worried anyway, would never forget the times when Roly had been her mainstay. She owed him a great deal, and the normal, dull card from him had done much to put her mind at rest.

'I do hope something comes of the widow,' she said, sipping her coffee. 'I'm pinning my hopes on her.'

After six weeks of therapy, Roly was told to take a holiday. The idea frightened him when it was first put to him; he did not think he was far enough advanced in recovery for such a step. At the beginning he had been frightened of everything, from venturing outside his own front door to answering the telephone or meeting people. Before his first appointment with the analyst he had had to have a double whisky in order to keep it. He had not intended to say much, but the analyst, a man in his fifties, had been curiously silent apart from the occasional question, and Roly had found it almost imperative to talk out of politeness. Since then, he had not stopped; every aspect of his strange malaise had come pouring out, even his murderous feelings for Kate, although he never mentioned her by name. Gradually, as the weeks went by he began to feel a lifting of the spirit as if a weight had been shifted from his shoulders. He was able to walk down a crowded street without the nightmare of seeing Kate's face on every woman he passed, start to meet up with friends again and go back to work three days a week. He was getting better, much better; eventually he came to accept the thought of a holiday.

Alicia Tate had sat next to him on the flight to Pisa. He had not been immediately attracted to her; she was full-busted, middle-aged and fresh-skinned without make-up, and she talked, which was not what he wanted, or so he thought. But something about her, a combination of her comfortable size and her Yorkshire accent perhaps, he found relaxing, and by the end of the journey they had arranged to meet for dinner. From then on they saw each other every day, sightseeing, eating and drinking and driving into the countryside around Florence. Her husband had died two years previously, she lived on the outskirts of Rochdale and owned, rather surprisingly, a boutique. She was, equally surprisingly, knowledgeable about works of art and architecture; there was a great deal to Alicia that was not immediately obvious. Roly, when he tried telling her about himself, realized how little his life amounted to, apart from the last unhappy year which he left unmentioned. He told her he was recovering from an illness and was grateful to her for not enquiring about its nature, and found himself at some point describing his childhood. She was a good listener.

There was no sex attached to their ten days of friendship; the question never arose, although Roly had wondered once or twice what it would be like. Alicia was returning home two days earlier than he, and he drove her to the airport. Watching her neat ankles disappearing through the barrier, it struck him forcibly how much he would miss her; the two remaining days of his holiday would be less enjoyable for her absence. It also occurred to him how seldom he had thought of Kate since he had been away, and that when he had recalled her, it was without the terrible, feverish malice. Alicia and

247

he had exchanged addresses and telephone numbers, promised to keep in touch and left it at that. He liked her for not insisting on a firm commitment as some women might have done; but after he was home he continued to miss her and began to regret not having made a definite arrangement for the near future. He telephoned her one evening, and her voice was warm and welcoming. 'I hoped you'd ring,' she told him. 'I thought of phoning you, but decided that you might have had enough of me after ten days.' And she gave the robust laugh which might have been irritating, but he found spontaneous, a part of her charm. After a prolonged chat they arranged that he should stay with her for a long weekend at the end of the month and before the weather deteriorated. 'It can get chilly in Yorkshire; bring plenty of sweaters,' she said. 'I light the fire in autumn; we'll be warm enough, don't worry.'

He wondered, when he had rung off, whether her words held a hidden invitation and if so, what he really wanted to do about it. He was not in love with her; at least, not in the half-crazed way he had loved Kate. But Alicia had qualities that put him at ease, motherliness and warmth, and he craved peace at all costs. Above all, she took him seriously and appeared to reciprocate his feelings, which was the deciding factor. There would be many worse things than burying his head in her cushiony bosom and drifting to sleep. If she wanted to take their friendship a stage further, he was willing; although the decision brought its own nagging worry. He could not remember when he had last been to bed with a woman; his whole being had been concentrated on Kate. Supposing he was impotent, the trauma of rejection having emasculated him? Imagining making a fool of himself with Alicia, he took his fears to his analyst who, rather than laying them to rest, issued a warning.

'I hadn't envisaged you starting a relationship immediately,' he said. 'It's early days yet; I don't want you to set yourself back if things go wrong for you. I'd advise waiting; but if you must embark on it, take it gradually.'

Roly had come to trust the analyst implicitly. Now, for the first time, he decided to ignore his advice and go his own way. He realized that he had begun to think of Alicia as an important part of his recovery; she would do him good, not harm, and if he failed, he knew instinctively she would understand. Despite that fact, he preferred to be certain for his own peace of mind, and he had friends who would help him. On a Monday evening, when the Teddy Bear Club was particularly quiet, he walked to the main road and took a taxi to Shepherds Market.

The girl who had taken him back to her flat was small and dark, and named, quite unsuitably, Virginia; Ginny for short. He knew her; he knew them all. It made no difference; it hadn't prevented him from losing his nerve. He realized the moment she dimmed the lights that he was incapable of making love to her – if it could be called that. She had been nice about it, said it didn't matter, which he supposed to her it didn't; probably a bit of a relief. She had given him a drink and they had talked for a while, she on the king-size double bed and he in an armchair. He told her about Alicia but not about Kate; he had talked enough about Kate in therapy sessions, and the compulsion had left him.

'Shouldn't worry about your problem,' Ginny said. 'Most likely, you haven't got one; it's all in the mind.' She stifled a yawn and swung her legs off the bed. 'And now, if you'll excuse me, Roly, I've got to be moving. I've enjoyed our chat.'

All in the mind; he wished she had not chosen the

phrase. It recalled everything that had happened to him in the past year. 'May I help myself to a drink while you're getting ready?' he asked.

'Go ahead.'

He watched her as she sat at the dressing-table in a black slip and did things to her face and hair.

'Don't you want the lights turned up? You can't see properly,' he said.

'No, thanks. The less I see of myself the better,' she answered.

There was a childlike quality about her; her limbs slim and fragile as a prepubescent girl's. It had not occurred to him before that she bore a resemblance to Kate; it was only in the muted lighting that she had a look of her, with her arms raised. She was brushing her hair, sweeping it up to fasten it on top of her head. With a sickening lurch of his stomach, Roly was carried back in time to the semi-darkness of a theatre, and Kate beside him with her own hair up, exposing her neck like the stem of a flower.

'Hey, Roly.' Ginny was speaking into the mirror. 'Be a love and fasten this hairclip for me, would you?'

He moved towards her as if in a dream and stood behind her, his hands hovering over her head in perplexity.

'It should snap shut,' she told him.

He fiddled with the clip, his fingers trembling, trying to concentrate, feeling her hair slippery to the touch, until the fastening clicked into place. 'It's fixed,' he said, glancing at her reflection.

'Thanks,' she said, smiling at him.

Kate's smile, Kate's face looked back at him from the subtle lighting of the mirror, her expression teasing, provocative. I shall always be with you, it was saying, I shall never leave. It filled him with an uncontrollable panic; lifting his hands, he placed them to lightly circle Ginny's neck, felt the cold metal of her thin gold chain and the warmth of her skin in comparison. She laughed.

'Changed your mind?' she asked softly, and catching hold of one of his wrists, pulled it downwards into the cleavage of her slip.

'No.' He drew back sharply.

'Something I said?'

'No, nothing like that.' He turned to retrieve his jacket from the chair. 'Sorry, Ginny, I have to go. Thanks for everything.' He drew some banknotes from his wallet and put them on a table.

'There's no need for that. I haven't exactly earned it.'

'You've been understanding,' he said.

She laughed again. 'You're a funny one, Roly.'

He left her block of flats like a man escaping from a nightmare, which in a way was the truth. Ginny did not realize how close to assault she had been; within a hair's breadth of his tightening his hold on her. All the pre-therapy horrors had returned to him in that moment, despite his certainty that he was free of them at last. He should have listened to the professional, not taken things – literally – into his own hands. He walked a long way without bothering to hail a taxi, until the tremor in his limbs had left him and he could think more clearly. By the time he reached Hyde Park Corner, Alicia stood out in his mind like a shining beacon beckoning a distressed mariner to safety; she had become his salvation. He wondered why he had not realized this sooner, instead of dithering about trying to prove himself as a man. With Alicia, there would be no fear of failure, and without the fear, he doubted he would fail. It was her very ordinariness that drew him to her, and her openness and warmth. In a strange way she reminded him of Elaine, the gardener's daughter with whom he had spent an afternoon in the shrubbery all those years ago; she, too, had been without guile. It seemed suddenly and overwhelmingly imperative that he should talk to Alicia before his courage deserted him; he leapt into the first available taxi and headed for home.

It was eleven-thirty by his watch when he telephoned her; late by civilized standards, but he did not hesitate. She answered immediately, her voice questioning but not perturbed.

'Hello?'

'Alicia, it's Roly.'

'Roly!'

'Sorry it's late, but I have something terribly important to ask you. Will you marry me?'

He was half-expecting her laugh; instead there was a pause. 'I probably will,' she said finally, without a hint of surprise. 'I'll need time to think about it, though.'

'How long?'

'Let's see how the weekend goes, shall we? You're jumping the gun a bit,' she told him comfortably.

He sighed. 'I suppose I am. It's just that I'm so sure about it.'

'That's nice. I can't pretend it hasn't crossed my mind, too.'

'It has?' he said, feeling his spirits soar. He added with an effort, 'I haven't been entirely open about myself. There are things I have to tell you.'

'Yes,' she said. 'I know that. We'll sort it all out when we see each other.'

'Don't run away, will you?'

'Nowhere to run to,' she said, laughing.

'Alicia,' he said, 'I love you.'

'No, you don't,' she replied calmly. 'But you'll come to do so one day.'

On a cold but sunny day in February, Kate and Matt stood on the steps of Chelsea Register Office and watched Roly and Alicia depart in a chauffeur-driven limousine.

'What a relief,' Kate said with a sigh of satisfaction.

'That it's over?' Matt asked, taking her arm and guiding her to the pavement.

'No, the fact that he found someone like Alicia to marry. She's exactly right for him, don't you think?'

'Perfect, if she banishes your guilt complex about him for ever,' Matt replied. 'And now let's get out of this freezing wind and go and drink their health.' There was to be a small gathering of friends at Roly's house.

'I shan't stay for long,' Kate said. The baby was due in three weeks. 'I feel the size of an elephant.'

'A very pretty elephant.'

In the back of a taxi they held hands. Kate said, 'I don't think I've ever seen Roly look so contented, kind of at peace with himself and genuinely happy. Did you notice?'

Matt hesitated. Behind the beaming smile Roly had bestowed on them after the ceremony had been a look of pure triumph. His eyes resting momentarily on Kate had held an unmistakable message: I no longer need you, I can live perfectly well without you. So it had seemed to Matt. Kate was best left with her own illusions.

'Yes, I noticed,' he said. 'What an incurable romantic you are, my darling.'

'I do like happy endings,' she confessed.

'Don't you think happy beginnings is a more appropriate description,' he suggested, 'for all of us?'

THE END

OUT OF THE SHADOWS

Titia Sutherland

The house was one of the most enduring influences in Rachel Playfair's life. It was really too large for one woman, but she liked the memories it held, the graceful garden, and even the amiable resident spirit who lived on the top floor. When Rachel's authoritative and somewhat pompous son tried to persuade her out of her house, she decided to make changes in her solitary life. With three children who needed her only spasmodically, and a small lonely granddaughter who needed her quite a lot, she made plans, first of all to take in a lodger and then, with the help of the unhappy Emily, to research the past of her house. Both decisions were to shatter the structure of Rachel's tranquil life.

The lodger proved to be a beguiling but disturbed man who was instantly fascinated by his cool landlady, and the delving into the past reopened a moving and poignant wartime tragedy that held curious overtones of events in Rachel's own life.

'THIS SENSITIVE PORTRAYAL OF A MIDDLE-AGED WOMAN'S UNEXPECTED SEXUAL PASSION TURNED INTO A GHOST STORY I COULDN'T PUT DOWN'
David Buckley, *Observer*

'AN EVOCATIVE STORY . . . GENTLY TOLD, ENVELOPS YOU COMPLETELY'
Company

0 552 99529 0

BLACK SWAN

ACCOMPLICE OF LOVE

Titia Sutherland

'A SENSITIVE, SENSUOUS STORY, BEAUTIFULLY TOLD'
Hazel Martin, *Prima*

When Leo Kinsey bought 'Girl with Cat' – the painting of a
nude whose auburn hair was the same colour as the cat's fur
– he had no idea how deeply involved he was to become
with both the artist, and the model. Josh Jones was a huge
rugged bear of a man. He was also one of the most talented
painters Leo had ever discovered and, very quickly, Leo and
his wife, Josh and Claudia – the girl with the auburn hair –
formed an uneasy friendship. Leo was to give Josh a one-
man exhibition in his elegant and distinguished gallery, and
Josh invited Leo down to their cottage in the country. In
spite of Josh's heavy drinking and the tension between him
and Claudia a careful *status quo* was preserved.

It was when unexpected tragedy smashed Leo's comfortable
and orderly life, that the relationship changed. For Claudia,
Josh's volatile, exciting, exotic wife, became all-important to
Leo. Between them flared a dangerous spark that threatened
to disrupt the lives of everyone about them.

'SHE MAKES US WANT TO TURN THE PAGES'
Maeve Binchy

'A BEAUTIFULLY WRITTEN ACCOUNT OF AN ARTIST,
HIS MODEL, HER LOVER AND THEIR EROTIC TRYSTS'
Living

0 552 99574 6

BLACK SWAN

A SELECTION OF FINE WRITING
AVAILABLE FROM BLACK SWAN

THE PRICES SHOWN BELOW WERE CORRECT AT THE TIME OF GOING TO PRESS.
HOWEVER TRANSWORLD PUBLISHERS RESERVE THE RIGHT TO SHOW NEW
RETAIL PRICES ON COVERS WHICH MAY DIFFER FROM THOSE PREVIOUSLY
ADVERTISED IN THE TEXT OR ELSEWHERE.

☐	99564 9	JUST FOR THE SUMMER	*Judy Astley*	£5.99
☐	99565 7	PLEASANT VICES	*Judy Astley*	£5.99
☐	13649 2	HUNGRY	*Jane Barry*	£6.99
☐	99648 3	TOUCH AND GO	*Elizabeth Berridge*	£5.99
☐	99537 1	GUPPIES FOR TEA	*Marika Cobbold*	£5.99
☐	99593 2	A RIVAL CREATION	*Marika Cobbold*	£5.99
☐	99587 8	LIKE WATER FOR CHOCOLATE	*Laura Esquivel*	£5.99
☐	99622 X	THE GOLDEN YEAR	*Elizabeth Falconer*	£5.99
☐	99610 6	THE SINGING HOUSE	*Janette Griffiths*	£5.99
☐	99590 8	OLD NIGHT	*Clare Harkness*	£5.99
☐	99503 7	WAITING TO EXHALE	*Terry McMillan*	£5.99
☐	99561 4	TELL MRS POOLE I'M SORRY	*Kathleen Rowntree*	£5.99
☐	99606 8	OUTSIDE, LOOKING IN	*Kathleen Rowntree*	£5.99
☐	99598 3	AN ANCIENT HOPE	*Caroline Stickland*	£5.99
☐	99529 0	OUT OF THE SHADOWS	*Titia Sutherland*	£5.99
☐	99460 X	THE FIFTH SUMMER	*Titia Sutherland*	£5.99
☐	99574 6	ACCOMPLICE OF LOVE	*Titia Sutherland*	£5.99
☐	99620 3	RUNNING AWAY	*Titia Sutherland*	£5.99
☐	99130 9	NOAH'S ARK	*Barbara Trapido*	£6.99
☐	99056 6	BROTHER OF THE MORE FAMOUS JACK	*Barbara Trapido*	£6.99
☐	99492 8	THE MEN AND THE GIRLS	*Joanna Trollope*	£5.99
☐	99549 5	A SPANISH LOVER	*Joanna Trollope*	£5.99
☐	99636 X	KNOWLEDGE OF ANGELS	*Jill Paton Walsh*	£5.99
☐	99495 2	A DUBIOUS LEGACY	*Mary Wesley*	£6.99
☐	99592 4	AN IMAGINATIVE EXPERIENCE	*Mary Wesley*	£5.99
☐	99639 4	THE TENNIS PARTY	*Madeleine Wickham*	£5.99
☐	99591 6	A MISLAID MAGIC	*Joyce Windsor*	£4.99